HER
FAMILY
SECRET

Melissa Wiesner

HER
FAMILY
SECRET

Bookouture

Published by Bookouture in 2021

An imprint of Storyfire Ltd.
Carmelite House
50 Victoria Embankment
London EC4Y 0DZ

www.bookouture.com

ISBN: 978-1-80019-557-8
eBook ISBN: 978-1-80019-556-1

This book is a work of fiction. Names, characters, businesses,
organizations, places and events other than those clearly in the
public domain, are either the product of the author's imagination
or are used fictitiously. Any resemblance to actual persons, living or
dead, events or locales is entirely coincidental.

For Anjali and Indy.
I can't wait to watch you follow your dreams.

CHAPTER ONE

When the phone rang at 10:45 that morning, Juniper Westwood knew before she answered that the call was going to ruin her day.

The phone played a cheerful salsa beat—her daughter Emma's choice of ringtone—that didn't match the dread doing a slow waltz in her stomach. June could see the sign for the airport up ahead. All she had to do was park her car, get through Security, and board her plane. It would take an hour, tops. And then, freedom. She'd be on her way to New Orleans, where—after eight years of making excuses, eight years of getting her husband David to agree to watch the kids only for him to back out a few weeks later when he realized he'd actually have to parent his children—she was finally going to meet her college roommates for a weekend away.

For a wild second, she considered sending the call to voicemail, getting on the plane, and letting David deal with the fallout. But no, she couldn't. June didn't leave messes for other people to clean up.

With one finger, she hit the button on the steering wheel, answering the call with the BMW's built-in Bluetooth system. "Hi, Mom."

Her mother Esther's voice reverberated through the car's speakers, as bright and loud as her bohemian scarves and turquoise jewelry. "Junie, honey, I'm glad I caught you. I was worried you might be in another one of those boring meetings and too busy to talk to your own mother."

Did they really need to do this right now? Esther always had to complain about June's corporate job before she'd get to the real point of calling, but June wasn't in the mood for it today. "Mom, when you call me in the middle of my workday, sometimes I have to work," she snapped.

"That's silly. You're the boss's wife. If you need to take a few minutes for the woman who gave you life, well, nobody's going to object."

"I'm *not* just the boss's wife. I have an actual role in the company—" June abruptly stopped talking and took a deep breath, like she'd learned in the yoga class she'd attended twice before dropping out because all that mindfulness stressed her out.

Three counts in. Hold for three counts. Three counts out.

Or was it supposed to be four counts? She should've paid more attention to the teacher's gentle instructions, instead of drafting her grocery list and reviewing the girls' school activities in her head. *Another fundraiser? Can't I write a check and be done with it? And Costume Day in the middle of May? Seriously?*

June blew the air from her lungs and gave up on mindful breathing, dragging her thoughts back to steering the BMW toward the airport and moving this discussion with her mother along. Why did she bother to argue about work with Esther anyway? Her mother had never held down a job in her life, unless you counted tarot-card reading and selling yoni eggs at the flea market. Which June most certainly did not.

"Mom, what's up?" Please let her be calling with one of her whacky ideas for an activity she wanted to do with the girls, and not to cancel on them.

"Honey, I'm calling with great news! Wolf's painting was accepted into the Santa Fe Artist Collective's annual showcase."

June sighed in relief. "Oh… that's… great." She hit her turn signal. Four miles to go and the airport would be in sight. Who was Wolf again? There were so many people in and out of her mother's life, Wolf could be anyone. A boyfriend, a roommate, the person at the next flea market booth. For all she knew, Wolf might be an actual wolf. But who cared, as long as her mother was on her way to Greenwich, Connecticut to babysit for the long weekend.

But her mother kept talking. "The final judging is on Sunday, and we're packing up the van and heading there now."

June's lungs squeezed, and she gripped the steering wheel tighter. "You're headed to Santa Fe." It was a statement, not a question. Because if her mother was supposed to pick up the girls in Greenwich in five hours, well, of course she was headed to Santa Fe.

The only reason why David had agreed to her New Orleans trip was if June arranged for help with the girls. There was no way that was ever going to be David's mother: Clarissa couldn't stand it when children made noise or messes. So, June had called her own mother, who was fine with noise and messes. But, unfortunately, she was less fine with details—like showing up. June wouldn't have asked if she'd had any other options.

"Juniper, this painting is a big deal for Wolf. An award of this caliber could alter the trajectory of his career. And he can't go without me—I'm his muse, remember? I sent you the photo."

June pressed a palm to her forehead as a vein began to pulse there. She vaguely remembered a text from her mother of a painting depicting a naked woman sitting in a lotus position in the desert. The woman was draped in a red cloth that thankfully covered the graphic bits and June hadn't done more than write back a generic, *Amazing*, before promptly shutting off her phone and going back to making dinner for the girls. Now that June thought about it, the woman in the painting did have her mother's long, blond hair. But she'd also had glowing blue skin, so how was June to know?

This Wolf must be another one of her mother's boyfriends. Esther had probably met him in the art scene in Philadelphia, where she met most of her boyfriends. Or maybe at her weekly drum circle.

"Mom, I'm about to get on my flight. You *promised* you'd be here to get the girls."

"Can't David pick them up?"

"Maybe he can *today*." Although he'd whine about being too busy to leave work early. "But tomorrow's the first day of summer break, and someone needs to be home with them while David goes to work. The nanny can't start until next week."

"I'm sure you'll work something out, honey. I mean, it's not like you're a struggling single mother."

Here we go again.

June heaved another breath. Damn it, she wished she could remember if it was supposed to be *in for three counts* or four. Maybe it was *in for three counts, out for four?* God, she hated yoga.

"You're lucky you have a husband to support you. I had to do everything myself. Three daughters, all on my own…" It was the same refrain Esther always came back to when June expressed frustration at her mother's failure to show up for graduations, or weddings, or the girls' birthday. *All the sacrifices she'd made.*

June's jaw clenched and her stomach began to burn. "*You* did everything yourself?" she snapped before she could stop herself. "I seem to recall it was *me* doing everything while you were off with your latest boyfriend. Looks like nothing much has changed." Damn it. How many hundreds of hours, and thousands of dollars, had she poured into therapy to learn there was no point engaging with a narcissist when they were rewriting history and making it all about them? And yet, here June was, arguing with her mother again. She sucked in another marginally cleansing breath.

"Well, aren't you the most ungrateful…"

"Mom, I've got to go." There was no point prolonging this conversation.

"Well, you could at least wish Wolf good luck before you hang up."

Oh, good Lord—June smacked the steering wheel with her palm to shut off the phone. Deep down, she'd known her mother would bail, but she'd wanted this trip so badly she'd ignored all her instincts. What an absolute waste.

What was she going to do now? As the airport terminal came into view, June pulled over onto the side of the road and flipped on her hazard lights. Her flight was in an hour and a half. Maybe she could still work this out.

She called David's cell phone, but it went to voicemail.

She tried a text: *CALL ME.* She wasn't an all-caps kind of person, so hopefully he'd get the message. Then she tried his office phone, his assistant, and his cell again. Still nothing.

June growled in frustration. For a second, she suspected David was deliberately ignoring her calls because he knew she was about to dump this problem on him. But, more likely, he was in the middle of a project he deemed more important than whatever she had to say.

Somehow, that was even worse.

As she sat and stared at the phone on her lap, waiting for David to get back to her, the clock on the dashboard slowly ticked toward noon, the time her flight was supposed to leave. What if she got on the plane anyway? When nobody came to pick up the girls at 3:30, the school would call David. David might be self-absorbed, but he loved the girls and he'd answer when the school called.

But June pictured Emma and Izzy standing by the building entrance, watching all their friends leave with their parents.

Waiting for someone to show up.

Her stomach churned at that painfully familiar image. It had been more than twenty-five years, but June could still remember the sinking in her chest as she hovered by the school gates while all the other kids filtered out. Of slowly realizing her mother wasn't coming and wondering if she'd *ever* show up. She could picture her younger sisters' faces looking to her to reassure them that everything was going to be okay. *Mommy will be here any minute.* She used to say it even though she had no idea if Esther had been delayed by traffic, or if she'd forgotten to pick them up entirely.

June's eyes burned, and she knew she couldn't do that to the girls. Instead, she called David one more time, and when he didn't answer, switched over to her text messages.

Esther flaked. I can't make it.

At least her college roommates knew her mother was unreliable. She'd spent pretty much every parents' weekend and graduation event with one of their families when Esther no-showed.

The replies came in quickly.

We'll miss you!

Aw, so sorry to hear.

Damn it, Esther! ☹

She had to wonder if they'd been expecting this text from her all along. June didn't know what she'd been thinking, expecting Esther to step up when she'd shown time and time again—

June's phone buzzed in her hand, and she clicked over to her work email. Twenty-two unread messages, just in the hour since she'd left the office. So much for unplugging from work this weekend. June typed in answers to the most pressing inquiries, swearing under her breath at a couple of questions forwarded by her assistant, Keith. Why did she even have an assistant if he couldn't deal with the most basic of tasks?

Probably because David had insisted. Keith had recently graduated from Yale, and that was good enough for David. Too bad she couldn't ask Keith to pick up the girls. And there really was nobody else she could call. Both her sisters had shut her down before she'd even asked them to come and help out. Typical. June hadn't seen either of them in over a year, despite the invitations she'd extended at Thanksgiving and Christmas.

June tossed her phone onto the car seat next to her as her chest began to burn. She dug around in her purse for the antacids her doctor had given her, along with a warning that she needed to get her blood pressure under control. *You're only thirty-eight, June. You have the blood pressure of an octogenarian.* But after pulling out a flattened granola bar, a naked Barbie, and two tampons that had lost their paper wrappers, she gave up on the medicine.

June turned the key in the ignition and headed back the way she'd come. When her phone rang a couple of minutes later, she glanced at the clock. Well, David's timing was perfect. It was too late to make her flight now. She slammed her hand on the steering wheel to answer the phone with Bluetooth.

"David, I've been calling for the last forty-five minutes. What if it had been an emergency?"

An unfamiliar male voice rumbled through the car speakers. "I'm sorry, there must be a mistake. My name isn't David. I'm looking for Juniper Westwood. Is she available?"

June's first thought was that something had happened to Emma or Izzy, and her hands began to shake on the steering wheel. "This—this is June Westwood. Who's calling, please?"

"Ms. Westwood, my name is Will Valencia, from the law firm of Valencia and King. I'm calling about your father."

Relief flooded through her. The girls were okay. She grabbed her coffee from the console and took a long swig to wet her parched throat. But on her second sip, the man's words began to register. She sucked a gulp of air and breathed in the coffee right along with it. "My—who?" she gasped, between fits of coughing.

"Your father, Ms. Westwood."

June's heart pounded in her ears. Was this the call she'd been waiting for? Had her father finally decided to get back in touch with her after all this time? It had taken years for her to stop looking for him, and even longer to let go of the notion that he'd come back and find her. But he was always there in the periphery of her memory. That strong, smiling man who'd always known how to dry her tears or patch up her scraped knees.

At every milestone and important event, and sometimes even in the small, insignificant moments—when she had a fight with David, or when Esther flaked on her again—June's thoughts would drift to her father before she could stop them. What would he say? What advice would he give?

Her head might have stopped waiting for him, but deep down, her heart never had.

"Did he—" June swallowed hard. "Did my father ask you to reach out?"

"Ma'am, does the name Jasper Luc mean anything to you?"

June shook her head as her mind grasped at the image of a painting depicting two people standing in the middle of a city street, their bodies facing each other in an almost-embrace. Maybe they were about to kiss, but nobody would ever know, because the viewer watched them through the blurred windshield of a car recently smeared with washer fluid.

"Jasper Luc, the artist?" She'd studied his work, along with several other contemporary artists, in her freshman year painting class. That was before she'd switched to major in accounting. What did Jasper Luc have to do with anything?

"Yes, the artist." The caller paused for a moment. "Ms. Westwood, are you unaware Jasper Luc is your father?"

Was this a joke? Some kind of prank? June squeezed the steering wheel until her knuckles turned white. All she'd ever known about her father was the meager information she and her sisters had managed to pry out of their mother.

Esther had met him in Philly and they'd had a whirlwind romance that left her pregnant. From the less-than-complimentary things Esther had to say about the father of her children,

June suspected the relationship had been volatile. The rapid arrival of Sierra and then Raven after June had probably been Esther's way of trying to hold the relationship together. The ploy backfired on her, though, when whoever their father was took off after Raven's birth.

June had always held the memories of her father like precious heirlooms, and when she was in high school, she'd created a series of paintings to immortalize them. A dark, curly-haired man with a proud smile on his face, standing next to a little girl balanced on a stool to face him. A scene at Christmas-time, when he'd given her a set of her own oil pastels: not one of the cheap brands they made for kids, but the real ones.

June had shown the series at her high school art show, and it was one of the few times her mother had shown up. In the end, June had wished Esther hadn't come, because she'd rolled her eyes and told June they were better off without him in their lives. And how could June dispute that? How could she say her father had loved her at all? After all, he'd taken off and never came back.

June had always believed her mother didn't know where to find her father. But Jasper Luc? Esther could have tracked him down anytime she wanted.

All of a sudden, June was shaking with cold, even as beads of sweat pricked her forehead. Cars zoomed by on both sides, giving her a sense of vertigo. She stared out the windshield; everything had a strange, blurred quality to it.

The irony wasn't lost on June.

"Is it true?" June managed to whisper. Was it possible that her father was Jasper Luc, and after all this time, he wanted back in her life? Maybe it hadn't been him who left, but Esther who'd forced him out all along.

On the other end of the line, the attorney cleared his throat. "Jasper named his three children—Juniper, Sierra, and Raven—in his will."

"In his…" June trailed off.

"I'm sorry to tell you your father passed away earlier this week."

The attorney's words kicked her straight in the gut. Her father was dead. Before she'd even known who he was. Before she could ever see him again. Her heart pounded like she'd been sprinting up-hill, and she couldn't quite suck enough air into her lungs. June plunged one hand into her purse, digging around for her antacids again.

"Ms. Westwood." The caller paused for a moment. "Jasper Luc left everything to you and your sisters. His house, studio and artwork in Wishing Cove, Washington."

June's foot hit the brake, and the car screeched to a stop. From somewhere far away, a horn blared. A second later, she heard a loud, metallic crunch, and then everything went black.

CHAPTER TWO

Caleb Valencia wasn't in the mood for visitors. Especially visitors in the form of his twin brother, Will, who was about to step out of his Mercedes and start spouting positivity like some kind of motivational speaker. Caleb looked around for a place to hide, but the only haven along the rocky path leading to the main house and driveway was the door to Jasper's studio. And there was no way in hell he was going in there.

Caleb sighed and dragged his feet through the gravel as he made his way up the hill. Will had already spotted him, anyway. His brother stood in front of Jasper's porch in a charcoal gray suit, crisp white shirt, and pale blue tie. Caleb's gaze skated down to his own paint-splattered jeans and frayed T-shirt. Man, if looking at Will's face wasn't like looking in a mirror, he'd have bet money one of them had been switched at birth.

"Hey, bro, how are you?" Will asked.

Caleb shrugged in response. Nobody was going to accuse him of being the talkative twin.

Will held out a hand and Caleb grabbed it, getting that awkward back-slap hug out of the way. Will had come home one day in his senior year of high school having adopted the bro-hug. On a better week, Caleb would give him shit about it. But this wasn't a better week.

"Listen, Caleb. I don't want you to start thinking there was something you could have—"

"Thanks for coming. Was there something you needed?" Caleb already knew what his brother was going to say. He'd already heard it from their mother on Tuesday, after she'd seen Jasper's obituary in the *New York Times*.

Will paused, giving him that appraising look that said he knew his brother was doing his 'avoidance thing' again. Caleb didn't know what was so terrible about avoidance. Bottling up his feelings had worked far better than letting them explode. Besides, his parents had spent good money when he was a kid to make sure he had a team of therapists and a cabinet full of drugs to keep him from exploding. He was thirty-nine years old now. The ship had sailed on blabbering about his emotions like a Real Housewife.

Will picked up a dark leather briefcase from the porch steps and pulled out a pile of papers. "Yeah, actually, I'm here on business."

Caleb nodded. Jasper had died five days ago. As Jasper's attorney, it was Will's job to deal with the fallout, at least from a financial perspective. Estates, wills, that kind of thing. Caleb was living on the deceased man's property in Wishing Cove, and he knew at some point that he'd have to figure out what the hell he was going to do next. He wasn't a backup plan kind of guy; over the past two decades, he and Jasper had co-existed on the five-acre estate just south of town, overlooking Everett Bay, with Jasper living in the main house and Caleb across the field in the smaller guesthouse.

Caleb turned his eyes westward, past the wildflower-dotted meadow to the edge of the cliff dropping off to reveal an expanse of sea below. He and Jasper had shared the studio space overlooking the water. But now he'd have to leave it all.

Caleb couldn't imagine where he'd go, and what it would do to his work. But he couldn't imagine no longer having Jasper to challenge and confront and push him to be a better artist, either.

Will nodded toward the wicker chairs on the porch. "Is it okay if we sit here? Or should we go down to your house?"

Caleb gave a wave of his hand and trudged up the steps. "Nah, this is fine." *Better to get it over with.* He settled into a chair and watched his brother shuffle the stack of papers.

"Right, so. I guess I should tell you Jasper had three daughters."

"Yeah." He'd figured Jasper would leave the estate to them. But still, it stung.

Will's head jerked up, eyes wide. "You knew?"

Caleb nodded. He'd started working as Jasper's apprentice when he was practically a kid, mostly doing menial tasks like washing brushes and stretching canvases. But as he'd developed as an artist in his own right, their relationship had evolved from master and student into colleagues, and then friends. After twenty years, Jasper had been family, in many ways closer than Caleb's own parents, who'd never understood his art; or his brother, who'd always been his polar opposite.

"I didn't know Jasper told you. When he came to me to draw up his will, he said nobody knew. He didn't want it ending up in the press, or reporters stalking them for interviews."

"Yeah, from what Jasper told me, I don't think *they* know he was their dad. So good luck with that."

Will leaned back in his chair and set a shiny leather shoe across his opposite leg. "Oh, they most definitely don't know. Or they didn't until I talked to one of them today. The oldest."

"Juniper. What did she say when you told her?"

"She sounded really stunned, and before I could give too many details, she hung up on me." Will shrugged. "I'm not sure she believed me, to be honest. The other two sisters didn't answer their phones."

Caleb nodded. "Raven's a photojournalist who could be anywhere in the world right now. But Sierra's a writer in Northern California, so she probably checks her messages."

Will raised his eyebrows. "For someone who didn't want a relationship with his kids, Jasper sure kept tabs on them."

Caleb ran a palm across the week-old stubble on his cheek. "Yeah, well…" Jasper had had his reasons. Caleb understood them.

Will went back to shuffling his papers. "So, he left the house, his studio, and most of his artwork to his daughters." His eyes flicked up from the page, as if he were measuring Caleb's reaction to the news.

Caleb leaned back in his chair, nodding slowly. He hadn't expected Jasper to leave the property to him, but the news confirmed he'd have to pack up and move on. In one brutal moment, he'd lost his mentor, his best friend, his home. Everything that had saved him, back when he was a runaway train careening toward a cliff.

"But," Will continued, "the terms of the will dictate the property should be divided at the path leading to the studio. The guesthouse and your part of the studio go to you."

Caleb's head jerked up. He wouldn't have to move. He could stay in the place where he'd grown from an angry, undisciplined kid into an artist.

"I'm sorry I didn't tell you sooner." Will leaned in, resting his elbows on his knees. "As his lawyer and the executor of his will, I wanted to make sure I did things by the book. Especially with someone as high profile as Jasper."

"Yeah, I understand." Caleb ran a hand over his face. "This is… wow." Out across the property, purple lupine gently waved in the meadow in front of his little gray clapboard house on the hill. "This means a lot."

"I'm happy for you, bro. I know how important this place is to you."

They both knew it wasn't just the house, or the view. It was the stability, the routine. He'd always struggled most when he felt adrift. This place, and Jasper—they'd anchored him. Sometimes he wondered if they'd saved his life. Caleb blew out a breath and stood up. He paced to the edge of the porch and leaned his weight against the railing as the enormous loss of his friend hit him.

Will shuffled around behind him and, a moment later, Caleb felt his brother's hand on his arm. "You okay? You want to grab some dinner later and talk about it?"

"No." Caleb pulled his arm away. "I'm fine." He didn't need Will hanging around here, worrying about him. "Let's get this over with so you can go, and I can get back to the studio."

Will took a step back, his eyes darkening.

Shit. His brother was trying to help, but it only added to Caleb's irritation. Will's perpetual look of disappointment served as a constant reminder of how Caleb had managed to fail everyone. This was exactly why he was better off hiding out in the studio alone. Why was that always so hard for Will to understand? Caleb rubbed his temple, trying to massage away the buzzing in his head.

"Okay…" Will backed off and went back to his seat. He picked up the papers on the table and flipped through them. "Caleb, Jasper left you *Girl in the Trees*."

Caleb whirled around.

Holy shit.

Girl in the Trees was arguably Jasper's most famous painting. It depicted a far-away woman standing in the center of a forest. The woman gazed off into the distance and held her arm above her head as if she were stretching. The shape of her body in an earth-toned dress resembled the curve of the tree trunks and branches encircling her, so much so a casual observer might not notice her standing there at all. *Girl in the Trees* had been exhibited in every major museum and gallery in the world.

"It's in a show at the Whitney until January," Will added. "I wonder what the daughters will end up doing with his other work." Will shook his head.

"I hope they appreciate the importance of what they inherited. That they don't sell it all to the highest bidder." The buzzing in Caleb's head grew louder. "I'd hate for Jasper's work to end up next to a gold toilet in some billionaire's bathroom."

He wished he could talk to Jasper just one more time, and understand what he'd been hoping for when he'd left his work to the three daughters he never knew. But, more than that, Caleb wished he could understand how Jasper had mixed up his medications and in a senseless accident, ended one of the most influential painting careers of this century.

And ended the most important friendship of Caleb's life right along with it.

CHAPTER THREE

When June woke up and saw David standing above her with a worried look on his face, her first thought was she'd forgotten to set the alarm. The girls were going to be late for school again. And was today the drama club performance? Had she remembered to pick up the mouse and elephant costumes earlier this week? Plus, she still needed to finish the PowerPoint for the board presentation. Please don't let today be the day they started construction at the Greenwich Metro North station. It was going to be a mess trying to get to work.

June tried to sit up, tired before she even started her day. Why did she always feel like she'd been shot out of a cannon and had to accomplish a million tasks before she hit the ground?

Something tangled around her chest, holding her down on the pillow. A knife twisted into her temple and she gasped at the pain.

David put his hand on her shoulder, gently pressing her back into the bed. "Lie down. You have a concussion."

June blinked at him, trying to process his words. Where was she? And why did she feel like she'd been thrown over Niagara Falls in a barrel? Her head ached, something in her chest felt like it had taken a blow from a golf club, and her whole body throbbed.

"What's this?" she asked weakly, pulling on a cord that disappeared into her gown.

"Don't yank it out. That's to monitor your heart rate."

"Why?"

"Why? Because you were in a car accident and when the paramedics came, your blood pressure was through the roof. At first they thought you'd had a heart attack or a stroke."

A car accident? June grabbed the side rails on the bed and struggled to sit up. Her chest was on fire. "Where are the girls? David, are the girls okay?"

"The girls are fine. Priya went to get them from school."

June sank back into the pillow. She didn't like David's assistant picking them up. Priya was twenty-five and childless. She'd probably let them talk her into buying ice cream, and she wouldn't know how to check the girls were clicked into their booster seats correctly. But thank God they weren't in the car during the accident.

Another pain shot from her left shoulder to her ribs. "What's the matter with me?" She poked gingerly at her sternum. "Why does my chest hurt? *Did* I have a heart attack?"

David sighed, and for a second, June thought his eyes rolled, the tiniest bit. "No, that's probably your broken collar bone hurting. There's nothing wrong with your heart. They're monitoring it just to be safe." He ran a hand through his close-cropped blond hair. "The guy who hit you said you slammed on your brakes and came to a dead stop in the middle of the highway."

June's eyes widened. She didn't remember any of this. "Oh my God, was anyone else hurt?"

David grabbed the knot in his tie and loosened it with a hard yank. "Thankfully, no. That doesn't mean he won't sue, though."

From her hospital bed, June looked up at the man she'd spent the past nineteen years of her life with. Other than a few streaks of gray around his temples, he still resembled that twenty-two-year-old fraternity boy she'd literally crashed into in the library her freshman year. She'd been at Yale on a scholarship, still an art major at that point, and he was a legacy student finishing up his business degree and moving on to his MBA. They couldn't have been more different, but that had been part of the attraction. Everything about David—from his preppy clothes, vacation house in Nantucket, and ancestors who'd come over on the Mayflower—was the complete opposite of her background.

David's life represented stability and security. His parents were still married after thirty years, and they worked side by side in the family's thriving healthcare company. David didn't have to worry about losing his scholarship if his grades slipped, or about holding down a part-time job to send money home to his siblings. When he took June out to dinner, he didn't even glance at the bill before plunking down his credit card.

At Yale, David had called his parents every Sunday and drove into Manhattan once a month for a visit. He'd always returned with his laundry washed and folded by the family's housekeeper, and a stack of homemade meals packed by his mother for his freezer. When June was able to scrape together the train fare to visit her family, half the time her mother forgot she was coming.

In the beginning, David didn't seem fazed by their differences. He thought the pink streaks in her wild, curly hair were "charming," and he used to joke that he'd be happy to pose if she ever needed a model for figure drawing class. But all that first semester, she'd had a vague feeling David wasn't really serious about her, and that he was just having a little fun before he settled down with someone his family would find more suitable.

The following semester, June switched from art to accounting. A more practical major was her only hope of providing for the two younger sisters back home relying on her.

June swapped the pink in her hair for caramel highlights, invested in a straightener to wrestle out every last curl, and shopped at the Goodwill in the wealthier part of town for twinsets and flats.

David took her home to meet his parents that summer.

June pressed her head back against the pillow and eyed her husband pacing in front of her. Had they always been like this?

They'd never had the kind of devotion that would send David flying to her bedside in a panic, tears in his eyes, declaring his love. Truth be told, she'd never wanted that kind of passion. Her father leaving had taught her to keep a strong grip on her heart. But did David really care more about whether he might be sued than if she were okay?

June closed her eyes, shutting David out. He was upset. She would be too, if she'd answered a call saying her spouse had been in an accident.

A middle-aged woman in blue scrubs appeared at the foot of the bed. "Hi, Juniper. I'm Dr. Howard. How are you feeling?"

June pressed a hand to her temple. "Like I was hit by a car."

Dr. Howard smiled. "That sounds about right. I'm glad to see you're awake. We didn't have many concerns about long-term brain injury, but it's great to see you alert and talking."

"Can I go home now?"

The doctor approached the side of the bed. "Not just yet. Besides a lot of bumps and bruises, you have a minor fracture in your clavicle, which we'll treat with Motrin, and you'll have to wear a sling for a couple of weeks. You had a pretty serious concussion, so we'd like to monitor you overnight."

June nodded. That wasn't so bad. Considering.

"You're going to have a killer headache for a couple of weeks. What do you do for work?"

"I'm an accountant."

Dr. Howard cringed. "I don't imagine you can do that job without staring at a tiny spreadsheet on a screen all day?"

June shook her head and winced at the chisel gouging her brain.

"Is there any chance you have some sick days saved up? I'm going to recommend you don't go back to work for at least a month. Maybe two. Trying to do a job like that will make your headaches significantly worse. You'll need to rest as much as possible."

David stepped up to the other side of the bed. "It's a good thing I own the company where she works. I'll have a talk with the boss." He gave the doctor a wink and June's face flushed with embarrassment. Even at a time like this, he had to mention he owned the company. If she had a dollar for every time David puffed out his chest and joked about being her boss she'd be able to afford... *a divorce.*

June's body tensed. *Where did that come from?* Her brain really *had* rattled around in her head in the accident.

Dr. Howard's expression remained unchanged. "That works out." She pulled a cell phone from her pocket and glanced at the screen. "Excuse me, I need to take this. You've got a heavy-duty painkiller in your IV tonight. I'll have the nurse put an order in for extra-strength Motrin tomorrow."

As the doctor pushed through the curtain and stepped out the door, June heard voices in the hall. A second later, two little girls burst into the room, dark brown ringlets bouncing around their faces. June's heart lurched at the sight of them. Her babies: seven-year-old Emma and six-year-old Izzy. What would they have done if she'd been seriously injured, or killed in the accident?

"Mommy! What happened?" Emma demanded, shoving past David to get to the bed.

Izzy hung back, staring at all the machines and wires with wide blue eyes. June did her best to smile. "Come here, baby." She held out her hand. "Mommy's okay. It was only a little accident."

Izzy silently crept closer while Emma climbed right up onto the foot of the bed. "Priya says you went in an ambroo-lance to the hospital. Was it fun? Whooo-wheeee!"

June winced at the noise, and her irritation at Priya grew. Did she have to go into all the details? Didn't she know car crashes and ambulances could be scary to a little kid, especially if their mother was involved? June shot a glare at the pretty, dark-haired woman who'd followed the girls into the room, but Priya was gazing at David and missed June's ire entirely.

June beckoned for Izzy again. "Come up here with Em, baby."

Izzy climbed onto the bed, much more delicately than her sister, and crawled up near the top. June wrapped an arm around her daughter and settled her against the unbroken side of her chest. "I'm fine. I've got a couple of bumps, and that's it. There's nothing to worry about, okay?"

Izzy nodded and grabbed a corner of the sheet, twisting it in her palm the same way she did with her baby blanket at home. June's heart tugged again. She hated that the girls had to go home without her tonight. They were already upset—or at least Izzy was—and David didn't know any of the routines to comfort them: what they liked to eat, what books they read before bed. He usually worked late, and left the parenting to her. Once, when June was away at a PTA meeting, he'd even forgotten about Emma's strawberry allergy, and she'd ended up in the ER. How a parent could forget something like that was unimaginable to June.

Priya stepped up to the bed and rested her hands on the bedrail. "I'm sorry about the accident, Mrs. Westwood. Let me know if there's anything I can do."

June nodded. "Thanks." Priya was only trying to help. She didn't have kids; it wasn't her fault she didn't know what to say to them.

David put a hand on the rail next to Priya's, and leaned in. "What I don't understand is why you were going north on the interstate instead of south. I thought you were headed to the airport for your trip."

June stared at David and Priya's hands lined up on the bedrail, David's left with his gold wedding ring, and Priya's right with a pretty silver knot on her third finger. It all started coming back to her: the call from her mother, a guy named Wolf, a text to her friends backing out of the trip. After that, things got a little fuzzy.

"My mom flaked. There was nobody to pick up the kids. I tried calling you." Her eyes skated past David and Priya's rings, tracing their arms up to their shoulders, where they almost touched. "I tried calling both of you, a bunch of times. Nobody answered."

Priya shot a quick, almost imperceptible glance at David, and pulled her hands off the bedrail. She stared down at them, twisting her ring around her finger.

David cleared his throat. "We were in meetings all morning." His eyes met hers and then flickered past to the opposite wall.

A dark, slippery dread began to seep into June's chest like oil pooling in the driveway. There was an intimacy to the way he and Priya had stood next to each other, like they were two people so used to touching they forgot about leaving a space between them.

But then David smiled at June, and reached down to push a lock of hair behind her ear. "I'm so glad you're okay. I don't know what the girls and I would do without you."

A minute later, Priya was on her phone in the corner, texting someone. The girls protested when they heard June wouldn't be going home with them, and Emma negotiated with David for a TV show before bed. June watched her husband agree to their child's demands, shooting her a grin that said *What kind of monster have we created?*

She'd been imagining things. Priya was probably texting her friends to make plans for after she ditched this boring family. And she, David, and the girls were fine. Maybe this accident would even help them appreciate each other a little more.

As David rounded up the girls to head home, the painkillers kicked in, and June closed her eyes and drifted off to sleep.

CHAPTER FOUR

Four days later, June got out of bed to send the girls off with the nanny, took an extra-strength Motrin for her throbbing collarbone, and wiped down the counters. She wandered into the den to pick up a book she'd been meaning to read, but discovered the tiny print made her head ache.

David had taken her laptop and hidden it somewhere, claiming he didn't trust her to follow doctor's orders and stay away from it, which left her with a hollow pit in her stomach. She wasn't a child: she could monitor her own computer use.

He'd also tossed out all the regular coffee in an attempt to limit her caffeine intake after the doctor mentioned her elevated blood pressure, so June brewed a cup of herbal tea that tasted exactly the way she imagined dirty, wet fall leaves the kids tracked in from the backyard would taste. She dumped it down the drain and then slowly limped around the house, looking for a project. But everything in the house was sleek, austere, and spotless. Mess and clutter irritated David, so at some point it had become easier to keep the kids' toys contained to the playroom in the basement, and to shove her collection of books and pottery into an unused bedroom closet.

June stumbled to a stop in front of the door to one of the guest rooms. There was another box in that bedroom closet, too. Buried deeper, in the crawl space behind the Christmas decorations. The box she'd hadn't touched since her freshman year of college, but for some reason, had dragged around to every place she'd lived for the past decade and a half.

Her art supplies. Charcoals, pastels, oil paints. There might even be an old bottle of linseed oil in there, surely rancid by now. But while the paints might be dried up, the oils separated long ago, the charcoals would be fine, maybe the pastels too, and of course the heavy canvas paper in the sketchbooks. *Could I—*

June backed away from the door, her feet sinking in the plush, white carpeting.

No.

David's head would explode if he came home to find her coated in the fine, black powder that charcoals seemed to distribute on every available surface. And the sharp, waxy scent of oil pastels had a way of permeating the air and lingering for days. Not to mention that white carpet. There weren't enough drop cloths in the world to protect a carpet like that.

No, this was the sort of house where you hung artwork— preferably something modern and minimalist—not where you created it.

When she was a kid, she'd overheard her mother criticizing developers for tearing up the beautiful old farmlands outside of Philly and building McMansions in their place. June had imagined giant castles serving hamburgers and fries from a window on the side. To a kid in Section 8 housing, McMansions had sounded wonderful.

What would that nine-year-old girl think of all this?

June gave herself a mental shake. She had the security she'd always wanted. Where was this sudden longing for her old creative life coming from?

It was only boredom talking. What the hell had David done with her laptop?

She made her way to his office, sat at the mahogany desk, and turned on his massive desktop computer with the double screens. June wasn't supposed to be working; she had permission not to be working—*doctor's orders*—and yet, she didn't know how to shut it off. All her adult life, June had gone into the office early, stayed late, and once the girls were born and had to be picked up from daycare by six, answered emails after bedtime when other moms were probably binge-watching Netflix.

And lately, the more she accomplished, the more there was to do, like a whirlpool churning her round and round and never sending her back to shore. Yet here was a life raft offering a reprieve, and she couldn't even reach out her hand and take it.

As the computer monitor powered on, a window popped up on the screen with a list of names and messages. David liked to use messaging apps, and she was staring right at his texting history with Priya.

A memory of the two of them standing shoulder to shoulder in her hospital room flashed in her head, and a the same feeling of dread washed over her. June clicked over to David's online calendar and checked Thursday morning. Sure enough, 10 a.m. to noon was blank.

They'd said they'd been in meetings all morning, and David was meticulous about updating his calendar.

Before she could change her mind, June clicked back to David's texts and scrolled up a couple of months. At first, the messages appeared to be professional: Priya reminding David of his appointments, and suggesting he ask about a client's kids or compliment someone on their golf game. Little things to make David look attentive, and make the client feel special. But then the comments became more personal.

Why don't I take you for dinner on Tuesday?
You look great in that color.
Couldn't concentrate on the meeting with you in the room.

And then, there it was. That trip to Chicago when David didn't want her tagging along, even though it was their anniversary. He'd said he'd be too busy working to have any fun. Priya had gone, though. And texted David her hotel room number at midnight, along with a very detailed description of what she was—or more accurately, *wasn't*—wearing.

Head throbbing, June shut down the computer and limped into the kitchen to find her phone. Before she could think about it, she texted David the most straightforward question she'd asked in a long time.

Are you and Priya having an affair?

For once, David wrote back immediately.

Where is this coming from?

Are you?

I think we should discuss this when I get home tonight.

June's head snapped back from the phone, sending another shot of pain through it, and a wave of vertigo overtook her. He didn't deny it. If he wasn't having an affair, he would have said so. She gripped the phone in her shaking hand and managed to type out—

I read the texts on your computer.

A gray ellipsis popped up, indicating David was writing a response. June held her breath. And, finally—

Are you serious?

June leaned on the counter for support. Her head pounded and her body ached all the way down to her bones.

Are you in love with her?

She stared at the screen, watching as one minute and then two minutes ticked by on the clock. No response. The longer she stood there with the silent phone in her hand, the more her anger and shock began to dissipate, supplanted by another emotion entirely.

Fear.

What have I done? By confronting David like this, she may as well have poured gasoline on her life and lit a match. What if he came home and said he was leaving? Or wanted a divorce? What would she do? And what about the girls?

Fix this, a little voice in the back of her head whispered. *Hold together the safe, secure life you've worked so hard to build.*

But she didn't know how. And then came the text that imploded it all.

Yes.

And a moment later, another one.

We have a lot to talk about. I'll be home in a few hours.

June sank to the cold tile floor as a freight train roared in her ears. Was this really happening? Nineteen years of doing everything right, of supporting David while he launched his business—*giving up my own dreams,* a tiny, bitter voice whispered—being the perfect wife and mother, only to have it all come crashing down over some text messages.

When June's phone rang a minute later, she jumped and automatically answered it.

"Ms. Westwood," came a male voice. "This is Will Valencia from the law firm of Valencia and King."

Had David hired divorce lawyers already? But no, it would've been impossible for him to move that quickly.

"I'm calling to follow up on our conversation from last Thursday," the voice continued. "About your father's estate."

"My father…" June pressed her hands to her forehead. There must be a mistake. "I'm sorry, I don't understand."

The man paused. "Is this June Westwood? We spoke last Thursday about your father's estate."

Last Thursday—that was the day of her accident. June closed her eyes as a memory she couldn't quite grasp flitted around her consciousness. *A windshield blurred by washer fluid.* Was that what had caused the accident?

Suddenly she remembered. "Jasper Luc," she gasped. This man had claimed Jasper Luc, the renowned contemporary artist, was *her father.* How had she forgotten this conversation?

"That's right." The attorney spoke slowly. "Jasper left you most of his estate. There's a house outside of Seattle, his studio, and a number of paintings. I haven't been able to reach your sisters yet…"

Will Valencia kept talking, but June didn't hear another word. The hard tile of the floor dug into her tailbone and the edge of a drawer jabbed her spine as she slumped back against the cabinets. Her father was gone. Forever. She'd never know what she'd done to make him leave her.

There had to be something wrong with her. Why else would everyone leave her? It started with her father, but then her mother had checked out, and even her sisters were too busy to call her. And now David.

With that thought, June froze.

David would be on his way home soon. To talk to her about the affair he'd been having with his secretary. The secretary he'd just admitted he was in love with. David owned the company where she worked, he took care of all their finances. If their marriage was over, would he be reasonable and fair about it, or would he fight her for everything? He was ruthless at work when he was competing for a client's business; would he be the same in a divorce? She'd always gone along with it, grateful for the life he'd offered and grateful not to end up perpetually struggling like her mother. Grateful to be with a steady, reliable man who'd never leave her like her father once did. And now David held all the power.

Except—

"I'm sorry. Did you say there's a house? In Seattle?" What was she thinking, even considering this? Yet, as the idea took shape in her head, her heart rate slowly returned to its normal, steady rhythm. What would it be like to get away from everything? And everyone? Just for a little while?

It wasn't only the accident, or the affair. It was this vague sense of dissatisfaction that had seeped into her life, like smoke from a dive bar, over the past few months; maybe even the past few years. This feeling that there had to be more to life than shuttling the girls from activity to activity, rushing off to a job that gave her less and less joy, and coming home to a husband who had nothing to say to her.

The girls weren't babies anymore, and thanks to her supporting him for the past decade, David's business was a success. But where did it leave her? A cliché of the dissatisfied wife wandering around a cold, empty house while her husband was sleeping with his secretary.

If she had to stay in that house another day, had to see David's cheating face telling her how he wanted things to go, she was going to lose it.

"The property is about two hours north of Seattle, in a town called Wishing Cove," the attorney said.

"And it belongs to me and my sisters? We can go there whenever we want?" June's mind raced with everything she'd have to do in a couple of short hours. Could she get it all done, with a fractured collarbone and a concussion?

"Technically, yes. There's some paperwork, and I'd have to get you the keys. You can fly into Bellingham, it's about twenty minutes south-east of Wishing Cove. If you let me know when you want to come, I can make the arrangements. A couple of weeks should be enough—"

June cut him off. "Tomorrow."

"Did you say *tomorrow*?"

"Yes, my daughters and I will arrive tomorrow. Is this the best number to reach you? I'll let you know our flight time."

CHAPTER FIVE

Caleb closed the door to the studio and stepped out onto the gravel path, flipping up the hood of his sweatshirt to protect himself from the cold drizzle pricking his skin. Across the bay, gray clouds stretched to the horizon. What time was it? He couldn't remember the last time he'd eaten or taken his meds. Had he worked all day without looking up?

More than anything, he relied on regular routines—sleep, meals, reasonable work hours with breaks—to keep his mood stable. He and his therapist had spent hours talking about it. *Social rhythms therapy*, Emily had said.

As soon as the news had broken about Jasper, Emily had called him. But he'd let the call go to voicemail. He wasn't ready to discuss his feelings about Jasper's death, or to listen to the same platitudes his mother and brother had been giving him.

There was nothing you could have done.

Rationally, Caleb knew it was nobody's fault. Jasper had been sick with pneumonia a few weeks before his death, and hadn't been sleeping. From the investigator's initial report, they suspected the three sleeping pills he'd been prescribed had interacted with his mood stabilizers and stopped his heart in his sleep.

But who knew better than Caleb how important it was to monitor medications? He should have paid more attention, asked more questions; especially if he knew Jasper was exhausted and not thinking straight. Over the years, he and Jasper had developed an unspoken agreement to look out for each other. Few people understood the struggles of living with mental illness, so in a way, he and Jasper had become their own little misfit family.

It was easier that way. They respected each other's art, checked in if one of them was having an episode, and didn't judge beyond that. Jasper was the only person in Caleb's life he *hadn't* hurt or let down.

Until Jasper had needed him the most.

Caleb staggered up the hill to his house, gulped down his pills with a glass of water, and fell into bed.

When he woke, the sun was shining. He glanced at his phone but ignored the missed calls and voicemails from Will. He'd call his brother back later, after a shower and breakfast.

Caleb made a cup of tea—he tried to limit his caffeine intake—and carried the mug outside to the deck. The fog and rain from the day before had drifted out to sea, leaving behind a couple of fat white clouds in an otherwise clear blue sky, and the crisp outline of fir trees seemed even sharper against the shimmering water. For the first time since he'd been knocked on his ass by Jasper's death a week earlier, Caleb's haze dissipated. He'd drive into town to buy some groceries and, later, spend a few hours in the studio. Back on routine. Everything would be fine.

But as Caleb just happened to glance across the meadow toward the main house, the mug jerked in his hand, sloshing tea over the side. An unfamiliar car was parked in the driveway. After Jasper's death hit the news, Will had hired an art appraiser to assess the contents of the studio. One of the art world's best was ready to fly in and take everything to climate-controlled storage as soon as Will got hold of Jasper's daughters. He'd also hired a security guard to watch the estate's front gate, knowing reporters and rabid fans would show up, looking for a story or a small piece of the late artist's legacy. Flowers and artwork had started piling up on the shoulder of Pinecrest Drive in tribute but, so far, the guard had kept everyone at bay.

So, who was the owner of the SUV parked in the driveway?

Caleb spun around, to look toward the studio down the hill. He and Will had triple-locked the door, but now that door—to Jasper's side of the studio—hung open.

A shot of adrenaline exploded in Caleb's chest. He dropped his mug and took off down the hill. With each thump of his shoes on the gravel path, another burst of rage mixed with fear pumped through his veins. What if it was a thief trying to steal Jasper's paintings? Or worse, a vandal destroying everything? Even a fan who only wanted a look might touch a canvas with dirty hands, spill paint, drop something.

Those paintings were all that was left of Jasper. Caleb would do anything to protect them.

Caleb burst through the doorway and stopped short at the sight of a woman standing in the middle of the room with her arms wrapped around herself, staring at a canvas propped on an easel. The woman's wide, stunned blue eyes jerked from the painting to his face. Her expression shifted from shock to fear.

She'd better be afraid.

He took a step toward her. "Who the hell are you, and how did you get in here?"

The woman looked around wildly, and then scurried to the corner and grabbed a broom propped there. "Who are *you*? Don't come any closer." She pointed the stick at him as if brandishing a sword.

Caleb was about to take another step toward her when he registered the waver in her voice. Sweat beads had broken out on her pale forehead and a sling covered her left arm. She was injured. And clearly terrified. He caught a glimpse of his reflection in the windows behind her. His unwashed hair stuck out in messy spikes, the days-old stubble on his face had turned into a full-grown beard, and his paint-splattered clothes were wrinkled from at least one day of wear and twelve hours of sleep. He looked homeless—a portrait he was all too familiar with—and it wouldn't surprise him if he smelled like he was back to living on the street again, too.

He held up his hands, backing away from her slowly. "I'm not going to touch you. But if you don't get out of here right now, I'm going to call the cops."

The woman shocked him by standing up to her full height, taking a step toward him, and waving the broom. "If *you* don't get out of here, *I'm* going to call the cops."

Caleb let out a half-laugh, half-snort at her audacity. "Listen. I don't know who you are or what right you think you have to be in here, but I live here. I worked with Jasper for close to twenty years. Maybe you think you're Jasper's biggest fan or some bullshit, but let me be the one to tell you they *all* think they're Jasper's biggest fan." He waved his hand at the canvases lined up against the walls. "I'll do anything to keep these paintings safe. So why don't you walk out of here before there's any trouble."

As he spoke, the woman slowly lowered the broom. She leaned her forehead against the palm of her hand and took a deep, shuddering breath. "Oh my God, you're the protégé or whatever the lawyer called you. The apprentice."

He stared at her for a second, taking in this new development. "The lawyer? You know *Will*?"

"Yes. He told me about you. You live here and worked with my—worked with Jasper." Now that his shock at finding an intruder had begun to wane, Caleb saw Jasper's eerily pale blue eyes staring back at him.

Oh, shit.

"I have to admit, I wasn't expecting someone so—" she waved her hand at him but didn't finish her thought. With his unkempt appearance, Caleb could only imagine what she was going to say.

She shivered. "I thought you were a robber."

"You're one of the daughters." Caleb took in her forest-green flats, dark-wash jeans, and cream-colored cashmere sweater. *The accountant.* "You're Juniper."

"June," she blurted out so quickly, Caleb suspected it was a reflex. "We arrived early this morning. Will picked us up at the airport and had a rental car delivered."

He should have paid more attention to his brother's voicemails. But he'd seen Will recently, and he hadn't said anything about June coming to Wishing Cove. "Well, June, you sure move fast."

She blinked at him and shoved a lock of her hair out of her face. That hair was the same dark brown, almost black, as Jasper's. "Excuse me?"

"When did you arrange all this with Will?"

"Yesterday afternoon."

"And here you are today."

She hesitated, giving him the side-eye as if she were trying to figure out where he was going with this.

"Will told you about your inheritance. All these paintings are yours now. That must have gotten you pretty excited. They're worth a lot of money." A rabid fan breaking in would be better than this woman. At least a fan would care about Jasper's art.

"I'm aware they're valuable," she snapped, sounding every bit like a prim accountant.

"Oh, I bet you are." He'd been afraid of this. The daughters were only interested in the money. Why else would June show up this quickly, and make tracks directly for the studio? Had she even peeked into the house, or taken a second to admire the view? "So, you figured you'd fly out, grab the artwork, and cash it all in?"

"What? *No!*"

"Listen, I know you didn't have a relationship with your father, so maybe this doesn't have the same meaning for you as it has for me. But these paintings aren't some gold coins you can sell on eBay. They're cultural artifacts. You owe it to Jasper to take your time, make sure they're appraised properly. If you're planning to sell them, it shouldn't be to the highest bidder, but to museums or universities where they can be preserved and appreciated by everyone."

June's mouth dropped open and she straightened her spine. "First of all, I understand that Jasper was one of the pioneers of modern photorealism, and that his technique of using layers and barriers to disorient the viewer launched a whole movement—I am not some moron who would pack up Jasper Luc's paintings and sell them on eBay. And, for your information, I'm not even here for the paintings."

Caleb took a step back in surprise and, for a second, all he could do was stare. He'd seen pictures of June over the years, and had vaguely considered her attractive, not really thinking about it much one way or the other. He damn sure hadn't been expecting the woman in front of him. Now that June was no longer afraid, she faced him head-on, glaring defiantly as two pink splotches bloomed on her pale cheeks. The twist of annoyance on her face only emphasized her full lips and, inexplicably, his heart rattled against his sternum as her pale, angry eyes met his.

And then her words about Jasper's work sank in. Maybe she knew more about art than he'd given her credit for. That had him even more intrigued.

"Second of all," June continued, oblivious to the strange effect she was having on him. "The reason I didn't have a relationship with Jasper was his choice, not mine. I understand from your brother you were the son Jasper never had. Well, I was a daughter he *did* have and didn't bother with. So, I disagree that I owe Jasper Luc a damn thing."

"Wait a minute—"

She cut him off. "Now, if you'll excuse me." She took three furious steps past him toward the door before all of a sudden stopping short.

Standing with her back to him, she wavered, lifting the arm encased in the sling to the side of her head, and reaching out blindly with the other hand for something to grab on to. "Oh God," she muttered under her breath.

In two steps, he was standing next to her, reaching out to grasp her good arm and steady her. "Are you okay?"

For a second, she leaned into him, squeezing her eyes shut and breathing heavily. He wrapped an arm around her, pulling her against his chest and catching a whiff of vanilla. "Let's find you somewhere to sit."

June's eyes flew open and met his. Before he could react, she wrenched away from him and stumbled back into the middle of the room. "I'm sorry. I'm recovering from a minor accident and I sometimes get a little... dizzy." All traces of color had drained from her face.

"Can I walk you up to the house?"

A flash of what might have been surprise moved across her face before she smoothed it away. "No. Thank you. I can make it on my own." She shuffled toward the exit and stopped in the doorway, leaning against the frame. "I guess if you live on the property, I'll be seeing you around. I assume you can lock up here?"

Caleb nodded.

June stood up straight as color began to seep back into her cheeks. "Okay, well." That prim voice was back. "We'll have to do our best to stay out of each other's way." Before he could answer, she turned, more carefully this time, and marched out of the studio.

Caleb watched her walk past the window and turn onto the path leading to the main house. When she stepped out of view, he turned back to the studio, picking up the discarded broom from the middle of the floor and placing it back in the corner. Then he took a sweeping look at Jasper's paintings. For a second, he was tempted to dig through the stack of work Jasper had left. To search for—what?

A sign? A message?

Caleb shook his head. Those paintings belonged to June and her sisters. There were no hidden clues for him within their brush strokes, and nothing that would bring his mentor back. Nothing that would lift this heavy weight of guilt that pressed on him, reminding him every hour of every day that he could have prevented this.

No, he'd just have to learn to live with it.

Caleb picked up a heavy drop cloth from the folded stack on the shelf and gently draped it over several paintings to protect them from dust. Then he capped a couple of tubes of paint Jasper had left open on the table, and placed two brushes in a tray by the sink. When he was satisfied everything was as organized as it could be, he locked up the studio.

As he hiked up the path, his gaze drifted across the meadow toward the opposite trail leading to Jasper's house, and his thoughts turned back to June. She'd said she wasn't there for the paintings.

So, why *was* she there?

And, more importantly, when was she leaving?

CHAPTER SIX

June stomped up the porch steps of Jasper Luc's house and flung herself into a wicker chair. The walk up the hill had done nothing to tamp down the swirl of emotions that had kicked up like dust on the gravel path following her encounter with the apprentice, or protégé, or whoever that insufferable man was to her estranged father.

Caleb.

She certainly hadn't been expecting *him* when Will Valencia picked them up at the airport in his shiny black Mercedes and mentioned his brother lived on the property. Will had a type of pulled-together, movie star good looks—tailored suit and tie; short, dark hair combed back off his face; intense copper eyes; and slightly cocky smile set against perfect, golden brown, clean-shaven skin—which, after a long night on a plane with very little sleep, had momentarily left her tongue-tied.

No, Caleb had looked like he'd escaped from an institution and was there to rob her. Will said they were identical twins, but she hadn't even recognized Caleb with those dirty, rumpled clothes, that scraggly beard, and the dark circles under his eyes. And as he stood there yelling at her while his too-long hair slid out of the elastic band at the base of his neck... could anyone have blamed her for grabbing a broom and swinging at him?

When he'd finally calmed down long enough to have a conversation—if you could call hurling insults at her a conver-sation—he'd still been a total jerk. Accusing her of caring only about the money. Suggesting she was too dumb to take proper care of Jasper's paintings.

She gazed past the flowers in the meadow to the pine- and fir-covered islands dotting the bay. She hadn't asked for any of this. Not Jasper's house, or his land, or his paintings.

But, God—what she would have given to know her father.

June glanced at her phone and saw the time was a little after nine; the sunlight bounced off the screen and made her wince. The girls had been so excited about the impromptu adventure she'd sprung on them they hadn't slept a wink on the plane. Instead, they'd charmed the flight attendants into giving them extra orange juice and cookies, and embarked on a cartoon marathon.

On the drive from the airport to Jasper's house, the girls had finally crashed. Will—charming man that he was—had helped her to make the queen bed in one of the guest rooms and carry the girls upstairs. He'd apologized on three different occasions because he hadn't had time to hire someone to come in to clean and get the house ready for them.

Sitting outside on the porch now, June knew she should go inside, figure out where she was going to sleep, and take a look around the house. If they were really staying for a while, she ought to make herself at home. But something held her back. It felt invasive to creep around the house of a complete stranger, even if he did share her genetic material. So, she'd ended up wandering down to the studio. She'd only planned to peek in through the windows, but the keys were on the ring Will had given her, and curiosity had pulled her hand to the lock.

And, suddenly, right in front of her on a wooden easel, had been a real, honest-to-God Jasper Luc. Not hanging, unapproachable, in a cold museum, but warm, vibrant, and alive with the sun slanting across it and a tube of what was possibly the last paint color Jasper Luc would ever brush onto a canvas lying open on the stool next to it. She'd capped the paint tube, shoved it in her pocket and quickly backed away from the painting. For one intense second, she'd felt… something. A tiny thread running from her to that canvas, connecting her to her father. He'd left this beautiful painting, all these beautiful paintings, to her. And then that man had burst in, and as quickly as the feeling came, it disappeared.

Caleb had said he'd worked with Jasper for twenty years. *Twenty years.*

Twenty years ago, she'd loved painting with a passion that sometimes left her breathless. If Jasper Luc—her father—had shown up on her doorstep and asked her to come and work as his apprentice, it would have meant *everything.*

What would it have been like to spend the past twenty years talking about light and shadow and brushstrokes with Jasper? To see that smile he used to direct at her childish crayon drawings light up with pride for her first real art show? But, instead, her father had chosen Caleb as the object of his focus and attention and pride. And she'd spent the past twenty years building other people's—her sisters', her husband's, even her children's—dreams.

June ran her fingers underneath her eyes and wiped away the tears threatening to spill over. She wasn't a kid anymore, and her father had left three decades ago. This ache in her chest was only exhaustion from the accident, the long flight, and the lack of sleep. But it was time to pull herself together. What if the girls came outside and found her like this?

June's phone buzzed in her lap, and she looked down to find a thumbs-up from David, his response to her message that they'd arrived in Wishing Cove.

Yesterday, after she'd hurried to pack suitcases for her and the girls, June had called David and told him she was taking the girls on a vacation to the Pacific Northwest. To be honest, she'd expected him to argue, but he'd been remarkably calm about the whole thing.

It occurred to June that with her and the girls out of the way, David could do whatever he wanted right out in the open. Her chest ached at the thought. Never in a million years had she imagined her marriage ending like this. Or at all. Maybe she and David never had the kind of wild passion you read about in novels, but they'd treated each other, and their marriage vows, with respect. Or so she'd always thought.

At some point soon, she'd have to tell David about Jasper, and to deal with all of this. But now wasn't the time. She was going on more than twenty-four hours without sleep and wasn't in the mood for another contentious conversation with an unpleasant man.

With that thought, her phone buzzed. *Raven.* She quickly swiped to answer. Raven, her youngest sister, was someone June most definitely *did* want to have a conversation with.

"Raven? I can't believe you called back so quickly." June tried to tamp down her irritation over all the times her sister hadn't called her back.

"Of course!" Raven's voice mingled with all sorts of background noises buzzing through the phone's tiny speaker.

"Raven! Where *are* you? Tell me you're not calling from a war zone."

"No, I'm in Senegal, actually. I'm shooting a story on fashion, if you can believe it. Dakar is the Paris of West Africa."

"What is all the noise?"

"Train station."

"Ah, okay." June sighed in relief.

"I'm calling because I got three really weird messages in the last week. Some dude talking about Jasper Luc. You know, the artist?" Raven's voice faded as the loud squeal of what June could only imagine was a train braking pierced her eardrum.

So that explained why Raven had called her back right away. She'd gotten Will's messages. Raven never called her back this quickly just to check in and talk about the girls.

"But in the last message—no, I don't need a new phone!" Raven's voice drifted in and out as she seemed to be holding a side conversation with someone trying to sell her something. "I'm *holding* a phone, see? Sorry, Junie. Anyway. The guy said something about an inheritance. Is this some sort of scam? Is someone going to ask me to wire them a million dollars?"

From the corner of her eye, June spotted movement down by the studio. She watched as Caleb stepped outside, pulled the door shut behind him, and checked all the locks. From this distance, his clothes didn't look as bad as they did up close. They fit his tall, lean frame at least. And maybe they weren't actually dirty. Now that she thought about it, he *was* an artist. It was possible those smudges were paint.

How could she explain all this to her sister when she was half a world away? "It's not a scam."

"Okay, so…"

"Jasper Luc died last week. Apparently, he was our father. He left us… some things."

The phone went silent. Her sister didn't speak a word, and it almost seemed as if the trains and vendors peddling phones in the background paused to let the news sink in, too. Finally, Raven's voice, muted this time, came through. "June, seriously, this is a joke, right? Jasper Luc? Where did you even come up with that?"

For the first time since her accident, June had an inexplicable urge to laugh. She wished she'd come up with this story. She wished she could go back to last week when she was rushing to catch her flight to New Orleans and had crashed her car, learned her husband was cheating, and ended up with a dead father. She wished instead that she'd pulled off one of those *Sliding Doors* moments and gotten on the plane, and her life went on as usual.

"Raven, I swear I'm not making this up."

"*Jasper Luc* was really our father? Did Mom know?"

"I don't know, actually. Everything has happened so fast, I haven't had a chance to call her."

"What did he leave us? Like a painting or something?"

"Um, yes, he left us a painting." It was probably best to rip off the Band-Aid. "Sort of… all the paintings. And a house, and some land, and his studio in Wishing Cove."

"Are you serious?" Raven screeched along with another train pulling into the station.

"I'm sitting on Jasper's porch right now. Or I guess it's *our* porch, which is so weird. Raven, you should see it here." June's gaze skimmed across the estate to the studio at the edge of the cliff. She deliberately avoided looking in the direction of Caleb's gray clapboard house on the opposite hill, where he was now sipping from a mug on the back deck. "I peeked in Jasper's studio this morning, and it was amazing."

"You're *there*? With David and the girls?"

"No, just the girls. David—uh—had to work." This wasn't the time to get into it. "Listen, Raven. Is there any chance you could come here? The estate—there's a lot to sort through…" June trailed off, suddenly exhausted. It was probably pointless to ask her sister to fly in all the way from—where did she say? Senegal? Raven had already canceled on them twice this year when she couldn't say no to an assignment.

"How long are you staying?" Raven asked.

June had no idea; she and David needed to discuss it. "A while. For the summer maybe." That just popped out. She definitely hadn't discussed the whole *summer* with David.

"Well, maybe I could come next month. After this Senegal assignment, I'm supposed to head to Kenya and—"

"*Next month?*" June interrupted, standing up and pacing across the porch. "Surely there's someone else who can stand in? Just this once."

"I'm a freelance photographer. If I say no, the editors will stop asking me, and move on to the next guy."

"But you never say no." June leaned against the porch railing. She was *not* going to feel guilty because, for once, she wanted to be more important than Raven's next assignment.

A tiny, petty part of June wanted to point out that Raven wouldn't even be in high demand if it weren't for June's support—from her first accounting job—back when Raven was struggling to make a name for herself as a photographer. And Sierra might not have found success as an author without June's help paying for rent and the other expenses that her undergraduate creative writing program scholarships hadn't covered.

But June would never say that to her sisters. It wasn't Sierra's and Raven's fault their mother had checked out, leaving the burden on June. And deep down—in normal times—she didn't really resent the sacrifices she'd made. But at that moment, June was just... exhausted. "Please, Raven. I really need you."

Raven sighed. "I'll try to work it out and be there soon."

"Try hard, okay?"

"I said I will," Raven said, an edge creeping into her voice.

June backed off. "I appreciate it."

"Listen, don't touch anything in the studio. I want to take some photos first. Of how Jasper left it."

That was classic Raven. The world would cease to exist if it wasn't properly documented by her camera. Was that why she'd agreed come? Because she saw an opportunity to take photos of something special? June shook off the negative thoughts. Raven had agreed to come, it didn't matter why.

Suddenly, the idea of her dazzling, energetic baby sister blowing in like a warm breeze off the ocean filled June with a sense of excitement she'd been missing. Raven would tell outrageous stories about her exploits all over the world, chase the girls around and make them laugh, and curl up on the couch for a chat.

It occurred to June she'd been lonelier than she realized. She and David spent long hours at the office, and when they talked, it was usually about work or the girls. She'd never really made a lot of close friends in Greenwich. The working moms at the girls' school were too busy to meet up, and the stay-at-home moms got together while she was at work.

The loud screech of another train brought June back to her phone call.

"I've got to go." Raven's voice reverberated above the din. "This is my train."

As they said their goodbyes, June couldn't quite ignore her twinge of envy at Raven's freedom to pick up and go anywhere she wanted at a moment's notice; to follow the next big story or her latest creative whim without having to worry about anyone but herself.

June shook her head. This trip to Wishing Cove was the most spontaneous thing she'd ever done. Maybe it would be a new beginning, a step closer to finding the kind of life she wanted, on her own terms, just like her sisters had.

She sent Sierra a text. *Call me. Very important.* Hopefully, she could convince her middle sister to fly in while Raven was here. It had been so long since the three of them were in the same place.

Filled with renewed energy, June hopped up off the wicker chair and headed inside to take stock of the sleeping situation. And to look for coffee. God, she hoped Jasper had left some coffee. She paused in the doorway and glanced back over her shoulder at Caleb lounging on his deck, mug in hand. Perhaps she'd overreacted when she'd swung the broom at his head. How bad would it be to slink over there and beg for a cup?

As if he sensed her gaze, Caleb turned his head in her direction. She knew he was looking at her by the way her body reacted; the same way it had reacted when he'd grasped her arm and pulled her against his chest to steady her. Hot followed by cold, with a fuzziness in her brain that had nothing to do with her concussion.

June quickly looked away and ducked into the house. She didn't need coffee that badly.

CHAPTER SEVEN

After a quick shower, Caleb stepped out onto his deck where he found two freckled little girls fishing a lost soccer ball from under the bushes below. They stared up at him with wide blue eyes that looked exactly like their mother's. And exactly like the man who'd been like a father to him for almost twenty years. Those eyes tore at his insides.

"Hello," the girl in the green T-shirt said in a loud, clear voice.

The other girl, this one in blue, grabbed her sister's arm. "Emma," she whispered. "Mommy said not to bother him."

"We're not bothering you, right?" Emma looked at him without flinching, almost as if she were daring him to disagree with her.

Caleb sighed. "Not yet."

"See?" Emma gave her sister an exaggerated shrug. "We're not bothering him." She turned back to Caleb. "I'm Emma, I'm seven. And this is my sister Izzy, she's six. What's your name?"

Caleb eyed the girls. "Didn't your mother tell you?"

"No." Emma shook her head and her ringlets bounced like hundreds of tiny springs. "But she did say you were in-suff-er-a-ble when she thought we weren't listening. What does insufferable mean?"

Caleb pressed his lips together to hide his smile. "It means charming and handsome." He crouched down to their level. "My name is Caleb. What are you two doing here?"

"We're on vacation." Emma seemed to be the talkative one.

"How long are you staying?" It was shameful, he knew, pumping these innocent little girls for information about their mother's plans. But it wasn't like he could ask her. She might try to bash his head in with another broom.

"Mommy says for the whole summer."

Caleb's muscles stiffened. *The whole summer?* He had to put up with them for the whole summer? June lurking around Jasper's studio, watching him from the front porch, shooting glares across the meadow?

Distracting him with the curve of her mouth.

No, this was never going to work. He needed to get her out of there. "Doesn't your mom have to get back to work?"

Izzy shook her head. "Mommy was in a car accident, so she can't work."

So that explained the sling, and the dizzy spell in the studio. Maybe it also explained what she meant when she said she wasn't there for the paintings. Maybe she was there to recover from her accident. But that didn't mean she was completely off the hook for heading straight to Jasper's studio when she arrived. He'd withhold judgment until he saw what she decided to do with the paintings.

Caleb saw movement by the side of the house and stood up as the woman in question came into view.

"Emma, Izzy, there you are. I told you not to bother Mr. Caleb." The sun glinted off her long, dark hair, showing off her fancy salon highlights. The girls' hair was as wild as Jasper's had been, but June's didn't hold even a tiny wave. The curls must have skipped a generation.

"He says we're not bothering him, Mommy." Emma turned to him with her arms crossed. "Tell her we're not bothering you."

"They're not bothering me," Caleb blurted, holding his hands up in mock surrender.

June's lips quirked. He tried not to stare.

Crimson Lake mixed with Cadmium Orange and a touch of Titanium Zinc White.

She turned to give him an appraising look, and he could almost feel her gaze sweep over him, taking in his clean pair of jeans, T-shirt, and recently washed hair waving around his ears. Suddenly he was glad he'd shaved and thrown on something other than his usual paint-spattered work clothes.

He didn't know why he cared.

"Girls, we should go. I want to run into town and find a grocery store."

"Actually, that's where I'm headed now. I could drive you." The words were out of his mouth before he thought about what he was saying.

From the way June's body stiffened, his offer had left her equally surprised. What was he thinking, suggesting they ride into town together? Now, instead of going their separate ways, they'd be spending half the afternoon together. If June and the girls were really going to spend the summer here, it was even more reason to shut this down now, and establish clear boundaries.

He had an important gallery show this fall and his latest painting was a disaster. The light, the movement, none of it was right. Every time he tried to work on it, a million distractions poured in his head like water from a broken dam, sweeping his focus downstream.

Jasper. The estate. Will stopping by every goddamn day to check on him, wanting to talk. His mother calling to ask if he'd seen his therapist lately—trying to casually slip it into conversation, like he couldn't see what she was doing from a mile away.

Thinking about it now started those familiar gears cranking in his head. He needed time alone and space to focus. Not two little girls and their mother hanging around thinking they were friends.

Before he could come up with a way to back-pedal, June blew out a breath and nodded. "That would be really great." She straightened the sling on her injured arm and looked like she was about to say something else, but stopped.

Well, he was stuck now. Better get it over with. "Let me grab a few things. I'll meet you on the driveway in five?"

Seven minutes later, Emma and Izzy were strapped into their booster seats in the back of his Jeep, each clutching a ratty pink bunny. As their mother slid into the seat next to him, Caleb noticed June had a tiny dusting of freckles across her nose that didn't match her expensive hairstyle or Connecticut-lady-who-lunches clothing.

Caleb cleared his throat and started the car. Those freckles, and that mouth… they were exactly why he shouldn't be driving her places.

As he eased the car onto Pinecrest Drive in the direction of town, the pink bunnies in the backseat struck up a conversation in Emma and Izzy's little girl voices. June stared out her window at a grove of trees, pressing her forehead to the glass and craning her neck to look upward. Then she shifted, leaning forward to watch the ocean slide past. "God, it's so beautiful here."

"Is this your first time in the Pacific Northwest?"

"Yes. I grew up in Philly and went to college in Connecticut. I'm embarrassed to say that except for my honeymoon in Italy, I've never left the east coast."

"What about vacations?" She seemed like the kind of woman who took expensive holidays.

"My husband—" She paused, and Caleb wondered if she'd lost her train of thought. Maybe a result of the accident the girls had mentioned. "Um," June finally continued, "my—David's family has a beach house in Nantucket, so we end up spending most of our vacations there. David always thought it was easier to go somewhere comfortable and familiar since neither of us are able to take much time away from work."

"The girls mentioned you've taken off for the whole summer. How'd you pull that off?"

"Doctor's orders. I had a concussion and I'm not supposed to stare at a computer screen. David owns the business."

If her husband owned the business, why couldn't he get the time off to travel somewhere she wanted to go? Or come out to Wishing Cove with her? Caleb gave a shake of his head. He didn't know anything about their situation, and he didn't want to.

"You've finally made it to the Pacific Northwest, so maybe the accident was life's way of telling you to slow down."

"Yeah. Maybe." June's mouth turned up into a smile as she watched the trees flying past. She'd been giving him wary looks since their encounter in Jasper's studio, but with that smile, an unexpected warmth filled his chest.

"What about you?" June asked. "Are you from around here?"

"I'm not really from anywhere." He shrugged. "My mom grew up outside of San Francisco, and my dad came to the US from Spain for medical school. My parents met at Stanford."

Caleb clicked on his signal to turn onto a smaller road leading them into the area of town with the grocery store. "They're surgeons who spent most of Will's and my childhood working all over the country, filling in as temporary physicians when there were shortages. Usually in poor, rural areas, so Will and I grew up in places like Meade, Oklahoma and Spring Bluff, Alabama."

"It's a good thing you had a built-in friend in Will, with all the moving around," June said.

"Yeah, I was lucky to have Will." He still was, even if sometimes he didn't want to admit it. "I'd never lived in one place for longer than two years until I came to work as Jasper's apprentice. I've been here for almost twenty years now." He could sense June looking at him, sizing him up.

"So, Jasper was—what? Your mentor, or something?"

Caleb nodded. "I was a lost kid in need of direction." An understatement. "He gave me a job and he helped me to focus, to find my perspective as an artist."

"So, how did he pick you out of the long line of young artists who would've killed for that gig? Did you send him a portfolio?"

"No, I met Jasper at one of his shows."

"Oh." June blinked. "But there must have been a reason he chose you, right? Does your work lean toward contemporary realism too, or…" She trailed off.

"Abstract."

"Really?" June bit her lip. "So, why do you think he—"

Caleb stopped at a red light and turned to look at her. "Jasper and I had a lot in common." As soon as he said it, he realized his mistake. She'd want to know what he and her father had in common. But telling Jasper's story meant revealing his own.

"Yeah? Like what?" There was a gravel to her voice that hinted at pain underneath. And suddenly it occurred to him that maybe what she really wanted to know was why Jasper picked him, *instead of her*.

Caleb opened his mouth to respond, but he closed it again. What could he say? How could he tell her that Jasper left her because she deserved better, and picked him because he didn't? "Nothing. Forget I said anything."

She shifted in her seat. "Please? I have so few memories of him. It would be nice to understand a little more about my father and the people who were important to him after he left us." June twisted the strap of her purse in her hands.

The naked longing on her face tugged at Caleb's heart, but he did his best to shrug it off. *She's fine.* Married and well-off with two adorable children. Growing up without a father hadn't seemed to do any long-term damage, and from what he could tell, her sisters were doing okay, too.

Of course, he knew better than anyone that what you saw on the surface didn't always reflect what was underneath.

June watched him, clearly waiting for an answer. The girls chattered in the backseat, but it didn't mask the silence echoing through the front.

Finally, June gave him a wry smile. "Well, I hope that whatever you had in common with Jasper, it wasn't that you picked up and left your family behind!" From the lilt of her voice, he knew she meant it as a joke, to lighten the mood. But the statement slammed into him like a wrecking ball and, for a second, left him breathless.

Goddamn it, he'd been fine up until now. Well, not fine, but… okay. He hadn't been overcome by this suffocating guilt over all the ways he'd destroyed everyone who'd cared about him in *years*. And now he couldn't stop these thoughts from tearing through his head.

June stared at him, probably wondering why he looked like he wanted to puke. "Oh, I didn't mean to imply—I just meant—"

"Green light!" a voice screeched from the backseat.

Caleb jumped and shifted his body to face the front of the car. He pressed the gas and turned into the parking lot of the grocery store. "Why don't we do our own thing and meet back here in half an hour?" he said, after he'd eased the car into a spot.

Caleb hopped out of the car, but before he could head into the store, the passenger door opened and closed.

"Caleb, wait," June called to him, rounding the front of the Jeep and stopping in front of him. "I'm sorry. Back there, I didn't mean to—it was a very bad joke. I figured you were young when you came to work with Jasper, you probably didn't have a wife or kids… not like Jasper did before he came here…"

"I didn't." It came out more harshly than he intended, and June took a startled step backwards. "I didn't have a wife." Not by the time he came to Wishing Cove. The knife twisted in his gut.

"I'm just trying to understand… there's so much I don't know about Jasper," June said, wringing her purse strap again. "Why he left us and came here, or even how he died. But you knew him. I was hoping you could answer some questions for me. Maybe this evening, after the girls go to bed? Please?"

Caleb hesitated, watching June nervously chew on her bottom lip. People thought they wanted the truth until they dug it up and found out they couldn't bury it back in the ground again. "If you have any questions about Jasper, you should ask Will. He can fill you in on the details of the will and estate." Caleb turned and headed toward the grocery store.

"I don't understand, Caleb," June called to him, her voice hoarse now. "I thought Jasper was your friend. Why don't you want to talk about him? Why did you even invite us along if you were just going to shut down and walk away?"

Caleb hesitated, turning slowly. Why *had* he invited June along? A light breeze teased a lock of shiny hair across her face, and he clutched the keys in his hand to keep from reaching out to push it behind her ear. He was drawn to her in a way he hadn't been drawn to anyone since... it didn't matter. It was a long time ago now.

From what Jasper had said, June used to have an interest in art. Caleb could imagine spending an evening with her, could imagine telling her about working with Jasper and finding his voice as an artist. Talking with June would be infinitely better than his current plans to heat up leftovers for dinner and spend a few more solitary hours in the studio listening to the buzzing in his head grow louder. But that was exactly why he needed to shut this down now. He needed to get his shit together, not introduce more complications.

"I guess it was temporary insanity," he told her, before he could change his mind. And with that, he turned and headed into the grocery store—alone.

CHAPTER EIGHT

As June unpacked the groceries onto the granite counter in Jasper's kitchen, her phone buzzed. She shoved a carton of milk into the refrigerator and swiped to answer.

"*June.* I'm so glad I caught you." June's sister Sierra's voice carried through the phone. "I finally listened to my messages," Sierra said. "Is it true?"

June rounded the kitchen island to the other side, where she slid onto a battered wooden barstool. "It's true. All of it."

"The lawyer—Will?— said in his message you're there at the estate, in Washington?"

"It's a long story. Raven is going to come here soon. I'd love it if you could come too. There's a lot to figure out with Jasper's estate. And the girls would be so thrilled to see you." June took a deep breath, waiting for Sierra to turn her down as usual. She tended to disappear when she was writing a novel, and often didn't resurface until it was finished. "Maybe you could come just for a few days—"

"I don't know. I've got this deadline—"

"Please?" June cut her sister off before Sierra could launch into excuses that would only make her feel guilty for asking. "There are a lot of decisions to be made with the house and paintings."

"June, you know I totally trust you to take care of everything."

Of course Sierra trusted her to take care of everything. June had been taking care of everything for their entire lives. Didn't it ever occur to her sister that she might like a little help? "Sierra, that's not the point. Just because I can make the decisions doesn't mean I should always have to—" Hearing the sharpness of her tone, June abruptly stopped taking. She couldn't remember speaking to her sisters like this before. But she couldn't remember being this tired and wrung out before either.

Sierra was silent for a moment, and then finally, she said, "Okay, I can come."

June slumped on the counter as the exhaustion of the past few days pressed on her. She hadn't realized how much she'd been holding it together until the relief of sharing the burden sank in. "You know I wouldn't ask if it wasn't important."

"I'll send you my flight details. Do I fly into Seattle?"

"Bellingham has an airport just fifteen minutes from here." She probably shouldn't get her hopes up until Sierra actually arrived. Similar to Raven, June's middle sister could be difficult to pin down for a visit, and she and the girls had been disappointed on more than one occasion.

"I can't wait to see you." Sierra sighed, for a moment, sounding as weary as June felt. As a novelist, Sierra's job could be solitary, almost to the point of reclusive. June worried about her all alone in her cottage in Northern California—Sierra never mentioned dating, or friends aside from her neighbors. When June brought it up, Sierra waved her off, saying it was the price she paid for creativity.

June wouldn't know, so she didn't argue.

They hung up and June continued unpacking the groceries. Will had said he hadn't had time to bring someone in to clean Jasper's house, so she hadn't expected everything to be so orderly.

The whole house had been a surprise, really. Clean, modern, and comfortable, but with rustic touches, like the refurbished vintage stove and apron-front sink in the kitchen, iron bedframes in the guest rooms, and a claw-foot tub in the bathroom. The living room had twelve-foot ceilings, overstuffed couches draped in hand-knit throws, and a fireplace as the centerpiece, with a neat stack of logs next to it. A shelf on one wall overflowed with stacks of well-loved books, and a basket full of pinecones and stones sat on the entry table, as if it were the spot where someone stopped to empty their pockets on their way into the house.

It was all so strange, living in the house of a man she only knew from a few hazy memories. A man she knew so little about. *Her father.*

She'd imagined him a thousand times, conjured up those moments of connection from three decades ago, but the reality in Wishing Cove was something else entirely. June still didn't know how Jasper had died—if it had been the result of a long illness or something more sudden. His obituary hadn't revealed a cause of death, and Caleb wasn't talking.

She resented Caleb's reluctance to talk about Jasper. If he'd truly been like family to Caleb, why wouldn't he *want* to talk about him? So what if Jasper had been a private person? It wasn't like she was going to sell his story to the tabloids. Didn't she deserve to know about her own father? And deserve to know why he'd spent the past twenty years nurturing the creative ambitions of a complete stranger, when one of his own children had once dreamed of being an artist herself?

Didn't she deserve to know why Caleb was worthy, and she wasn't?

With that thought, June's back straightened. *Where are these feelings coming from?* She'd given up painting her freshman year in college and made the choice to pursue a more practical profession: she'd chosen David and the stability he offered with her eyes wide open, knowing they'd never share a great passion, and feeling nothing but relief over that fact. She'd seen her mother fall in and out of love, and nursed her through the heartbreak and devastation more times than June could count. June was attracted to David's steadiness, and that was enough.

And if she'd had to give up painting, well, it was a small price to pay. Or at least it seemed that way at the time. So why was she brooding over lost artistic opportunities now? Why did it feel like Caleb had stolen something that was rightfully hers?

Maybe it was because, suddenly, her whole life was a sham. Steady, reliable David was nothing but a fraud. And Jasper Luc, the *artist*, was her father and she never knew.

She never knew.

Would she have sought him out when she was young? Convinced him to let her come here and work with him, instead of Caleb? If she'd known who her father was, maybe she wouldn't have given up her artistic dreams in favor of a life with David. Especially when the stability he offered ended up being nothing but an illusion.

And now, everywhere she turned, she found reminders of all she'd given up. Reminders of what she might have had. Jasper's studio. Caleb's paint-splattered clothes. Above the mantel in the living room hung a gorgeous abstract painting that she'd been staring at every time she walked through the room.

June abandoned the groceries on the counter and wandered upstairs. She'd claimed an empty bedroom in the front of the house for herself, and put the girls in the room next door. But she'd pulled the door shut to the bedroom in the back, the one that had clearly belonged to Jasper.

June paused outside the door and then, with a deep breath, she slowly pushed it open. A queen-sized bed covered in a slightly rumpled navy duvet took up the far wall next to a side table with an open book propped on it. There was a simple bureau opposite the bed and, in one corner, a leather club chair with a plaid shirt draped over it.

June stepped inside the room slowly, almost cautiously, and made her way over to the chair. As she sat down, her shoulder brushed the shirt, and the woodsy smell of soap mingled with the slight sharpness of oil paint had unexpected tears pricking the back of her eyes. It had been over thirty years, but that unique combination of scents was as familiar as if she'd encountered it yesterday.

A memory of sitting shoulder to shoulder with her father on the front steps of the old brick row house where they'd lived on the first floor floated into her consciousness. They'd gone there to sketch—her father with his artist's pad and charcoals, and six-year-old June with a sparkly notebook and unicorn pencil.

He'd leaned over to comment on her work, remarking on the lines and shading, taking it as seriously as if her work hung in a gallery. With each of his movements, that scent would wrap around her like a warm blanket. And strangely, it comforted her as much now as it had back then.

Across the room, June's gaze was drawn to a sketch pad and a handful of charcoal pencils, just like the ones she remembered from childhood, on the table by the bed. She'd seen a similar pad and pencils on the coffee table downstairs, and another in a basket in the kitchen. Jasper had probably left them lying around for when inspiration hit. Because when you lived a creative life like Jasper—or Raven, or Sierra—inspiration probably hit all the time.

June stood up, grabbed the pad, and stuck two pencils in her back pocket. She peeked in on Emma and Izzy who were parked in front of the TV, watching cartoons. June was trying to keep them awake long enough to get back on a normal routine. If they went to bed now, they'd be up at 4 a.m.

"Guys, I'm going for a walk. If you need anything, come outside and call for me."

The girls barely even glanced in her direction.

June slipped out the front door and took the gravel path down the hill. Passing the locked door of Jasper's studio, she rounded the corner to the front of the building and stopped short. It was larger than it looked from the vantage point of the house. Standing on the side of the building facing out to the water, she could see the sun slanting into Jasper's studio through the wall of windows. The easel Caleb had caught her staring at that morning was covered by a drop cloth, and so were the paintings lined up against the wall.

But past the opening to Jasper's workspace stretched another wall of windows, revealing a similarly shaped studio next to it. June gasped, stumbling backwards, and ducked out of sight of the expanse of glass. Because inside the other studio stood Caleb, glaring at a large canvas propped on an easel.

He'd changed back into paint clothes and pulled his hair into a messy ponytail, but all traces of the unkempt intruder she'd taken him for in their first meeting were gone. Earlier, when she'd seen him in the jeans and T-shirt he'd worn to the grocery store, with his hair still damp from the shower, she'd been momentarily speechless. He was every bit as attractive as his twin, but without Will's good-natured personality to put her at ease.

June peeked around the corner and watched him rake a hand through his hair and narrow his eyes at the canvas. Something told her he wouldn't take kindly to an interruption while he worked, and the last thing she needed was another run-in with that brooding man. Especially today, when all her old scars seemed like they'd suddenly split wide open again. June scurried away from the studio, following the split-rail fence separating the path from the scraggly weeds and wild blackberry bushes lining the edge of the cliff.

About fifty feet from the studio, she detoured down a set of steps built into the hill leading to a small, narrow beach below. Scattered around on the beach were a series of man-made stacks of rocks. Each rock was delicately balanced on top of the one below it so that they formed a sort of tower, some as high as two or three feet tall. June was afraid to investigate too closely and knock one of the towers over, so she lowered herself onto a large piece of driftwood and pulled a pencil from her back pocket.

A sailboat skated across Everett Bay, and June dashed off a quick sketch, using soft, rounded lines to capture the movement of the sails, and darker, cross-hatched smudges to simulate the downy texture of the distant trees. At first her muscles felt awkward, unfamiliar, a wobbly toddler taking her first steps; but soon, her shoulders relaxed and her hand moved with confidence and rhythm, like hearing a song she hadn't played for half her life, but could still remember all the words to.

June was adding shading for the water when an unmistakable sound broke her focus. "Mom-meeee."

The girls, calling her from the porch. They were probably hungry for dinner. After dinner, they'd need baths, and David would want them to call to say goodnight. June sighed and glanced down at her sketch. It was nothing special. Just an amateurish drawing of a boat on the water. She'd gotten the motion of the sails wrong and, if she were honest, those trees looked more like pubic hair.

June ripped the page out of the sketchbook, tossed it behind the driftwood where the tide would sweep it out to sea later that evening, and hurried back up the steps.

At the top of the cliff, she stopped short, letting out a little scream. A man towered over her on the path, only a few feet away. June blinked. Caleb. "God, you scared me. Again."

"The girls were calling." He scrubbed a hand across his cheek, looking vaguely unfocused, like half his brain was still back in his studio. "I didn't know if you could hear them."

Great, she'd dragged him from his work, and he seemed annoyed. "I'm sorry."

He shifted from one foot to the other, gazing past her out to the ocean. "What?"

"I said I'm sorry for disturbing you." Was he hearing a word she said?

He turned to her then, and the storm in his eyes took her breath away. Because that expression—the intensity, the darkness—it was so...

Familiar.

Slowly, a memory took shape.

She was maybe six years old, creeping out to the garage behind the row house to see Daddy. Maybe he'd let her use his paints again. They'd had so much fun last week.

The quiet creak of the door as she pushed it open.

The swish of Daddy's brush on the canvas.

He stood there, eyes narrowed, angry. Staring at the painting in front of him. Maybe she should go.

Turning, she winced as her flowered sneaker squeaked on the garage floor. Daddy looked up sharply. A chill ran through her.

She wasn't afraid he'd hurt her. But it was as if he was looking right past her, right through her.

Daddy wasn't in the garage at all. He'd gone somewhere else entirely. Somewhere she couldn't reach him.

Standing on the path with Caleb, that same chill ran through June now.

Jasper and I had a lot in common.

June backed away, but Caleb held out a hand to stop her. He blinked, and seemed to shake off whatever it was that had consumed him moments ago. "It's fine. They're not disturbing me. I got a little caught up in my work and needed to take a break, anyway."

June eyed him warily. "Oh. Well, thanks for coming to look for me."

Caleb turned his gaze on June. "What are you doing out here?"

"Just a little exploring." June shifted the sketchbook awkwardly, hoping he wouldn't notice her holding it—or worse, ask questions. But one of the pencils started to slide. The sling on her other arm prevented her from catching it, and the pencil fell to the ground.

Caleb picked it up and held it out to her, his eyes drifting to the sketchbook and back to her flushed face. His eyebrows raised, but to her great relief he didn't comment. As she grabbed the pencil, her hand brushed his and, unexpectedly, a wave of heat worked its way up her arm. She shoved the pencil inside the sketch pad. "I'll let you get back to work."

Before he could respond, she took off up the path.

CHAPTER NINE

The next morning, Caleb stepped out onto his deck, cup of tea in hand, and jumped when he found Emma and Izzy's little faces staring up at him again.

"Jeez, don't sneak up on people like that." He wiped his now tea-covered hand on the hip of his paint pants.

"We didn't sneak up. We're just standing here," Emma said, with wide-eyed innocence.

Caleb sighed. That was true. But *why* were they just standing there? He wasn't used to people—especially miniature ones—lurking around in his space, disturbing his focus. He'd planned to do a little sketching over tea before heading to the studio.

Emma eyed the sketch pad under his arm and pointed to the box in his hand. "Are those crayons?"

"No, they're oil pastels." Caleb opened the box to show her. "They're kind of—fancy grown-up crayons."

"We left all our crayons at home." She heaved a giant sigh, and her shoulders practically drooped to the ground. "We miss them, right, Izzy?"

Izzy nodded solemnly.

Despite himself, Caleb smiled at their dramatics, but quickly shook his head. He'd forced himself to eat a healthy breakfast of eggs and toast—even though every bite had tasted like cardboard—and today was the day he was going to get back on track. Spend the day in the studio and finally get the abstract lines of the subway train in his painting to feel like movement instead of scribbles. To finally quiet the buzzing in his head. These girls were not part of his plans for the morning.

"Your mom is probably looking for you, so why don't you head home?"

"No, she's not," Emma said. "Mommy said we could play outside as long as we stay where she can see us."

Caleb sighed. Maybe the quickest way to get rid of them was to let them draw for a few minutes, until they got bored. "Okay, look, I need to work, so if you stay, you have to be quiet."

Their mournful faces did the fastest one-eighty he'd ever seen, and they clambered around the table on the deck. He put the oil pastels in the middle, handed each girl a sheet from his sketch pad, and took a seat across from them.

He'd barely drawn three lines on his own page when Emma's voice cut into his thoughts. "Why don't you have any pink?"

His head jerked up. "What?"

"You don't have any pink pastels. Crayola always has pink."

He sighed, dropping his sketch pad on the table. This set of oil pastels had cost him forty bucks at the art shop in town. They were the highest-quality crayons the kid had ever seen. And she wanted Crayola. "You have to make pink. By mixing red and white."

Emma picked up the two colors and banged them together. "How do you mix them?"

He gestured for her to hand them over. Might as well show her and then he could get back to work. "Like this." Caleb sketched about a dozen lines of red on the page and cross-hatched a dozen lines of white over top. He continued the pattern with another few red lines, white, red again. Then he took his thumb and smudged the colors together until they blended into a frothy cloud of pink.

"Ohhhhh!" the girls cooed.

Caleb looked back and forth between them. Didn't June ever have them play around, learning about colors? "Haven't you tried this before? Maybe with paint? Your mom never showed you?"

The girls shook their heads.

"Mommy doesn't like to do art," Izzy said.

Caleb begged to differ. He'd seen her sketching on the beach yesterday, and he knew from Jasper she'd been an artsy kid in high school. But even if the girls didn't know anything about that, didn't June ever do art as an activity with her children? His own mother could barely draw a stick figure, but when he was a kid she used to do crafts with him.

"And Daddy doesn't like paint all over the place," Emma chimed in. "Too messy." Ah, that explained it.

"Pay attention, girls. I'm going to teach you something."

They experimented with color combinations, making orange, purple, light green, magenta, and brown. Caleb settled back in his chair, his own drawing forgotten, and watched the girls try different shades. Seeing the wonder on their faces, Caleb couldn't help but think about Jasper.

Jasper had been the best mentor Caleb could've asked for, especially in the early days when he was insecure about his work and finding his voice as an artist. Jasper always had time to help him work through a painting he was struggling with, to push him to try harder techniques, or to encourage him to look at something in a new way. As he'd progressed, Jasper had seemed as pleased about Caleb's success as he was about his own.

Jasper had left his own family behind and chosen to focus his attention on Caleb. *And thank God he had.* But sitting here now, with the man gone forever and his charming granddaughters grinning up at him, Caleb ached on Jasper's behalf for all he'd missed out on. Jasper would have loved teaching these eager little girls about colors and shading and light. And he would have been good at it. Patient. Encouraging.

Caleb shook his head. There were reasons Jasper had moved out there to live a solitary life. It was easy to romanticize it with the girls sitting there looking adorable, but what would they look like when their grandpa had a relapse? When he spiraled out of control? People always got hurt, and Jasper had done the right thing keeping his distance.

Caleb needed to believe that.

He turned to the girls. "Okay, time to pack it up. Your mom probably wants you home."

"Oh," Izzy murmured, her shoulders slumping.

They moved slowly, but the girls did what he asked and carefully placed his oil pastels back in the box. He was about to send them home when he caught the little frowns on their faces, this time for real.

"Listen," he told them. "Tell your mom to check out the Starlake Arts Center in town. They have classes and camps for kids. Can you remember the name?"

The girls nodded and thanked him politely before they took off across the meadow. He watched until they clambered up onto Jasper's porch, and June opened the door to usher them inside.

Caleb sank back in his chair, grateful for the silence so he could get back to his drawing. But, after a moment, he looked up from his sketchbook. He'd lost the thread of what he'd been working on. It was too quiet. And his earlier regret over Jasper missing out on his grandchildren hung around the edges of his consciousness.

He and Jasper were the kind of people who were meant to be loners. They were meant to focus their passion and energy on their art instead of their relationships. It was one of the most fundamental lessons Jasper had taught him, right up there with the painting techniques that helped the art world take notice of Caleb's talent. It had worked for the two of them to live a solitary life out there on the property. Both of their careers had taken off in Wishing Cove. And, equally importantly, both of them had kept their mental health relatively stable.

It wasn't like they'd been monks. He and Jasper both dated women in town on occasion, but they knew better than to let anything get too serious. Jasper had gone down that road decades earlier. And he'd carried the guilt over the incident that had compelled him to leave Esther and his daughters until the day he died.

Caleb understood because he harbored his own regrets.

An image of a blond woman with her eyes closed flashed through his head. For once, she'd looked so peaceful, calm; without that wild battle raging beneath the surface. A tiny smile had grazed her lips as if she were immersed in a beautiful dream.

If only she'd been sleeping. If only he'd been able to save her.

Caleb pressed his elbows into the table and rubbed his temples, as if that would release the memories thrashing around in his head. He picked up his sketchbook and focused on the task in front of him. But still, the memories stayed put, nudging his hand every time he pressed a mark on the page. When he finally looked up, a drawing had formed.

Kaitlyn.

His wife for such a short time.

His wife, who had died two decades earlier.

Why was she in his head now?

Caleb tossed the pastels onto the table and scrubbed his hands across the tingling skin on his forearms. His lungs squeezed, and his left leg began to twitch with agitation. A familiar vibration took up space in his head.

Before he realized what he was doing, Caleb gave the table a hard shove, sending it crashing into the porch railing and knocking his sketch pad into the grass below. The pages fluttered and bent as they hit the ground at an awkward angle, and the noise tugged him back to reality.

He needed to get up, to move, to get out of there.

As Caleb stood, he spotted motion across the meadow. June, on the porch, staring back at him. Their eyes met. Swearing under his breath, he turned and headed inside, leaving his sketchbook, and drawing of Kaitlyn, soaking up the dew in the damp grass below.

*

One hour and a run through the woods later, Caleb jogged down the road toward the estate entrance. The gears grinding in his head had slowed, quieting the cacophony of intrusive thoughts. He felt almost back to normal again.

As he approached the gate, the security guard waved him over to the small RV he sat in to keep watch.

"Hey, James, how's it going?" Caleb asked.

"A package was delivered for Juniper Westwood. FedEx. I signed for it. If you're headed back to the house, would you mind dropping it off so I don't have to leave my post?"

Caleb took the flat, rectangular box. "Sure."

He headed down the hill toward the main house, wiping the sweat from his forehead. June had seen him looking worse on the first day.

Anyway, he didn't care what June thought.

"Oh! Caleb," June said, when she saw him standing on the other side of the screen door. He liked the way his name sounded coming from her mouth. "I'm glad you came by."

His life had been so solitary out there on the estate that sometimes he'd go for days without seeing another soul. He and Jasper used to make sure they got together for dinner a few times a month, and Will would stop by from time to time to check up on him, but often those visits seemed more like an obligation. Caleb didn't think of himself as lonely, but something about hearing June say she was glad he was there warmed him more than he wanted to admit.

"The girls told me you taught them to mix colors with your oil pastels." June stepped out onto the porch. "They can't stop talking about it. Thank you for your patience with them."

Caleb wanted to ask June why *she* hadn't been the one to teach the girls about mixing paint colors, and why they mistakenly thought she didn't like art. But then he'd have to explain what he knew about her, what Jasper had known. That would open up even more questions, and Caleb definitely didn't want to go down that road. Instead, he held out the package. "Delivery for you."

"Ah, my new laptop. I wasn't expecting it until tomorrow. Thank you, I'm so out of the loop at work."

Laptop?

"You're working? I thought screens were off-limits because of the concussion."

She still wore the sling on her arm, and the purple bruise on her temple stood out against her pale skin.

A flush moved up her cheeks. "You sound like David. He hid my lapto—" She paused and shook her head slowly. "Never mind."

What? Was she going to say her husband hid her laptop? Because that was a pretty controlling thing to do to another adult, even if she wasn't supposed to be using it.

"I'm not really working," she declared, almost as if she were trying to convince herself. "I only want to check in on some people. I'm sure I have a million emails piled up, and my new assistant only started a couple of months ago. I feel bad leaving him hanging. And the nanny—we left abruptly. I want to make sure David is still paying her."

Caleb didn't know the whole story, but if June were out here to recover from an accident, maybe David should be reassuring her he'd take care of things, rather than hiding her laptop. Couldn't he check in on her assistant, and deal with the nanny himself?

June suddenly looked tired, balancing her new laptop under one arm. Caleb almost reached out to carry it for her, but held back. The last thing he needed was to get any more involved with this woman and her daughters. His outburst on the deck earlier reminded him that he had his own issues to deal with. Nothing good could come from the lurch in his chest every time June smiled at him, or this desire to linger on her porch talking to her. It was better if they stuck to their separate sides of the property. "Okay… well. Don't work too hard."

"I'm not really working," she repeated.

Not my business. He turned with a wave and headed down the porch steps.

"See you later," she murmured.

Something in the way her voice dipped had him wondering if maybe she was sorry to see him go, and he almost turned around. Instead, he forced himself to keep walking. Because if he turned around, he might have to acknowledge his urge to put his arms around her and ease some of her burden. But he didn't want to think about the emotions she stirred in him. Numbness was so much easier. So, he kept walking.

He had a painting to work on.

CHAPTER TEN

Two days later, June and the girls were growing restless. She suspected it was a combination of the rain keeping them indoors, and the fact that back in Connecticut, they were used to having every minute of their lives scheduled. She still had a job, committees, and volunteer projects she'd signed on to coordinate. But in between emailing her assistant, brainstorming ideas for the next PTA fundraiser, and her board responsibilities, June had more downtime than ever.

When she wasn't sketching in one of the notebooks Jasper had left lying around the house, June was staring at the painting over the fireplace, slowly uncovering the bustle of people walking home under the glow of streetlamps in its swirls of color. Who was the artist? She could see a signature on the bottom corner, but the letters were as abstract as the rest of the work. And every day, June wandered down to Jasper's studio to imagine the man—*her father*—standing in that very spot in front of the easel.

The girls seemed to have caught the artistic bug in Wishing Cove, too. They'd come home from Caleb's house the other day buzzing with excitement over the color mixing technique he'd taught them, and they'd been begging to go to art camp at a place he'd told them about in town. All of it added to the little thorns of regret scraping at her like the blackberry bushes on the hill. Not only had she erased art from her own life, but she'd denied her daughters the opportunity to appreciate and enjoy it, too. Emma and Izzy were descendants of the great Jasper Luc, and she hadn't even taught them how to mix paint colors.

Back in Connecticut, she'd blamed it on David, and told herself it wasn't worth it to hear him complaining about the chaos and mess. But the truth was it had terrified her to think about art. June knew she couldn't go back to painting only halfway, which meant she couldn't go back at all. Her life in Connecticut didn't have any space for an impractical hobby, and art was a slippery slope that could too easily turn into an obsession. Before she knew it, she'd be shirking her responsibilities and letting the girls down.

Before she knew it, she'd end up like her mother.

But now, after spending most of her adult life convinced pursuing art would be selfish and impractical, it was hard to wrap her mind around the fact that she shared genetic material with the person who'd created some of the greatest works of the twenty-first century.

Each day she spent in Wishing Cove, confronted by Jasper's creative life, made it harder not to second-guess her own choices. So, when she woke the third day in a row to cold rain dripping down the window panes, June decided to take the girls to check out the Starlake Arts Center in town, to see about the art camps for kids.

If she was being really honest about it, maybe going to the arts center was as much for her as it was for the girls.

The problem now was figuring out how to get there. The doctor had said June could drive whenever she was ready, and Will had arranged for a rental company to drop off a car. But with the occasional dizzy spell and her arm still in a sling, she wasn't sure it was a good idea to get behind the wheel. Maybe she hadn't entirely thought through the logistics when she moved herself and the girls to a remote stretch of land in a small town where she didn't know a single soul.

She peeked out her bedroom window as Caleb made his way down to his studio through the rain. Okay, it wasn't true she didn't know *anyone*, but she and the girls might as well have been completely alone out there for all the attention he'd paid them in the past few days. Caleb hadn't even glanced across the meadow to wave since the day he'd delivered her laptop.

But what did she expect? Caleb probably lived out there because he wanted to be left alone to paint, and he hadn't signed on to be a tour guide for an injured mom and her two kids.

It was just that there'd been a couple of moments when she'd thought maybe they'd had a connection. When he'd relaxed, and she'd felt an awareness between them before he closed off again.

Something about him drew her in, despite every instinct that warned her away. He had an intensity that seemed to simmer under the surface, waiting to boil over like it had the day she'd watched him shove the table across the deck. Or the moment on the cliff top when he'd awakened that strange memory of her father. It had to be his passion for painting, and frustration when he had a creative block, that inspired him to react so strongly. She remembered those feelings from her own long-ago days as an art student, and because of that, Caleb intrigued her even more.

And scared her half to death.

June backed away from the window. It was only the isolated surroundings causing her preoccupation with Caleb. Once her sisters arrived, she'd stop looking across the meadow for a glimpse of him, and her heart would quit somersaulting every time she spotted him on the path to the studio. Her husband had left her for another woman, and she was *not* about to develop a sad, lonely crush on her new neighbor. Especially when her new neighbor was an aloof, brooding artist. She'd be skating way too close to her mother's territory.

No, she was there to focus on her own life and, right now, she needed to get herself and the girls to town. June glanced up at the sky. It seemed like maybe there'd be a break in the rain soon, something the weather app on her phone confirmed. They could walk. Jasper's estate was only a couple of miles outside of town and the exercise and fresh air would do them good.

An hour later, June and the girls set off on their adventure. The rain had fizzled out, leaving a pleasant, earthy scent in the air. The road had a wide shoulder for walking, and the girls skipped ahead, excited to be outside after being cooped up for days. They stopped to collect pinecones and pick the wildflowers growing along the road. But about thirty minutes in, the shoulder narrowed around an uphill turn, forcing them off the pavement. They trudged along through the damp, prickly weeds on the side of the road, and soon their sneakers were soaked.

After another five minutes battling the brambles, the girls began to whine. June assured them they were almost there, although she wasn't entirely sure it was true. She'd set her phone on the table by the door when Izzy was having trouble with her shoelace, and she'd forgotten to pick it up again. But they'd been walking for over half an hour, and it was only supposed to be three miles to the arts center.

At that moment, the gray cloud overhead opened up, despite the weather app's assurances it would be partly sunny for the rest of the day. June pulled the girls' raincoats from her backpack— good thing she'd grabbed them at the last minute—but if the rain kept up, it would only be a matter of time before it soaked through the lightweight material. And, of course, she'd forgotten to pack a raincoat for herself.

June pulled her flimsy canvas jacket more tightly around herself and looked up at the sky, hoping to see a hint of sunshine breaking through. Nothing but gray stretched beyond the trees. What had she been thinking dragging the girls out like this? What had she been thinking coming to this isolated place away from everything she knew? She'd left Connecticut hoping this would be a chance to slow down and figure out what she really wanted in life. To figure out who she was outside of being David's wife, accountant at his company, and mother of his children.

To find herself.

But being here only left her more lost. It only highlighted all the ways she was losing control of everything—her marriage was in a shambles, work was a million miles away, and now here she was on the side of the road in a downpour. It was her own fault she couldn't drive them into town like a normal person.

She didn't belong here. Jasper's silence for the past thirty years made that clear, underscored by the irritated looks from Caleb whenever he bothered to look at her at all. Guilt stabbed her as she thought about all the work waiting for her back at the house. This idea she could come to Wishing Cove and magically pick up sketching and painting where she'd left off—after over a decade and a half—was childish and irresponsible.

But she didn't belong in Connecticut either, and the thought of going back there and spending another decade or two staring at spreadsheets and helping David build his dream while he cavorted with his secretary made her want to sit down on the embankment and cry.

At that moment, a familiar black Jeep pulled up next to them. The window rolled down and there sat Caleb looking rumpled and irritated, but most importantly, *dry*.

"Get in," he said, gruffly.

June hustled the girls over to the car and into the backseat. Then she rounded the front of the car and slid in next to Caleb. "Oh my gosh, thank you."

"What were you doing on the side of the road?" he asked, with more than a hint of annoyance in his voice. "With all these sharp turns, a car could have come out of nowhere and the driver might not have seen you."

When he put it like that, it really did highlight how bad an idea it had been to drag the kids out on this poorly planned adventure. June leaned back into the seat and crossed her arms over her chest, shivering as much from the image of a car careening into her and the girls as from the wet fabric stuck to her skin.

Caleb reached forward and switched the heat to high with a vigorous twist of his wrist.

"We were going to Starlake to check out the art camps."

Caleb shot a glance in her direction, but his expression remained impassive. "Don't you have a rental car sitting in the driveway?"

"I thought walking would be good exercise." Would he roll his eyes if she admitted she was too afraid to drive? June already felt conscious of being in his space on Jasper's property; she didn't want him to think he'd have to start rescuing her and the girls. Even if that's exactly what he was doing right now.

"In a downpour?"

"Mommy's app said it wouldn't rain," Emma chimed in from the backseat.

Caleb slowed the car and turned the steering wheel to the right, pulling off the road into a driveway.

"What are you doing?" June asked.

"I'm turning around so I can take you to Starlake."

He'd been driving away from town toward Jasper's estate when he'd pulled over to pick them up. For the first time, June noticed the bags of art supplies by her feet, and her battered heart took another blow. It was just another reminder—in a long series of reminders—that Jasper had picked Caleb's painting career to nurture, instead of his own daughter's. Never mind that Jasper had probably never even known she'd wanted to be an artist.

He'd never known anything about her at all.

Suddenly, the Starlake Arts Center was the last place June wanted to go. She was cold and wet, and tired from somewhere deep in her bones. "Thanks, but we're pretty soaked," June said, around the lump in her throat. "Let's go back to Jasper's."

Caleb's hand stilled on the gearshift and he gave her a sideways look. "Are you sure?" he asked, his voice gentler now. "You were almost there. It's only a half a mile up the road."

"Yeah." She shifted in her seat. "Like you said, we have a rental car."

But he still didn't move. June forced herself to turn and give him what she hoped came off as a casual smile. "We'll dry off and drive into town like normal people."

He looked at her for another moment before he put the car into reverse.

A few minutes later, Caleb parked his Jeep in the driveway next to Jasper's house. As June climbed out of the car, the rain stopped, and a couple of tentative sunbeams peeked their way through the clouds. *Oh, great.* Just when she'd rather the rain pour down to match her dark mood.

The girls headed down the path toward Jasper's porch. All June wanted was to join them and run into the house, but politeness won out. She turned to face Caleb. "Thank you for the ride." Maybe he wouldn't notice the tiny wobble in her voice.

"June." Caleb took a step toward her, and his presence filled her senses. He smelled like oil paints mixed with the rain that had fallen on him when he'd hopped out of the car to help buckle the girls in. His damp T-shirt clung to his broad shoulders in patches, and she had to tilt her head back to look him in the eye. He reached out and took her gently by her good shoulder. The heat from his hand warmed her, and her heart stuttered in her chest.

"You've been upset since you got in my car," he said, softly. His dark eyes roamed over her, softer now, brows furrowed with concern.

For one crazy second, the concern on his face tempted her to lean into him and spill everything. David cheating, the shock of learning Jasper was her father, the way Wishing Cove stirred up her longing to paint again, even her embarrassing crush on him. But what good would that do? He couldn't fix any of it, and he certainly wasn't harboring a secret attraction for her. They had to co-exist out here for the next few months. The worst thing would be if he felt sorry for her.

"I'm fine." June stumbled backwards, and Caleb's hand slid off her arm. "Just tired. The girls woke up at the crack of dawn—we're probably still getting used to the time difference."

Something like disappointment flitted across his face, but it was gone so fast she'd probably imagined it. "Right." He shoved his hands into his pockets.

"Thanks again for the ride." June turned toward Jasper's house.

"Hey, wait," Caleb called to her, as he swung open the Jeep's passenger-side door. "This is for you." He pulled out one of the bags from the art store.

"For—me?" June stared at the bag of art supplies Caleb held out to her. Did he really buy her... How did he know...?

"Yeah, the girls loved those oil pastels."

June pressed a hand to her forehead. Of course. He'd bought art supplies for *the girls*. "Oh. Thank you."

"You're welcome." He paused in front of her and looked like he wanted to say more. June held her breath, waiting. Finally, he seemed to change his mind, looking away. "See you around." With that, he turned and headed down the path toward his cottage.

June peeked inside the bag and found three sketch pads of heavy canvas paper, and three sets of oil pastels—the same professional brand her father had bought her all those years ago.

She was about to go into the house when she stopped short. *Wait.* Caleb had bought *three* sets of supplies, not *two*. He'd seen her carrying a sketch pad down by the beach earlier that week, so maybe he'd assumed...

June gave herself a mental shake. For all he knew about her, she could have been making a grocery list that day. He'd probably grabbed an extra set for the girls, or maybe it was a mistake. She glanced in Caleb's direction, but he'd already disappeared into his cottage, and she wasn't about to go knock on the door. She shoved the art supplies back in the bag and headed for the house.

CHAPTER ELEVEN

For the next few days, Caleb managed to avoid his new neighbors, lying low in his house when he wasn't putting in long hours in his studio. It helped that the Pacific Northwest drizzle kept the girls inside and prevented their mother from taking them on any more hikes along the side of the road.

Or sneaking off to sketch on the beach.

For about the hundredth time since he'd followed June's footsteps down to the shore, Caleb glanced at the drawing on his worktable. He'd seen June rip it from her sketchbook and toss it aside. Out of curiosity, he'd crept down later to rescue it before the ocean could drag it out to sea. He'd wanted to catch a glimpse of what Jasper Luc's accountant daughter was capable of.

Apparently, she was capable of more than he'd expected. A lot more.

Technically, the drawing was excellent. She'd used a two-point perspective to convey the height of the sailboat in the foreground and the row of islands disappearing on the horizon in the background. Her lines were confident, a mix of soft and firm strokes capturing the texture of the sails, the water, and the trees. But more than technical skill, the drawing evoked a sense of story, a suggestion of depth beyond a simple boat on the water. Caleb wanted to keep looking, to know more about where the sailboat was racing off to, and where it had come from.

In all his years as an artist, he'd rarely encountered an amateur with that level of raw skill. How had June ended up as an accountant?

He was becoming increasingly preoccupied with that drawing, and with the woman who'd created it.

Hearing a shriek from outside his studio, Caleb shoved the drawing into a drawer and hurried to the back window. Will's Mercedes came to a stop in the driveway next to the main house. A moment later, June and the girls flew down the porch steps and ran toward it. The passenger-side doors opened and two women tumbled out, jumping up and down, hugging everyone, and letting out more high-pitched squeals.

Will exited the car slowly. Caleb watched him circle around to the back where he opened the trunk and pulled out a ratty backpack and a large black suitcase, before carrying them up onto the porch.

So, June had visitors? Delivered by Will, of all people?

Caleb grabbed his jacket off the hook by the door and headed out into the drizzle. He made his way up the hill to where Will stood at the front of the house. Caleb climbed the porch steps and stopped next to his brother, watching the reunion play out in the lawn below.

"Care to fill me in?"

"I texted you. When was the last time you checked your phone?"

Caleb wasn't actually sure. He was often so wrapped up in his work he forgot to charge his phone for days at a time. It wasn't like many people needed to reach him. There were a couple of women in town who he'd casually dated, but the ones who expected him to be available at a moment's notice eventually learned to move on and find someone else. His parents no longer worried about him as long as he called them once or twice a week. And then there was Will, who lived in town and more often than not just showed up.

"They're the sisters. Raven and Sierra."

Caleb took a closer look at the women in the yard. He should have recognized them. The blond in the chambray button-up had been wearing a similar shirt in the picture Jasper had shown him online, only there, she'd been standing on top of a mountain with a camera in her hand and a satisfied smile on her face. Raven, the photojournalist. Her boots slipped in the wet grass and wisps of her hair fell out of its bun as she picked Emma up and spun her around.

Caleb's gaze drifted to the other sister. Even if he hadn't seen her picture before, he knew her from the picture on the back cover of her novels. There, she sat composed with her red hair flowing over one shoulder and pair of black-rimmed glasses giving her the vague look of an attractive librarian. But now those glasses had fogged up, and her hair was frizzing from the rain as she picked up Izzy for a hug.

"How'd you end up being their driver?"

"June called me last night." Will shrugged. "She said ever since the accident, she's nervous about driving and asked if I'd mind getting her sisters from the airport. Of course, I said I'd be happy to. I don't think she has any other friends, or even *acquaintances*"—Will sized him up—"here in Wishing Cove who she can call if she needs something."

That grated on him, as Will probably knew it would. Was June really so wary of him she'd call Will before she'd walk a hundred feet across the meadow?

Caleb watched June's sisters gather around her, exclaiming over the sling on her arm and the yellowing bruise on her temple. She smiled and shrugged, probably insisting she was okay. But he could see her eyes soften and the rigidity ease from her shoulders at their concern.

Damn it, she was Jasper's daughter. But more than that, she was all alone here with two kids, injured, and he'd seen her dizzy spells for himself. He'd found her trudging through the rain trying to get to town and all he'd done was berate her for how dangerous it was. No wonder she'd looked like she was about to cry as she'd shivered in his car, and had practically run from him when they got home.

He couldn't have stopped by once this past week to ask her if she needed anything? No wonder she was wary of him—he hadn't done a goddamn thing to make her feel otherwise. For about the millionth time since they were kids, Caleb wished he could be more like his brother. That he could move through the world with Will's openness and ease, and not be stuck in his own head all the time.

Will hitched his chin at the women in the yard. "You know, Jasper's daughters are a blond, a brunette, and a redhead." He paused and flashed Caleb a grin. "There's a joke in there somewhere."

"Please stop. You're embarrassing yourself."

"Okay, I'm done." Will laughed. "The redhead is the author, Sierra. She was pretty reserved on the drive over. Unlike the loud-mouthed, blond one. She had no problem expressing her opinions about everything." Will's voice had an edge to it. Caleb turned to look at his brother.

"You two didn't hit it off?" It was rare that women were immune to Will's charms.

"Not so much."

Caleb studied the disgruntled look on his brother's face. "You couldn't charm her, huh?" Caleb pressed his lips together to hide his grin. This was *very* interesting.

With that, the women made their way up the porch steps to where Caleb and Will stood. Emma tugged at Raven and Sierra's hands, pulling them toward Caleb.

"Mr. Caleb, these are my aunties!" She turned to her aunts. "Mr. Caleb and Mr. Will are identical twins."

"That's right, Emma. Hi, I hope you had a good trip." Caleb held out his hand.

"It's nice to meet you, Caleb," Sierra said, giving his hand a delicate shake.

Raven reached out and took his hand with a firm grasp. "Hi, Caleb. You know what, you two really don't look anything alike." She glanced back and forth between Caleb and Will.

Will flashed her one of his signature smiles. "We're sort of like the before and after on one of those make-over shows." He gestured at Caleb's paint-splattered pants and tugged at the lapels of his custom-made suit.

Raven's eyes flickered down to Will's shiny leather shoes and then back to his face. "Yeah, well. There's something to be said for not trying so hard."

Caleb did his best to turn his laugh into a cough, ignoring the glare his brother shot him. "Nice to meet you, Raven."

Suddenly the air around him changed, and he looked up to find June standing in front of him. Her eyes shone and her cheeks had flushed bright pink, probably a combination of the cold and the excitement of seeing her sisters.

"Will, thank you so much for picking them up."

"It was no problem," Will said, with a smile. "Call me if you need anything."

A heavy, acrid unease rolled through Caleb's gut as Will turned, giving Caleb an unmistakable *Take that, bro* raise of his eyebrows as he pushed past him to take the handle of the suitcase from Sierra. "Let me get that for you." He reached for Raven's backpack, but she swung it out of his reach.

"No, thanks, I got it," Raven huffed, yanking it onto her back and pushing open the front door of the house. Sierra and Will followed with her luggage, and the girls hopped over the threshold behind them. June turned toward the door, but Caleb reached out a hand to stop her.

"June."

She swung back around. "Yes?"

He shifted his weight and scrubbed a hand across his forehead. God, he was so bad at this sort of thing. "Listen, I'm sorry for how I acted in the studio when we met. I know we got off on the wrong—" He trailed off because it felt like an understatement.

"Wrong foot?" June supplied.

"More like the whole leg."

Her lips quirked into a smile and she took a step toward him. He could smell vanilla again. Was it her shampoo? The rain must have brought out the scent.

"Caleb," June's blue eyes met his, "Will told me he arranged for an appraiser to help us with Jasper's paintings. He said before she comes, it might be a good idea to take an inventory and log everything." June twisted the fabric of her sling in her hand. "Nobody knows Jasper's work like you do. Would you help me?"

Caleb tore his eyes away from June and looked out at the rain dripping over the eaves of the porch and pinging on the edge of the railing. He'd been a lost, angry kid when he'd met Jasper at that gallery twenty years ago. Off his meds, estranged from his family, and truly hitting the basement floor of rock bottom.

Jasper had seen his potential as an artist at a time when it felt like everyone else in his life only saw his illness. For a kid who'd spent his whole life feeling like he was nothing, earning the respect of Jasper Luc had meant everything.

June shifted in front of him, dragging Caleb's attention back to the present. Now that Jasper was gone, what would it feel like to sort through his work and remember all the times they'd spent talking about art? Would it be a painful reminder of everything he'd lost?

But it meant too much to leave it to anyone else. Jasper should never have gotten to the point he did. Caleb should have noticed, should have called the doctor weeks earlier. He hadn't been able to save Jasper; the least he could do was make sure his paintings were preserved.

"Sure. I can help."

CHAPTER TWELVE

June stood at the kitchen island chopping vegetables for a salad and relishing the chaos swirling around her. A smile tugged at her lips as she watched Raven wave her arms and spin around the room, acting out the story of when she was chased by an elephant on safari. The girls squealed in excitement, jumping up and down. Sierra added commentary and elephant noises as she sipped her wine. Steam rose from a pot of pasta on the stove, and garlic and tomatoes sizzled in a pan next to it, filling the room with their aromatic scent.

June couldn't remember the last time she and her sisters were all in the same place like this. Maybe not since the girls were born. Sierra occasionally made it out to Connecticut for Christmas, and Raven breezed through whenever she was in the States, but finding a time to all get together had proved impossible. It seemed unbelievable now that work or school events could ever have been more important than this. Why hadn't she insisted they make more of an effort to get together regularly?

After a loud, chaotic dinner, June put the girls to bed and went downstairs to join her sisters. She found Sierra sitting alone on the couch in the living room, a crease bisecting her forehead as she read something on her phone. As June sank down next to her, Sierra looked up, blew out a breath, and tossed her phone on the coffee table.

"Everything okay?" June asked.

"Oh, fine. Just catching up on an email from my editor." Sierra shrugged a slender shoulder, and June envied her sister's toned biceps and the flatness of her stomach, visible beneath her slim T-shirt. June crossed her arms over her own midsection, which, two kids later, would never be the same.

"Where's Raven?" June looked toward the door to the kitchen.

"Bathroom." Sierra cringed. "Tummy troubles from something she ate in Dakar."

"I don't know how she does it." June reached for her glass of wine on the coffee table. "Sleeping in a different bed every night, never knowing what time zone she's in, eating questionable street food."

"It's funny how different our lives turned out to be." Sierra flashed her a wry smile. "After growing up with you two in that one-bedroom apartment, plus Mom's boyfriends coming and going, all I ever wanted was a quiet place to write."

June shuddered, remembering the three of them huddled in the bedroom while their mother went through another loud break-up with her latest boyfriend out in the hall. Remembered consoling her frightened sisters and knowing she'd be doing the same for her mother as soon as the guy slammed the front door, never to be seen or heard from again.

"I'm so glad you finally got your *room of one's own* in your little cottage," June said, and she *was* happy for her sister. But it was hard not to be a little resentful, too. For a brief moment, June closed her eyes and imagined *her* room of one's own. A little place all to herself. Maybe a studio where she could paint uninterrupted. But when would she even find the time for that?

"And then there's Raven." Sierra's voice cut into her reverie. "I didn't think it was possible to have a life less predictable than our childhood, but somehow she managed it."

"She thrives on it." June said. "Not me. I get thrown for a loop if the café in my office building runs out of my usual salad."

When she said it out loud, it sounded kind of pathetic. What would it be like to have the kind of freedom that Raven did? To roam where she wanted, to never be tied down? June had never let herself imagine it.

Sierra eyed her over the top of her wine glass. "Yet you up and moved to Wishing Cove on a whim. For the summer, anyway. This isn't exactly your regular routine."

Raven appeared in the doorway with one hand on her stomach. She shuffled over to the couch and flopped in between her sisters.

"You okay, honey?" June rubbed her leg.

Raven waved her hand. "Yeah, yeah. I'm used to this." Her head wagged back and forth between them. "What are we talking about?"

"June says she's predictable, but here she is on a spontaneous Pacific Northwest vacation." Sierra raised an eyebrow. "And in less than a week, she found a gorgeous set of twins to do her bidding. I couldn't believe it when Will showed up at baggage claim. I was a little speechless."

"I was the same way when he came to pick me up." June's shoulders shook with laughter. "I was exhausted and still dizzy from the concussion. I practically swooned into his arms."

Raven leaned back, kicking her feet up on the coffee table. "Ugh, no thanks. I much prefer the other twin, with the tortured-artist brooding thing he has going on."

Sierra elbowed Raven in the side. "What's your problem with Will? You were snarky with him from the minute he picked us up. I mean, the man was doing us a favor."

Raven shrugged. "He rubbed me the wrong way. He was so slick and charming, calling us *ladies*, insisting on opening the door for us. He reminded me of the rich guys in high school who used to make fun of us because our clothes came from Value City. Or those men I meet traveling, who hit on me in hotel bars and probably have a wife and kids waiting at home."

June's stomach lurched and she grabbed her wine glass. "I didn't get that feeling at all. Will has been really nice to me since I got here. His brother, on the other hand... the man is moody, and difficult, and—" She paused. *And way too appealing.* June blew out a breath. "Give me an easy, charming guy like Will any day."

Raven snorted. "Of course you like slick guys like Will. You married one."

"Raven!" Sierra gasped. "I can't believe you just said that."

Raven sat up straight and her feet slid off the coffee table, hitting the floor with a thump. "Oh, crap, I'm so sorry. I didn't mean it like that. You know I love David—"

June held up her hand. "It's okay. Raven, you're right. David *was* the rich kid who would've made fun of us for wearing Value City clothes in high school." She paused, pressing her palms to her burning cheeks. "And, unfortunately, he's also the guy who'd hit on you in the hotel bar while his wife and kids waited at home."

Sierra leaned across Raven and grabbed June's hand. "Oh, honey, David would never—"

"No," Raven cut in. "David loves you and the girls—"

"He's sleeping with his secretary," June blurted out.

The room went silent as both her sisters stared at her with wide eyes.

Finally, Raven whispered, "Are you sure?"

"I'm sure."

Raven jumped up from the couch and paced to the fireplace and back again. "Oh my God, I'm going to kill the motherfucker."

"Raven, you're going to wake the girls," Sierra shushed her. "This isn't what June needs right now."

Raven sat back down on the couch, more subdued now. "Did you leave him? Is this why you came out here?"

June stared down at her hands, noticing for the first time that the tendons beneath her skin were beginning to look more pronounced, and the skin rougher. She was over a decade older than David's girlfriend, and felt every minute of it. "He says he's in love with her."

She hadn't meant to blurt it out like this. June hadn't even been sure she was going to tell her sisters at all on their short visit, especially because she still hadn't talked to David, and nothing had been settled. With the time difference, and the girls always hanging around, it was hard to have a real conversation.

If June were really honest with herself, she was avoiding a conversation with David. It was much easier to focus on the present here in Wishing Cove than to face the wreckage back home. She'd have to go back there soon enough—she couldn't hide out here forever—but for now, she was happy to pretend this was nothing but a vacation with her sisters.

"What are you going to—" Raven began, before June cut her off.

"I don't want to talk about David. I'm so tired of David." June shifted in her seat and turned to face her sisters. "Let's focus on being together, okay?"

"But, June…" Raven trailed off as Sierra pressed a firm hand on her arm. Her sisters exchanged a sharp glance before Raven finally sighed. "Okay. Sierra, tell us what's going on with you. How's your latest book coming?"

Sierra scraped at some flaking nail polish with her thumb. "Oh… it's fine. I'm—well—I don't really want to talk about my book, either. This is my vacation, too. Let's not focus on work, right?"

June leaned forward. "Is everything going okay?"

Sierra dropped her hands in her lap. "Of course. It's fine. Going great."

June studied her sister. It didn't seem like it was going great. But what did she know about writing? It couldn't be easy to come up with all those stories year after year, and June didn't want to push. She'd asked them to back off about David, and she owed

Sierra the same respect. "I'm glad it worked out for you to be here."

"Me, too." Sierra was back to examining her manicure. "Actually, if you're going to be here for the whole summer, I might stay too. I can write anywhere…" She glanced at June. "I mean, if you don't mind having me. I can help out with the girls."

June opened her mouth, but she was too stunned to speak. She'd been a little nervous at the idea of staying in a place where she didn't know anyone for the whole summer. Will was around, but she didn't want to keep relying on him. And while she and Caleb seemed to have come to a truce, she didn't know how long that would last. There was nothing like having her sister there. All of a sudden, her accident and everything that followed seemed like it had happened for a reason. "Yes! Oh my God, Sierra! It would be amazing."

Raven looked back and forth between her sisters. "Wait. So, you're *both* going to be here for the whole summer?" She flopped back in her seat and crossed her arms like a petulant child. "I'm staying, too. I'm not missing out on all the fun."

This was even better, but June couldn't quite tamp down on her skepticism. Hadn't Raven said the editors would stop asking if she turned down too many jobs? And could Raven really stay in the same place for three whole months? June knew better than to get her hopes up. "But what about your work?

"I can take a couple of months off." Raven shrugged. "There will always be despots committing human rights violations and terrorists bombing innocent people. The one thing I can count on is the world will continue to be terrible long after I head back out there."

June had never heard Raven speak quite so bitterly about her job before. Raven saw some horrible things in her line of work, but from what she'd told them in the past, she'd always managed to keep a healthy distance. Maybe it was finally catching up with her. June was surprised it had taken this long.

Sierra must have been thinking the same thing because she reached out and squeezed Raven's hand. "It sounds like we could all use a little vacation."

June nodded. "I'm sorry it's under these circumstances, but I'm so excited to have this time with you."

"Me, too." Raven said, resting her head on June's shoulder like she used to do when she was a little girl.

Sierra picked up the bottle of wine on the coffee table and topped off their glasses. "So, are we going to talk about the elephant in the room? I don't mean the one chasing Raven's safari van."

"Do you mean the fact that *Jasper Luc* was our father and we had no idea?" Raven asked.

"I still can't believe we're in his house." June waved her arm around the room. "What are we going to do with all this?"

Sierra's gaze slid from the painting on the opposite wall to the shelf of books and settled on her sisters. "What do you two want to do with it?"

Raven was quick to answer. "Sell it. What else would we do with it? I mean, June's life is across the country, and Sierra, you'll want to go back to California to finish your book. And you guys know if it doesn't fit in my backpack, it's not something I need to hold on to."

June knew it didn't make any sense to keep the house. Raven was right. Her life *was* across the country. After the summer ended, they'd go back to their usual whirlwind of school and work and activities. They would never have the time to get out to the West Coast to really enjoy a place like this.

But for some reason, the idea of selling everything made June's stomach drop. Maybe it was because for the first time in her life, she'd found a small, fragile connection with her father. Or maybe it was the wild, unpredictable beauty of the Pacific Northwest that was so opposite to her orderly, refined life on the

East Coast. Spending time out there was doing something to her. June thought about the secret sketch pad of drawings she'd been scribbling in for the past week. "First we have to deal with Jasper's paintings. We shouldn't rush into anything."

"What do you think they're worth?" Raven asked.

"I'm sure they'd sell for tens of thousands, right?" Sierra looked back and forth between them. "I admit I don't know much about this stuff."

June shrugged. Sierra and Raven lived simply, and both made more than enough to support themselves, but neither she nor her sisters ran in the kind of circles that bought and sold the caliber of art Jasper produced.

"The value of Jasper's paintings probably went up since his death, but I hate the idea of selling them outright." June flashed back to that first argument with Caleb in the studio. He was right that Jasper's work belonged in museums and universities. They shouldn't just go to the highest bidder.

"Well, we don't have to decide today," Raven said. "But, Junie, the money could really help if you've left David for good."

June's heartbeat kicked up at the thought of being a single mother, of needing to rely on the unknown value of some inherited paintings to support herself and the girls. Was she an idiot for whiling away an entire summer here in Wishing Cove while David ran the business back east? Should she be rushing back to work as soon as possible? Those kinds of worries were enough to make her want to run upstairs and pack.

Raven made a face. "So, has anyone talked to Mom? Does anyone know if she knew about Jasper?"

"I tried calling a couple of times, but it went straight to voicemail." June shook her head. "She has no idea we're here."

"Let's call her now." Sierra grabbed her phone off the table and punched some buttons. The phone rang on speaker as she set it on the table in front of them.

Esther answered on the third ring. "Oh, hello Sierra, darling. I'm so glad you called. I saw a review of your latest novel last week. They only gave it three stars."

"Mom, you know I don't pay attention to reviews." Sierra rolled her eyes at her sisters.

"So, anyway Raven and June are here with me."

"Oh, hello, Raven! And June… Well, I hope you're calling to apologize for the terrible things you said to me last time we spoke. Raven, Sierra—apparently your sister resents all the time she spent babysitting you so I could work and support our family."

Her sisters looked at her questioningly, but June just shook her head and pressed her hands to her temples as her head began to throb. Nobody with a concussion should be forced to speak to their mother. Or at least to *her* mother. June conjured up her therapist's voice. *Don't engage. Don't engage.* If they didn't get to the point, Esther would do this all night. "Mom, we're calling to tell you we're at Jasper Luc's house."

The phone went silent. June and her sisters looked at each other, eyes wide, waiting for a reaction. Finally, Sierra leaned forward and touched the screen. "Mom? Are you there?"

"Yes, I'm here. Is *Jasper* there with you?" Esther practically whispered.

June exchanged glances with her sisters. Esther didn't know. "I guess you haven't heard. He died two weeks ago."

"Oh, no, I hadn't heard. Wolf and I have been staying on a commune in New Mexico while we're here for the artist collective's showcase." For once, Esther sounded subdued. "There's been no cell service. You happened to catch me in town." There was a pause. "I suppose Jasper's people contacted you."

"He left us most of his estate," June told her. "Mom, were you ever going to tell us Jasper Luc was our father? Didn't we have a right to know?"

"Don't be so dramatic," Esther said, a hard edge creeping into her voice. "*He* made the decision to take off, not me. *He's* the one who left me alone to raise three children without so much as a note or phone call for thirty years."

"But, Mom," June interjected, struggling to keep the edge out of her own voice, "didn't it occur to you to tell us who Jasper was? We could've reached out to him. Had a relationship with him. You always acted like you didn't know where to find our father."

Esther heaved a sigh. "Jasper was in and out of the art scene in the eighties. He was obviously talented, but so erratic. More tortured than most artists, and believe me when I tell you that's saying a lot. I had no idea he'd turn into the great Jasper Luc. He told me his name was Jack Lucas, for God's sake." Esther laughed, but it held a note of bitterness. "It wasn't until you girls were in high school that I found out your father had become a huge name. I read about him in a magazine. Can you imagine? All those years as a single mother and there he was, living his best life, rubbing elbows with celebrities, with his work in museums and galleries."

June paused as her heart tugged with a tiny thread of… compassion. It was an unfamiliar feeling when it came to her mother, and June wasn't sure what to do with it. She'd always placed the blame for her chaotic childhood solidly on Esther's shoulders. *Had* Jasper been rubbing elbows with celebrities while they'd been struggling to get by? If her own situation with David had shown her anything, it was that sometimes you could do everything right and still a man could leave you for a better offer.

"Was there another woman?"

"No. It wasn't about that." Esther sounded tired, resigned. "He left us, he didn't want anything to do with us. Why would I track him down, only to have him reject us again? It would have only ended in more heartbreak."

A silence settled around the room. Raven chewed on her thumbnail, and Sierra stared into the fireplace. June let this new development sink in. Would she make a similar choice to protect the girls? June hoped that even in a divorce, David would want to be in his children's lives.

"And see, I was right. He left you his estate, so he clearly knew where to find you. Why didn't he reach out *before* he died?"

Why hadn't he? It was the question that had been tugging on the edge of June's consciousness since she'd arrived in Wishing Cove. Why would Jasper ignore them when he was alive, only to leave them everything when he was gone?

June glanced at Sierra, who shook her head.

"I don't know why," June finally said.

"Well, I suggest you don't dwell on it. No sense wasting your time on a man who didn't care about you."

It was that simple, really. June pressed her palms to her eyes to hold off the tears that welled there. Since she'd come to Wishing Cove, warm memories of her father had been coming back to her in bits and pieces. And a little part of her had decided that he *had* cared about her. But when you broke it all down, Esther was right. Except for his will, there was little evidence he'd thought of her or her sisters at all. He hadn't even left a them note.

"So," Esther said, her voice lilting upward as if she were mentally brushing off the conversation. "Maybe Wolf and I should come over there when this show is over. Wolf would *love* to see where Jasper worked—maybe he could use the art supplies you're planning to get rid of."

Raven waved her hands wildly in front of her. "*Hell, no!*" she hissed.

Sierra shook her head vigorously.

"Oh, well," June said. "Now isn't really a good time to come…"

"Yeah," Raven added. "We can't even get into the studio. It's triple-locked and they lost the keys."

"But we'll call you again!" Sierra chimed in. "As soon as it's a good time. Okay? Oh, listen." She knocked on the wooden coffee table. "Did you hear that? It's the door. We have to get it. Give our love to Wolf. Bye!" She reached out and slammed her finger down on the red button to end the call.

Sierra blew out a huge breath and looked up from the phone. As soon as June met her eyes, they both started chuckling. Raven bent forward at the waist, her shoulders shaking with laughter.

"Give our love to *Wolf*?" Raven gasped.

"I know! I panicked!"

Raven shook her head. "Tell me they aren't going to suddenly show up here."

"Luckily, I don't think she knows where we are," June said. "Jasper kept his life pretty private."

Sierra looked between them. "Let's pinky swear to not tell her, okay?"

The three women linked pinkies, just like they used to when they were kids. June looked back and forth between her two sisters. "I love you, guys. I'm so glad you're here."

She shoved the nagging anxiety over David and Jasper out of her head. She was here with her sisters, and she didn't want to miss out on this time they had together.

Just like her mother had said: *No sense wasting your time on a man who didn't care about you.*

CHAPTER THIRTEEN

It took a tentative knock on the studio door to drag Caleb's attention away from his painting. Out the windows and across the water, a tiny break in the gray clouds revealed the sun drifting towards the horizon. He was grateful for the interruption. It could be an easy slide from painting all day, skipping meals and pulling a few all-nighters, to a full-blown episode where he didn't sleep, eat, or make rational decisions. He'd feel euphoric, like he could do anything, but he'd actually be out of control and not realize it. And the crash would inevitably follow.

Caleb dropped his brushes in the sink and opened the studio door. June stood there with the hood of her turquoise raincoat pulled over her head. The color made her blue eyes look even more luminous, closer to silver.

Cerulean Blue mixed with Titanium Zinc White.

"Hi, I'm sorry to interrupt."

"It's fine. I needed a break anyway." He took a step backward. "Do you want to come in?"

"Oh." June blinked as if that was the last thing she'd been expecting him to say. "Really? Okay." She stepped inside and flipped the hood off her head.

Now it was Caleb's turn to be surprised. "Wow," he blurted out, before he could stop himself.

"What?" June scrubbed a palm against her cheek. "What's wrong?"

"Nothing's wrong. I wasn't expecting that." He gestured at the hair curling wildly past her shoulders.

"Oh, yeah." She pulled her hair back from her face, gave it a twist, and let it go. It bounced right back into its unruly spirals. "With all the rain, I gave up straightening it."

"Why would you *ever* do that?"

"Do what?"

"Straighten it."

June flashed him a half-smile. "David always liked it straight. It looks more professional. And when it's curly, it's so frizzy and—"

"It's gorgeous. David is a moron."

She blushed, and for a moment he wondered what other sorts of things he could do to bring color to those pale cheeks. And then he realized that not only was he thinking inappropriate thoughts about a married woman, but he'd insulted her husband. "Shit, I'm sorry. I just called your husband a moron, didn't I?"

She surprised him by laughing. "You sure did, but you're not wrong."

Before he could spend too much time wondering what that meant, she took another step into the room. "I stopped by to ask if you might have a little time to help me look through Jasper's paintings tomorrow. Raven is going to take some photos of the studio in the morning, then she and Sierra are going to take the kids whale-watching. So, I'll have the whole afternoon free."

After their first argument in the studio, he hadn't worked up the nerve to ask June what she and her sisters planned to do with everything. He liked the idea of Raven documenting Jasper's space before it changed forever. It showed a reassuring level of respect for the man's work. "Sure, tomorrow works."

"Okay, thanks. I'll be there around one." She turned to leave but stopped mid-spin and blew out a breath. "Wow."

Caleb followed her gaze to the half-finished painting on his easel, and for a moment, his muscles tensed. He didn't usually share his work with anyone until he was finished. Well, except for Jasper.

She turned to face him. "*You* painted the abstract in Jasper's living room, didn't you? I've been staring at it for days. I love what you did with the reflection of light, and I keep finding more nuance. The crowd of people moving under the streetlamp, and the rain distorting the view." She glanced at the painting on his easel, this one capturing a tiny snippet of space between two subway cars racing by, the commuters blurred by the movement of the train.

He'd agonized over those trains for days. His first instinct was to jump in front of the painting and block June from looking until he had it perfect. But then he was distracted by the next thing she said.

"Your style is nothing like Jasper's, but I see his influence in your work. It captures the same kind of barrier between the viewer and subject. I want to stand here looking until the train pulls away or the rain stops." She took a couple of steps toward the easel and froze. "God, I'm sorry, look at me barging in here. I'm sure you're private about your work."

"No, it's—fine." And maybe it actually was fine. Caleb had admired June's drawing, the one still in his drawer. He'd always been a solitary person, but his friendship with Jasper had kept him from becoming too much of a recluse. Nobody could fill that hole in his life. But she had talent—he'd seen it for himself—and he'd missed these kinds of conversations now that Jasper was gone.

Maybe she could help him finally move past this creative block.

At that moment, a steady beat like a snare drum echoed from the roof. The clouds had swallowed up the sun and rivulets of water began pouring down the windows and pooling on the path below. In contrast to the cold rain outside, June brought a warmth to his studio that Caleb liked more than he wanted to admit. "Why don't you take off your coat?" He gestured toward a paint-splattered blue couch against the back wall. "You can have a seat if you want."

June hesitated. "Are you sure?"

Caleb took in the uncertain look on June's face. He liked to think Jasper would be happy to see a friendship develop between them. "You can't go back out in this."

"Okay." June tugged at her raincoat and winced as the movement bumped her injured shoulder. He reached over to help her slide it off her arms and smelled vanilla again.

"Do you want a drink? Something to warm you up a little?" he asked, as he hung up her coat.

"That sounds great, actually." She slipped out of her wet flip-flops and settled at one end of the couch with her feet tucked under her.

Caleb pulled a bottle of whiskey and two glasses from a cabinet, poured a generous splash in each, and handed her one. He sat down gently at the opposite end, careful not to jostle her injuries further.

"Tell me about your paintings," June said, taking a sip of her whiskey. "Has your work always leaned toward the abstract?"

Caleb paused as he settled back against the couch cushion. "No, believe it or not, I started out heavily influenced by contemporary realism, works by artists like"—he paused, giving her a wry smile—"Jasper, of course. Works that layer the images to create an abstraction of what's real. But as my art evolved, I found myself moving more toward the abstract." He glanced at the painting on his easel. "You're not wrong to say Jasper influenced my art, even more so in my early work." He gave June a lopsided smile. "It would have been hard not to be influenced by one of the greatest painters of this century."

June nodded slowly as she took in the other canvases in various stages of completion propped around the room. "Jasper's work is more controlled," she said. "He shows the viewer a calmness beneath the surface, while yours hints at chaos there. What I said earlier about wanting the train to pull away or the rain to stop... I'm equally fascinated to see the full picture come into view, and afraid that when it does, I'll miss the energy and chaos."

Caleb blinked. It was the sort of comment Jasper had made a dozen times before about his work. He'd encouraged Caleb to lean into the chaos, to dig deep into the feelings translating as turmoil on the canvas. Somehow it didn't surprise him June had managed to channel Jasper in her observation of his work.

The words she'd used to describe Caleb's art could also character-ize his feelings about her: *equal parts fascinated and afraid.* June intrigued him, and it wasn't just that he couldn't keep his eyes off her pretty face when she walked around the property. He was becoming totally preoccupied with the drawing he'd found, often pulling it out to look at it when he should be wrestling with his own painting. There was nothing more fascinating to him than genuine artistic talent. And from what he could tell, June had that in spades. The more he learned about her, the more time he wanted to spend with her, having conversations like this one, discovering what else there was to know about her. And learning whether she felt that same thrum of attraction growing slowly into a steady beat.

Caleb shifted in his seat. "So, it sounds like you have some knowledge about art."

She flashed him a rueful smile. "I don't know if I'd call it knowledge. More like an appreciation."

"Your father was a painter, your sister is a photographer, and your other sister is a writer. The creative gene clearly runs in your family." He took a sip of his whiskey. "I know you must have an artistic talent, it's just a question of what." Of course, he already knew, but he couldn't tell her that.

She looked into her glass, tracing a finger around the rim. For a second Caleb wondered if she was going to evade the question. But then she met his eyes. "Actually, I used to love to paint, and up until I was in college, I imagined having a life not very different from this." She gestured around the studio, and there was no mistaking the longing on her face. But in the next second it was gone. She dropped her hands in her lap and shrugged. "Anyway, it was a long time ago."

"What happened in college?"

"I quit painting to become an accountant."

"Why?"

June seemed to hesitate here, gazing out across the studio before she answered. "I needed to focus on something practical. We grew up in an unstable environment and it was important to have a job that paid the bills on time. So I could support everyone."

Caleb raised his eyebrows. Jasper had never mentioned the mother of his children. He'd only said Esther and the girls were better off without him. From Caleb's knowledge of how they'd turned out, he'd assumed June and her sisters grew up middle class, comfortable. That their mother had her shit together. But now, Caleb couldn't help wondering what June meant by *unstable*, and how much Jasper had been aware of. If Jasper had knowingly left June, Sierra, and Raven in a precarious situation, he was more selfish than Caleb realized.

Or more terrified of the impact his mental illness would have on his daughters.

"Yeah?" Caleb said, keeping his voice light. "Is your mom an artist, too?" If Esther had been a struggling painter, it made sense June would be wary of that kind of lifestyle.

But June slowly shook her head. "When she was younger, my mom was a model, but she never had a lot of success with it, and never managed to pivot to something else. She liked the spotlight, the attention. In order to make money, she sold cheap jewelry at local flea markets and craft fairs. That's how she connected with the art scene in Philly and met my father."

Caleb sat back against the couch. That didn't sound so bad. So, June and her sisters had grown up poor. Lots of people grew up poor, and it didn't always mean they had difficult childhoods.

"She liked dating artists," June continued. "Liked being the muse, and the whole tortured-artist drama of it. That's probably how she ended up having three kids with Jasper." June blinked at him. "Apparently, he was more tortured than most."

Caleb avoided her eyes and busied himself with grabbing the bottle of whiskey from the cabinet. A long silence stretched between them, and he knew June wanted him to tell her more about Jasper and his tortured artist tendencies. But sometimes the truth could hurt more than not knowing.

Finally, June looked down at her hands. "For my whole childhood, Mom was either madly in love and off with a new boyfriend, forgetting she had three kids until the school called because nobody was there to pick us up. Or she was going through a break-up, setting fire to some ex's clothes in the apartment courtyard, and becoming paralyzed with grief until the next guy came along. Either way, someone had to hold it all together."

"And you were the oldest, so that fell to you."

June shrugged, twisting the hem of her T-shirt in her fingers. "Even as a kid, I felt like the only responsible adult in the house."

Caleb sat back down on the couch and put the bottle on the coffee table. "So, you were the one who took care of things, and made sure your sisters' lives were stable. And you sacrificed your dreams to be an artist in the process."

"I—" June's eyes flickered to his and he saw a little flash that told him he'd hit on something painful and true.

Caleb thought back to the day he'd met her. Two kids, suffering from a concussion, and wearing a sling on her arm. And somehow, she had still looked completely pulled together, hair gleaming and straight, clothes fresh and unwrinkled. On his best day, he never looked that polished. He wondered again why her husband—*the moron*—hadn't come with her, at least to get her settled, to help with the girls. Even here on vacation—recovering from an injury—she still worried about the people at work, her kids' nanny.

His best guess was that June had spent her whole life taking care of everything and everyone, starting with her sisters when she was a kid. And even when they made it to adulthood, photojournalism and writing weren't easy careers to break into. How many years had June supported them while they pursued their passions? "I have a feeling you're good at hiding how much you do for people. I bet your sisters don't know you gave up painting for them."

June shook her head vigorously, and then winced, pressing her hand to the side of her head. "It wasn't like that. I don't have any regrets."

She'd probably convinced herself she didn't have regrets, but it was all over her face. "So, what about art as a hobby? Just because you're an accountant and a mom doesn't mean you have to give up painting entirely."

June watched the water streaming down the windowpanes, biting her lip as if she were debating whether to say something. Finally, she took another sip of whiskey, and said, "I've started drawing again, since I've been here."

"Yeah?" Had she been using the sketchbook and pastels he'd given her? He'd taken a chance, throwing an extra set into the bag when he bought them for the girls. "Would you let me take a look? I mean, since you've seen *my* work." He kept his tone light as he nudged her leg with his hand.

"It's so embarrassing. I'm not very good."

"I bet you are." He *knew* she was.

"I haven't picked up a pencil or paintbrush in more than fifteen years. I don't know why I mentioned my drawings." June's cheeks reddened. "I haven't told anyone else."

The warmth inside him had nothing to do with the whiskey. It meant something that she'd shared this with him.

June's leg stretched the slightest bit under his hand. He was still touching her. She was aware of it too, by the way she stared at her leg and then flicked her eyes to his face. But she didn't move, or look away, and something in the air grew heavy between them. All he'd have to do was shift slightly, and he could pull her across the narrow space of the couch cushions, into his arms. By the way June bit her lip, he could tell her thoughts were going in a similar direction. She nervously twisted the ring on her left hand.

Caleb blinked and yanked his hand away.

Jesus, what am I doing? She's married.

And even if she wasn't, June had told him all about her rocky childhood, and she'd made a life for herself that was the polar opposite. She'd have no interest in a *tortured* artist like him, and she didn't even know the half of it.

June cleared her throat and slid her feet to the ground, slipping them back into her flip-flops. "It looks like the rain is slowing down. I should probably go." She set her glass on the coffee table in front of her and didn't look at him. "The girls will need dinner." She stood up and walked over to the door where she grabbed her raincoat off the hook. Then she finally turned to face him. "I'll think about it, okay? The drawings, I mean."

"Okay. Thanks for hanging out."

"Thanks for the drink." She gave him a tiny smile and was out the door, running through the drizzle back up to Jasper's house. Caleb watched her through the window until she disappeared inside.

CHAPTER FOURTEEN

The phone woke June at 5:45 a.m., and she rolled over in bed to pick it up. David, probably on the train on his way into work. Her first thought, even in her half-asleep haze, was of course he wouldn't think about the time difference and wait until a reasonable hour to call. He was probably wearing his earphones, making calls on the train, not giving any thought to the people around him who might not want to listen to him *close the deal and double our ROI by going after the low-hanging fruit.*

"Hi, David."

"Hey. How are the girls?"

"They're good. They're, um, sleeping of course." June opened one eye. It was still dark out.

"You and I should talk."

June sat up in bed and rubbed her eyes. She knew they had to have this discussion. Better to get it over with. "Yeah."

"June, I didn't mean for any of this to happen with Priya. It just... did."

June punched a pillow against the wall and leaned against it. "So that's it? You're going to blow up fifteen years of marriage over an affair with your secretary?"

David cleared his throat. "Priya is an executive assistant, not a secretary."

"Really, David?" June lunged out of the bed and paced across the room. "That's what you're going to focus on right now? If Priya wants to be taken seriously as a professional, maybe she shouldn't have done something as clichéd as fucking her married boss."

David took a sharp intake of breath, probably because June had never in her life talked to him like this. She definitely hadn't ever hurled words like *fuck* at him in anger.

Well, times have fucking changed.

Finally, David said, "This isn't about Priya. It's about us. You have to admit things have been strained between us lately. You're so distant all the time… busy with the PTA and the girls' activities, and…"

"So, it's *my* fault you had an affair?"

"No." David sighed. "That's not what I'm saying. I want to have a reasonable conversation about this. I hoped you'd try to understand my perspective."

June's jaw clenched at the impatience in his voice. She could picture him looking at his watch, hoping they could wrap this up before the train went underground and they lost contact.

But as quickly as it had come, her anger vanished. Why would he expect any different from her? This was how it always went. David decided how he wanted things, and she went along. Of course he'd expect her to be as much of a doormat about this as she'd been about everything else.

Not anymore.

She took a deep breath. "I'd like to keep the girls here with me for the summer."

A silence stretched through the phone and, finally, David sputtered, "The *whole* summer?"

"Yes. Sierra and Raven both have some time off and are spending it here. I want the girls to be with their aunts. And you travel so much in the summer anyway, I doubt you'll really miss them."

"I don't even know where you and the girls are."

"David, I told you where we are. I even emailed you the address. My father died. He left my sisters and me a little bit of property."

Maybe *a little bit of property* was an understatement, but she didn't want David butting in and giving his opinions about what to do with Jasper's artwork. The decision was up to her and her sisters. She'd asked Will about inheritance law on the drive from the airport. Tried to keep it casual and slip it in with a bunch of other questions, and it sounded like David might not have any claim on Jasper's paintings in a divorce. A quick Google search on the subject had further reassured her, but maybe it was time to hire a lawyer.

"What's the house like?" David asked. "Seattle real estate is hot right now. Do you think it might be valuable?"

June's pacing stopped at this abrupt shift in conversation. Leave it to David to focus on what was really important. *The value of the property.* June shook her head. "It's north of Seattle, in a small town a couple of hours away. It turns out my father was an artist."

"Ah, well, I didn't expect Esther to attract an investment banker. Is the house even livable?"

Of course, David would assume if her father was an artist, he'd died destitute. She didn't see any reason to disabuse him of the notion. "Oh… you know. It's not too bad. It's an artist's house."

Through the phone, June could hear David blow out a breath. "All right, June, I expect the girls to be back by the end of August. I can't promise I'll continue to be understanding."

June shivered at the warning in his voice. David knew how much security mattered to her. He could make things difficult—fight her for custody of the girls, push her out of his company. In the past, she would have fallen over herself to smooth things over and be as agreeable as possible. But a little part of her—the part who'd been sneaking away to sketch on the beach—protested.

David is the one who had the affair. She was so tired of smoothing things over. And she wasn't totally powerless here—she had her sisters to back her up, and Jasper's estate had to be worth enough to support her and the girls, if she needed it.

"David, I have to go." June grabbed her robe from the back of her door. There would be no going back to sleep now. "I'll have the girls call you this evening." Before David could answer, she hung up the phone.

As June headed out of the bedroom, she paused in the doorway and looked down at her hand. Her one-and-a-half carat diamond engagement ring glinted back at her. She was always getting the stone caught on her clothes and constantly worrying she'd knock it loose from the setting. If she'd chosen the ring, she probably would have picked something more understated, maybe an antique, or a design by a local jeweler. But David had insisted she deserved the best, and if she were really honest with herself, a part of her had liked having that enormous rock on her finger at PTA meetings and work events, and when socializing with the other wives. That ring was worlds away from the cheap jewelry Esther used to sell at the flea market, and it showed that June belonged in David's world.

But the ring had no place in Wishing Cove, and not only because she might lose the stone stacking logs for the fireplace or dropping it in a tub of paint in Jasper's studio. June yanked it off her finger, and her wedding band too, and stuck them in the top drawer of the bureau.

June moved to the window and pulled open the curtain. Outside, the islands in the bay began to take shape as the morning light appeared to the east. She'd slept with the window cracked, and a cool breeze carried in the fresh scent of damp grass and pine.

June steadied her breathing. Today, she and Raven would take photographs in Jasper's studio. Then she'd meet Caleb to look through the paintings.

Her heart flickered as their conversation in his studio the day before came back to her. When they'd started talking about art, she'd felt that old exhilaration of connecting with someone on a creative level come rushing back. It was as if she'd known him for longer than a few weeks, and he seemed to understand her in a way that no one had in years. When the two of them were on the couch, that physical awareness had stretched across the small space between them…

June backed away from the window, shoving the memory from her head. She dropped her phone on the dresser and headed downstairs to make a pot of coffee so it would be ready when her sisters woke up.

*

A couple of hours later, June and Raven left the girls with Sierra and headed down to Jasper's studio so Raven could take photos.

"Wow." Raven sighed when June pushed the door open and they stepped inside. "Did I tell you I saw an exhibit of Jasper's work at the Guggenheim in Bilbao a couple of years ago? It's hard to believe this is where *Girl in the Trees* was created."

June pulled the canvas cover off the easel, revealing the half-finished work beneath. "I know. I studied him in college and always admired his work. Maybe deep down I felt a connection." Now wasn't the time to dwell on the sadness that washed over her at the memory of a young girl who'd loved to paint more than anything. A girl who'd had to give it up.

"So, this is how Jasper left his studio, right?" Raven set her camera bag on a table against the back wall and unzipped it. "Except for those drop cloths you said Caleb used when he covered the paintings? You didn't touch anything?"

June eyed the broom in the corner that she'd swung at Caleb's head. "Pretty much."

Raven pulled out her camera and set up an array of lenses on the table. For the next hour, June tried to stay out of her way, admiring the confidence in Raven's movements as she walked around snapping photos. Raven occasionally stopped to switch out her lens, and once she commented on how great the lighting was in the studio, but otherwise, she kept her face in the camera. June had seen thousands of Raven's photographs over the years, but this was the first time June had watched her work. The pride swelling in her chest at her sister's focus and professionalism reminded her of why she'd sacrificed so much.

While Raven finished taking her photos, June took another look around the studio. With the girls keeping her busy, she hadn't had much of a chance to explore yet, and it wasn't like she could bring them in there with her—they'd have paint all over the place in about five seconds flat.

June wandered to the back wall and the cabinet that sat against it. Curiously, she pulled on the door, but it stuck shut. June noticed a key hole and dug around in her pocket for the key ring Will had given her. Along with the keys to the studio and house, there was a smaller key she hadn't noticed before. She tried it in the lock and popped open the cabinet door.

In front of her sat a neat row of paint tubes with various amounts of color left in them. Beside the tubes were brushes, palette knives, and the other well-used supplies of a working artist. Why would Jasper lock a cabinet full of paint supplies?

The next shelf held sketches on heavy canvas paper—maybe that's why the cabinet was locked. These quick pencil drawings were the work of Jasper Luc and should probably be preserved along with his paintings. She was about to close the cabinet door when a flash of orange from behind the sketches caught her attention. Moving aside the papers, she saw a number of pill bottles hiding in the back corner.

June pulled them out one by one and set them on the counter by the sink. There were ten bottles there, all labeled with Jasper's name and different prescriptions.

June examined one of the bottles. *Aripiprazole.* She'd never heard of it. Then another. *Alprazolam.* It was like reading a foreign language. June looked around for her phone to google the names, but she'd left it up at the house.

Had Jasper been sick? There had to be an explanation for all these medications…

The click of Raven's camera slowed, and June felt her sister approach from behind.

"What's all this?"

"I don't know, I found it in the cabinet. Ever hear of 'alprazolam'?"

Raven shook her head. "This is a lot of drugs for one guy. You think Jasper died from some illness?"

June opened a bottle and peered at the peach-colored pills inside it, as if the answers to her questions were hidden in its depths. "It would make sense."

"You should ask Caleb."

"I did, once." June looked at her sister. "The day we arrived. I asked how Jasper died but Caleb snapped at me, and took off."

Raven picked up a bottle and gave it a shake. "Well, maybe it was painful for him to talk about. Especially if Jasper was sick for a long time and Caleb was the one caring for him."

June hadn't thought of it like that. She tried to imagine how she'd feel if her best friend died and some stranger came poking around asking questions. Maybe she'd pushed Caleb to talk before he was ready.

"And he barely knew you then," Raven continued. "But you said he agreed to help with the paintings, so he's obviously warmed to you. Maybe he'll talk now."

June started to gather up the bottles and shove them back into the cabinet where she'd found them. She'd try to talk to Caleb, but she had her doubts about how that would go. Raven hadn't seen the darkness in Caleb's eyes when she'd pushed him for answers.

Raven and June carefully re-covered Jasper's paintings, locked the studio, and headed back up the path to the house. Raven went inside and grabbed her laptop, and the two of them sat on the front porch while she transferred the photos over from her camera.

Just as the download was finishing, Will's Mercedes pulled into the driveway and he and Caleb got out. June couldn't help noticing that as Caleb laughed at something Will said, the creases around his eyes softened their usual intensity. He glanced in her direction, and a dozen different emotions picked up their weapons and waged a battle in her chest.

June waved and did her best to flash him a casual smile before turning back to Raven's laptop, staring at it without really seeing the photos on the screen.

A moment later, Caleb and Will appeared at the bottom of the porch steps.

"How did the photo shoot go?" Caleb asked.

"Great," Raven said. "You want to come and see?"

"Definitely." Caleb and Will climbed onto the porch and stood behind June's chair, looking at Raven's laptop over her shoulder. June couldn't see Caleb behind her, but she could feel him there by the way her body heated.

Photos flashed by on the screen, one at a time.

"These are beautiful," Caleb remarked.

Raven had an eye for details most people would have missed. Paint droplets on the floor. A tiny pencil sketch of fish bones taped carelessly on the wall. A series of seashells evenly spaced in a line on a shelf. Raven had adjusted the camera's depth of field to focus on elements in the foreground and leave the backgrounds blurred, highlighting the texture and light on the objects.

"You've really captured Jasper's personality in these," Caleb murmured.

June looked up, hearing a hoarseness in his voice. *Had* he nursed Jasper through a long illness? Maybe she should have been more sensitive to his loss. She wanted to reach out and squeeze his hand, but held back.

"You think so?" Raven looked up from the laptop with a proud smile. "Obviously, I never met him, but I think you can get a sense of people from the things they surround themselves with. I try to focus on the unique elements."

Caleb nodded, his eyes still on the photos flashing across the screen. "You really did. It's more than just the objects. It's the angles you chose. Like this one." Caleb waved at a shot Raven had taken of a handful of sticks left on a table. "You shot it directly overhead so it highlights the vertical lines. That's Jasper's signature style. You see vertical lines in *Girl in the Trees*, and if you look around, you'll start to notice it in other places."

"Huh." Raven nodded and looked back at the laptop. " Vertical lines have always been sort of my signature, too. Maybe I inherited it from Jasper."

Will leaned in, examining another photo. "I'll bet there are magazines that would buy these photos from you, maybe even the *New York Times* Arts section. Jasper's studio shot by Jasper's daughter. Someone would snap that story up."

Raven turned and gave him a withering look. "I don't need to say I'm related to Jasper to get my work noticed."

"I didn't mean—" Will shook his head. "Never mind. Forget it." He walked over to the porch railing and leaned on it, his back to them.

June gave her sister a warning look. "Raven, Will was only suggesting it might make an interesting story…"

A loud bang from above their heads cut her off mid-sentence. They all jumped.

"What was that?" June ran down the porch steps and out onto the grass, looking back at the house. Caleb and Will followed, and the three of them gazed up at the gutter hanging off the eave. It swung gently in the breeze and scraped against the porch roof.

"Oh, shit," Caleb said. "I guess we've found the source of a leak Jasper told me about. He never got around to calling a contractor to check it out."

"How bad is a broken gutter?" June never dealt with contractors and repair men at home. David was sure workmen would scam a woman, so he always insisted on being the one to talk to them.

Will pulled out his phone and began scrolling through it. "I've got a neighbor who can take a look at it. I'll text you his contact info."

At that moment, June noticed Raven standing at the top of the steps, gripping the porch railing so hard her knuckles had turned white. Her face was deathly pale, her whole body shook, and she gasped for breath.

June ran to her sister. "Raven, are you okay?"

Caleb sprinted up the porch steps behind her. He slid an arm around Raven and gently guided her down onto a step. "Put your head between your knees. Deep, calm breaths. You're okay."

Raven leaned forward, sucking in slow, deliberate breaths, while Caleb murmured to her.

June searched the porch for her phone. "Should I call an ambulance?"

"No." Raven shook her head weakly. "I'm fine."

Will walked up the steps and put a hand on June's arm. "She's having a panic attack. Caleb knows how to deal with these. You can listen to him."

He does? How? But of course, this wasn't the time to ask.

June clutched her sister's hand as Caleb quietly talked Raven through her deep breaths. The low tone of his voice washed over June, and she felt strangely soothed by it. By the way her shoulders relaxed, Raven did too. June wouldn't have known what to do in this situation, but Caleb seemed so calm, almost in his element, and she couldn't help but wonder how many times he'd done this before.

Will went into the house and came back with a bottle of water for Raven. After a few minutes, she sat up and rubbed a hand across her sweaty forehead. She took a few gulps of the water, and finally murmured, "I'm okay."

"Are you sure?" June tucked a lock of Raven's hair behind her ear.

Raven nodded. "Yes. Just mortified." She shot a tiny glance in Will's direction.

"What do you think happened?" June asked. "Was it the noise from when the gutter fell?"

Raven shrugged.

"Has this happened before?"

"Maybe." Raven shot another glance at Will, and then stared down at the toe of her sneaker. "It's actually happened a few times since last month." She rubbed her hands across her eyes. "I ended up in a rough situation in Uganda. You probably heard about the terrorist attack in the shopping mall? Where eighty people were killed?" Raven took a deep, shaky breath. "Well, I was there."

"Jesus," Will muttered under his breath.

"Oh my God, Raven." June's heart thudded in her chest. "You never said anything."

Raven shrugged. "I mean, I've photographed war zones before. I thought I was okay. But—this was different. This time I was a target."

"How terrifying." June's eyes filled with tears. No wonder Raven was bitter about the state of the world.

June felt a gentle hand squeeze her shoulder. Caleb, reaching behind Raven's back, offering a small bit of comfort. As she wrestled to keep her own emotions under control, part of her wanted so badly to lean on him. To hear him talk to her in that same calm, reassuring voice and, for once, to not have to be the one who held it all together.

But June knew this wasn't the time to fall apart. Her sister needed her. She mustered up a weak smile to let Caleb know she was okay. He must have gotten the hint because he gestured to Will and pointed at his house, letting her know they were going to sneak off and let her talk to her sister privately. She nodded. It was for the best.

Caleb hesitated for a moment, his dark eyes filling with worry, before he finally followed Will down the path.

June turned back to her sister. "Do you want to talk about it?"

"Not really."

"You can't bottle this up. Look what happens." June gestured at her sister slumped on the step.

Raven slowly stood up, brushing some nonexistent dust from her jeans. "I'm fine, honestly. I just need a little vacation." She headed across the porch to where they'd abandoned her camera and laptop on the table.

June followed her. "Is it okay if I tell Sierra? She needs to know."

Raven kept her head bent over her bag, shoving her camera inside and zipping it up with jerky movements. "Do what you have to do. But tell her not to get all weepy about it. You guys know my job is risky. This isn't news."

"I know, but—"

"Let's stop talking about it, okay?" Raven snapped her laptop shut.

"Still—" June had never seen Raven affected by an experience like this.

"June, I don't want to talk about it." Raven picked up her camera bag and slung it over her shoulder. "I'm *fine.* I swear. Let it go, okay?"

Raven's cheeks were still pale and her hair was a mess from bending forward to try to breathe. And she was clutching her stomach again. No wonder she'd been having stomach issues.

June wanted to throw her arms around her sister and protect her from the horrors of the outside world. To promise everything would be okay, just like she'd done when Raven was a little girl, and the way she did for Emma and Izzy now. But Raven wasn't a little girl anymore, and the barbed expression she leveled at June said she didn't want or need her interference.

June decided to give Raven some space. The last thing she wanted was to push her sister back to work before she was ready, and the surest way to do that would be to keep asking her to talk. "Okay. I'm here if you need me."

Raven nodded. "I know." Her mouth stretched into a smile that only looked a tiny bit forced. "Now, I've got to find my favorite girls to go whale-watching. And you've got a date in Jasper's studio."

"It's not a date," June blurted out, automatically.

"You sure?" Raven's eyebrows shot up. "I see the looks Caleb gives you."

"It's Caleb's brooding thing. He looks at everyone like that."

Raven crossed her arms in front of her. "He doesn't look at me like that."

June remembered his reassuring hand on her shoulder, and shivered. Raven shot her a knowing look before she grabbed the rest of her camera gear and headed for the front door of the house. June watched her sister disappear inside and sank down in a chair, suddenly exhausted. She and her sisters were quite the trio. Her marriage had crumbled, Raven was suffering from post-traumatic stress, and Sierra clammed up when questioned about her latest book.

A breeze blew from the direction of the sea, sending the purple lupine swaying across the meadow like a blanket unfurling. The gray clouds she'd grown to expect stretched to the horizon, but a tiny break let in the slanted lines of the sun's rays to graze the ocean like the crayon strokes of a child's drawing.

Why, after three decades of silence, had Jasper left them everything? Had he had any idea it would bring them together like this?

Whatever his reasons were, maybe they needed this place more than they knew. Maybe they needed each other, too.

CHAPTER FIFTEEN

At five minutes to one, June hurried down the path toward Jasper's studio to meet Caleb. Halfway down the hill, she spotted him leaning on the fence at the edge of the cliff, gazing out at the water. She slowed her steps and took a moment to admire his tall frame and the lean muscles flexing in his arms as he bent to grasp the fence rail.

It was hard to reconcile her first impression of him with the man standing in front of her. Watching him lean casually against the wooden rail, looking every bit as appealing in jeans and a T-shirt as his brother had in a three-piece suit, June couldn't deny Caleb was one of the most attractive men she'd ever encountered. Even in their first contentious interaction, she'd been drawn to him, and the feeling seemed to grow every time they were together.

She never would have imagined telling Caleb, of all people, about her secret drawings. But he'd asked about her sisters and had somehow understood she'd been the pillar that kept the roof from collapsing during their earthquake of a childhood. He seemed to view her as more than a mom to the girls, accountant, and wife of David. It had been so long since anyone had regarded her as her own person or thought to ask about her interests.

June shifted her sketchbook in her arms and, as if he sensed movement behind him, Caleb turned around. "Hey, how's Raven?"

"Acting like everything is fine."

"That was a pretty shocking revelation." Caleb shoved his hands in his pockets. "If you want to do this another time, I understand."

"No, it's okay. Raven is taking the girls whale-watching. She's done talking about it, so there's no use hanging around." June nervously spun the keys to the studio in her hand. "Unless you want to reschedule." As soon as the words were out of her mouth, she realized how much she'd been looking forward to spending this time with him in Jasper's studio. But she also knew this wouldn't be easy for him. Maybe he was hoping to put it off.

"Are you kidding? Don't think I didn't notice those drawings in your hand."

June gripped the sketchbook tightly for another second and then held it out to him. "You can take it, but only if you look when I'm not around." She couldn't bear to stand by nervously while he flipped through her work. If he hated it, at least she wouldn't have to watch while he struggled to keep a straight face.

He stepped closer. "Thank you for trusting me with this." His hand brushed hers as he took the sketchbook, and a warm current climbed up her arm and settled in her chest.

June turned away and concentrated on opening the studio door, doing her best to ignore the nutty scent radiating from where Caleb stood less than a foot away. It was probably the linseed oil he mixed with paint. She remembered how the smell used to permeate her own skin a lifetime ago. Maybe his effect on her had nothing to do with the man himself; maybe it was only the memories of being a young artist that he evoked.

June glanced up and their eyes met. No, it wasn't just old memories. Her heart slammed in her chest.

The key shook in her hand, and she almost dropped it before she managed to slide it into the lock. After an eternity, she pushed the door open and entered the studio, moving to the middle of the room to put a little space between them.

"Okay, I brought my laptop to log everything," June said. "How should we do this?" She wanted to jump right to asking about the pills in the cabinet, but what if he shut her down again, just like he had at the grocery store? What if he stormed off? This was her best shot to get the answers she'd been craving for the past three decades. She needed to approach Caleb carefully.

"Why don't you set up over there? I'll see what's over here." Caleb waved her over to a table on one side of the room, and June focused on her computer while he flipped through the canvases leaning against the wall. After a moment of sorting, he picked one and put it on the table in front of her.

Two people stood reflected upside down in a pond, their images blurred from the movement of a stone hitting the water and the waves rippling out to shore. The painting evoked a sense of stillness disturbed, and June found herself becoming strangely emotional, wanting to keep watching the scene until the water calmed and the figures came back into focus.

Caleb's voice floated into her thoughts. "This is an old one he painted right when I started working for him."

June looked up, surprised. "That long ago? Why is it still here? Shouldn't it be in a gallery or a museum?"

Caleb smiled and June couldn't miss the affection there. "Jasper never thought he got the movement right." He pointed to a corner of the painting where, to June's marginally trained eye, the water was slightly smudged. "He stewed over it for days, and finally gave up. So, this painting has been sitting here for years." Caleb shook his head. "It belongs somewhere people can experience it."

June turned back to the canvas in front of her, better under-standing Caleb's protectiveness over Jasper's work. If these paintings caused her to react so powerfully now, how must he feel after spending half his life invested in them?

He paused over the painting for one more moment before moving back to the wall of Jasper's work to select another. June snapped a photo of the canvas and logged it on the spreadsheet. While Caleb shuffled paintings across the room, June examined the section of water where Jasper had struggled. She probably wouldn't have noticed the slight imperfection if Caleb hadn't pointed it out. Almost twenty years ago, Jasper had already made a name for himself as a contemporary artist, yet he still had insecurities about his work that kept him from sharing it with the public.

June thought about her own drawings from the past week. One minute, she felt incredibly proud of them, and the next, the doubts seeped in. Maybe Jasper had wanted to throw his work in the sand and let the water sweep it away, just like she had. A cavern of longing split open in her chest, and she wished more than anything she could have known him, just a little. That she could have talked to him about all of this. Had he been a part of her life, would he have encouraged her work, mentored her the way he'd mentored Caleb?

Would he have been proud of me?

Caleb returned to the table with another painting and set it in front of her. He didn't speak, and she could feel his eyes on her, waiting for a reaction.

"Oh," June gasped. "A self-portrait."

Jasper had painted a close-up of his face gazing out of what looked to be the door of a shower. Steam gathered on the glass, blurring most of his image, but a casual hand-swipe across the surface had cleared a path, revealing half his mouth and nose, one intense blue-gray eye, and a patch of silver-streaked, wavy black hair.

With him staring back at her like this, up close and in full color, there was no denying Jasper was her father. She'd seen those eyes in the mirror for her entire life, and on the faces of her daughters.

She looked up to find Caleb watching her intently. "Is it painful for you to look at me? And the girls? We look so much like him."

Caleb cocked his head, and his gaze was a wool coat wrapping around her, heavy and warm. She resisted the urge to yank at the neck of her shirt. He shook his head. "Maybe it was a little, at first. But I think Jasper would've been proud of the girls. It's sad to think of him missing out on knowing them. And you…"

Caleb paused, his dark eyes tracing the brushstrokes of Jasper's portrait and then flickering back to June's face. "I have a confession to make. I found one of your drawings on the beach a couple of days ago."

Oh God. June's face flushed as she remembered the sketch of the sailboat on the water. Her mind grasped at all the flaws—the too-dark lines of the trees, the fabric on the sails that didn't hang quite right. She'd carefully chosen her best sketches in the book she'd given to Caleb. The sailboat would never have made the cut. Why hadn't she taken it back to the house and buried it in the trash?

"June, you're incredibly talented."

She shook her head. "I was only playing around… I didn't mean for anyone to see…" Her voice trailed off as he picked up her sketchbook from the table and flipped it open. "No, please don't look at it now—"

But it was too late. Caleb stood there with one hand on the table, leaning over a drawing she'd made yesterday of the girls playing on the beach during a break in the rain. "Look at this. You've so perfectly captured their individuality." He gestured at the page. "I swear, you can almost hear them laughing."

June had done her best to express the girls' unique personalities: Emma's bold gestures as she haphazardly dumped sand on a piece of driftwood and watched it slide to the ground; the exactness of Izzy's movements, gently pressing seashells into the soft sand to create a barrier around her carefully constructed castle. June was proud of that drawing… As long as she didn't spend too much time picking apart the flaws. "The rocks in the background still need work."

Caleb pushed himself off the table, shaking his head. "It's not about being technically perfect. It's about how people connect with your subject. The emotions you evoke. I don't think you have any idea how talented you are. And having you here, in Jasper's space…"

June grasped her left hand with her right and felt something missing. The rings she'd taken off that morning. She held her breath, suddenly nervous about what he might say.

"It sounds crazy, but I feel like you belong here," Caleb said softly. "Creating drawings like this one. Drawings that kick people right in the gut when they look at them. And if it took Jasper passing away to make that happen for you… well, it comforts me to think maybe something good came out of his death."

It should have brought her a sense of pride, and it did. A little. But there was something else there, too. She couldn't completely bury the pain the sentiment caused her. "I can't help but wonder why. Why did he have to die in order for me to come here, to get to know him? Why couldn't I have had this while he was still alive?"

By the way he blinked, the question surprised Caleb, or maybe it was the harshness in her tone.

It wasn't sadness over the death of her father causing her jaw to clench and her hands to shake. She was angry. At Jasper and, maybe, irrationally, at Caleb, too.

She couldn't tell Jasper what she was feeling, so she turned on Caleb. "Why did he leave us, move to the other side of the country, and live a whole life without us? Why didn't he want anything to do with his own daughters, but picked a total stranger to embrace like a son?"

Caleb took a step toward her. "June, that's not how it was. It wasn't a choice the way you're thinking it was. It wasn't you or me."

But it all came spilling out. "Didn't he care enough to find out anything about us? His own daughter is a successful photographer. He could have connected with her, seen the value in her work. And Sierra is a talented writer, she's even won awards. And as for my work—" She paused, remembering the few measly drawings she'd completed in the past few days. All those years she'd wasted, keeping her creativity all locked up. Suddenly, her anger dissipated. "I guess I probably didn't have much to offer."

"That's not true—"

"It is true. I squandered my talent to end up as nothing but a boring accountant with a cheating husband and a marriage that's fallen apart."

Caleb's eyes widened at the revelation and something shifted in the way he looked at her. It was probably disgust etched across his face. She'd thrown away her talent for a marriage and a life she couldn't even hold together. Maybe she was more pathetic than he'd thought.

"I keep thinking that if Jasper had been there to encourage me, I could have been something. I could have been doing what you're doing right now, spending my life in a place like this"—she waved her arm wildly around Jasper's studio—"painting every day and seeing my work in galleries where it could touch people. I could've had a life like this."

"*You still can!* June, you're not dead yet. You're what—in your mid-thirties? You have an entire life ahead of you."

"It's easy for you to say that when you don't have the responsibilities—"

Caleb slapped his hand down on the table. "Damn the responsibilities."

June blinked in surprise. Had her art inspired this kind of passionate response from him? It almost made her believe she really was good enough to go back to taking art seriously. But then she sighed. Even if she were good enough, there was so much at stake she had to think about. "The girls—"

"The girls are great. But you don't have to be an accountant for the rest of your life in order to be a great mother." He leaned in, both hands pressing down on the table. "Don't you want the girls to see you doing what you love? Don't you want them to grow up knowing it's possible to live your dreams?"

"But David—"

"You don't owe David anything. For once in your life, think about yourself. What do *you* want?"

She wished it were that easy. She wished she could be as sure as he was. June's shoulders slumped, and suddenly her head began to ache. "I don't know."

"Yes, you do. You want to be an artist, so *be an artist*."

June looked at Jasper's paintings laid out on the table. Their intensity gave her chills. That's what really good art did to you.

"I was so little when Jasper left." June closed her eyes, scouring the corners of her mind for memories of her father. She could see his dark curly hair spilling over silver-blue eyes that squinted at her with laughter. He'd cared about her. But was that something she remembered, or had her imagination conjured it up because she was so desperate to believe it?

She'd probably never know, and maybe it didn't matter. Jasper had left, and that told her everything she needed to know about how much he'd cared about her. June's eyes flew open and found Caleb. "Jasper picked up and moved across the country. He found *you* to invest all this time and energy into. Because you deserved it. I guess I didn't deserve it."

June knew it wasn't rational to say Jasper had picked Caleb over her. He'd met Caleb as an adult, while she'd only been a child. But she'd spent three decades recovering from her father's abandonment, and being in Wishing Cove had triggered a landslide of emotions.

"June, you didn't have anything to do with why Jasper walked away."

She stood abruptly, paced across the room and stopped in front of Jasper's easel. The canvas he would never finish gazed back, and its swirls of color, not yet fully formed, seemed to mock her. The painting was like her career as an artist: both had potential but neither would ever materialize.

"Why *did* he walk away?" June whirled around to face Caleb. "What right do you have to know so much about my father, but keep it a secret from me?"

"I'm not keeping—"

"Just stop it." June marched over to the cabinet in the back of the room and swung it open. "If you're not keeping secrets about my father, then tell me what *these* are." She grabbed a handful of pill bottles and waved them in Caleb's direction.

His face drained of color.

So much for approaching Caleb carefully. But sorrow and anger had been simmering inside her for so long, and building in her chest like steam in a pot since she'd come to her father's estate. Finally, the lid came flying off.

June came back to where Caleb stood. "Tell me what these are for." She flung the bottles on the table.

"I—these are—" Caleb cursed under his breath as he raked a hand through his hair and stared past her, out the window.

"Were you going to tell me about any of this?"

He took a deep breath. "No."

Just like that. No discussion, nothing. *Just "no".* Suddenly, June was so tired of these men and their secrets. Jasper. David. She'd wasted years of her life living in the dark, only knowing half the story from men who didn't care one bit about her. She wasn't going to waste one more second on Caleb.

"Get out."

At that, he met her eyes. "What?"

"Get out. If you're not going to tell me the full story, if you're going to keep a dead man's secrets at the expense of people who are very much alive, then I don't want you here. Go."

Caleb eyed her warily, as if he were afraid she might grab the broom from the corner and swing it at him again. She seriously considered it.

"Fine. *I'll* go. But I will find out what you're protecting him from." June turned on her heels and swung open the studio door. "Goodbye, Caleb."

CHAPTER SIXTEEN

Wiping his sweaty palms on his jeans, Caleb eyed the woman walking out the door with her arms crossed in front of her. *Shit, I thought I'd thrown all the pills away.* How could he have forgotten to check the cabinet in the studio? And now June was demanding answers.

Answers she deserved.

Except it wasn't only Jasper's story. Those weren't only Jasper's pills.

But how could he let her continue to think Jasper had left because there was something wrong with her? It hadn't just been anger slashed across her face. There was hurt in her eyes too. Heartbreak. She must have spent years agonizing over the father who'd left her, and in not knowing why, she'd blamed herself.

Caleb approached the bottles rolling across the table and picked one up. Before he could change his mind, he called out to June. "Okay. I'll talk."

She came back into the room cautiously, almost as if she were suddenly afraid of whatever was in the bottle Caleb held out to her. Finally, she took it and turned it around in her hand so she could read the label. "Lithium? What is it?"

"It's a mood stabilizer."

She looked at the next bottle. "Aripiprazole." She sounded the word out slowly.

"It's an antipsychotic."

June's eyebrows shot northward. "An antipsychotic? Why?"

Caleb sucked in a breath. He didn't know why he was so nervous. If she reacted badly, it would tell him all he needed to know. "Jasper had bipolar disorder."

"Bipolar disorder? What was that like?"

Caleb slid into a chair and indicated she should sit, too. "It's different for everyone, but many people with bipolar disorder go through episodes of mood swings, from depressed lows to manic highs."

June slowly lowered herself into a chair across from him. "And you're saying Jasper suffered from these mood swings—depressed lows and manic highs?"

"Yeah. The medications helped. But sometimes he'd try to go off them."

"And what would happen?"

"A couple of times he had manic episodes and stayed up working for days at a time. Became obsessed with getting a painting right to the point that he stopped eating and sleeping. But he had a really good psychiatrist who was very involved with his treatment."

June looked down at her hands as understanding dawned on her face. "I bet *you* were very involved, too."

Caleb shrugged. If only she knew how little credit he deserved. "Maybe a little. I tried, anyway."

"Is this how you knew how to help Raven earlier? Are panic attacks common in people with bipolar disorder?"

"They can be." Caleb shifted in his seat.

"Did Jasper ever have them?"

No. Jasper hadn't ever had a panic attack in the years Caleb knew him. But this wasn't only about Jasper, even if June thought it was. Caleb's life and Jasper's, they were so tightly woven, sometimes he forgot whose story was whose. "I guess."

June looked at him with her brow furrowed, and he knew she was waiting for an explanation. But he wasn't going there. Not today.

Not ever.

Finally, June blinked and sat back in her chair, focusing her gaze on the pills in her hand. "So—what? Jasper took off and left us because people with bipolar disorder can't have kids? I'm sorry, Caleb, but I'm not buying it."

"Of course, they can have kids. But—" He paused.

How could he explain what it was like to spend your life examining your moods under a microscope? To have to keep watch because looking away could mean losing control, screwing up your life, and hurting the people you care about the most? "Jasper said something happened to make him realize you and your sisters weren't safe. That you were better off without him. So, he left."

June nodded slowly, before asking in a measured voice, "What was the something that happened?"

"He never gave me any details. But it was something that scared him enough to leave for good. I think Jasper was ashamed, and that can be part of bipolar disorder, too. When you come down from a manic episode, you have to face the mess you made and the people you hurt."

June shoved her chair back from the table and stood up. She crossed the room and stared at the painting Jasper had left on the easel. Slowly, she turned toward Caleb, her blue eyes stark against her pale face. "How did he die?"

He should have known he couldn't avoid this conversation forever: of course she would want to know how Jasper died. Caleb just couldn't move past the feeling that he had a small part in it.

"Jasper had pneumonia a couple of months ago. He was sick for weeks, and even after he started to feel better, he couldn't sleep and had no appetite. It was affecting his work. His doctor gave

him some sleeping pills to help him get past the rough patch."
Caleb took a deep breath. "Primary care doctors are notoriously
bad about paying attention to drug interactions with bipolar
meds. He should have seen his psychiatrist to check the dosage. I
should have *made* him see his psychiatrist. But I was traveling—I
had a couple of gallery shows in Chicago and New York, and—"
Caleb shook his head. The gallery in New York was a prestigious
one. It had been an honor to display his work in their show. He'd
gotten caught up in all the recognition.

"They think the sleeping pills interacted with his anti-
psychotics"—Caleb forced the next words out—"causing his
heart to stop."

He glanced at June, who was staring intently back at him.

"It's not your fault," she whispered.

"Rationally, I know. But—"

"But you blame yourself."

"Of course I do."

"It was an accident."

An accident he should have prevented.

June pressed a palm to her temple. "I'm still trying to wrap my
head around it all. He didn't think my sisters and I were safe with
him—for whatever reason—when we were kids. But what about
when we were teenagers? Or adults? He could have contacted us
at any point in the last twenty years. Why didn't he? Jasper didn't
care about us. Maybe he only left us this inheritance out of guilt."

She's wrong.

Caleb had been hearing about Jasper's daughters for years.
And everything about their lives had seemed pretty damn perfect.
They were happy, well-off, successful.

How could Caleb explain to June the daily struggles of mental
illness, the lows and highs? How could he describe to her what
it was like to be a sinking ship trying not to drag anyone else
down with you?

How could he tell her Jasper had chosen him because they were alike in so many ways beyond art?

His vision blurred like the smear of a child's finger-painting. *I can't. I can't tell her.*

But he couldn't let her believe she hadn't mattered. That her art didn't matter.

"There's one more thing I need to show you." Caleb crossed the studio again, to another cabinet against the same wall.

"That cabinet is locked," June said. "Raven told me she tried to open it earlier, and neither of us could find the key."

Caleb pulled the key from his pocket. "Yeah, that's because I took it." He should have remembered the other cabinet too, the one with the pills in it. He hadn't been thinking straight.

June blinked in surprise.

Caleb inserted the key in the lock and yanked the door open. From the bottom shelf, he pulled out a cardboard box.

Behind him, he heard June ask, "What is it?"

Caleb moved over to the couch along the back wall. He set the box down on the coffee table and gestured for June to come over. She lowered herself onto the couch next to him and perched near the edge of the cushion with her back straight. Tense.

Caleb slid the box across the table toward her. "Open it."

CHAPTER SEVENTEEN

June wasn't sure she wanted to know what was in the box. All these revelations about Jasper had left her with more questions than answers. What had happened to make Jasper think she and her sisters weren't safe with him? Was it a convenient excuse he'd used to justify leaving them and never looking back?

She gave Caleb the side-eye as she reached for the box and slowly pulled off the lid. Inside, she found a stack of papers and newspaper clippings. At first glance, it looked like a bunch of junk someone didn't know what to do with. She shot Caleb a skeptical look and he waved a hand at the box, indicating she should look closer. June pulled a piece of paper off the top of the stack and flipped it over.

She gasped.

It was an article from the *Greenwich Gazette*. The local newspaper had interviewed her a year ago about how she juggled being a working mom and a volunteer at the kids' school. They'd used a photo of her and the girls selling tickets at the annual carnival fundraiser.

How did Jasper get a copy of this article? And why did he keep it in a box in his studio?

Caleb reclined against the couch, his expression impenetrable, so she turned back to the contents of the box and found her face staring back up at her. She recognized the photo from the company 'Meet the Team' page. Underneath the headshot, her bio listed her professional accomplishments—Master of Accountancy, job title, board appointments. Jasper must've printed it off and saved it.

June kept digging, pulling paper after paper from the box.

There was a picture of her at the company Christmas party, and a college newspaper story about the annual harvest party David's fraternity hosted at a local farm, with a photo someone had snapped of her picking apples. And many more, all the way back to a small pile of baby and toddler photos rubber-banded together. Looking in the box was like looking at a retrospective of her life.

June tore her gaze away from the papers strewn in front of her and focused on Caleb. "How did Jasper get all of this?"

Caleb leaned forward, picking up an article from the table. "Every few months, Jasper would google you and your sisters. He collected every photo or story and printed them out. There are other boxes in the cabinet for Sierra and Raven."

June surveyed her history, laid out in fragments on the table. Jasper had kept all of this, not only from her childhood, but recently, too. He'd cared about her and her sisters, had secreted away any details of their lives he could find. "Jasper did all this, and he never once thought about reaching out? Not in all this time?"

"I'm sure he thought about it. How could he not?" Caleb shook his head slowly. "He told me once, early on, that he thought about sending money, but by the time his work started to be recognized and he actually had money to send, you were in high school, well on your way to Yale, and he thought you wouldn't want to hear from him." Caleb reached for a photo of her from the college yearbook. "He did pay for your scholarship though, anonymously, of course. And Sierra's too."

June's eyes flew to his face. "He did?" She didn't think it could hurt any more, but she'd been wrong. Her thoughts immediately darted to her kids. What would it be like to only know them through photographs, or an occasional article printed in the newspaper?

Her heart ached for them all. She and her sisters had missed out on having a father, and her girls, a grandfather. But Jasper had missed out on his children. She still didn't completely understand why, but her eyes burned at what must have been the agony of that decision.

June blinked as a flash of a memory, hazy around the edges, formed in her mind. *An avocado-green stove with a silver pot on top. Fire lapping at a curtain hanging from a window. And then*—that was it. The image disappeared. Was it a memory, or just a figment of her imagination?

A drop of water splashed on the newspaper article in her hand, leaving a dark spot that bled into the headline. A second one fell right beside it. Her tears. She was crying. For everything she'd lost, for everything they'd all lost.

Caleb's hand gently pressed down on her arm, drawing her back to reality. "You okay?"

"Yes." June swiped at her cheeks with her palm. "Thank you for sharing this with me." She reached out and took his hand. "It means so much to know that—whatever the reason he left—at least he didn't walk away easily."

Caleb looked down at their intertwined fingers, and his gaze slowly flickered to her face. His dark eyes were inches away, searching hers with an intensity that sent a shiver through her. Without thinking, she pulled her hand away. Caleb blew out a breath and leaned back against the couch cushions, putting some space between them.

Regret washed over her, but she wasn't sure if it was for holding his hand, or for pulling away. She'd been with David since she was nineteen years old. David, who was safe, stable, and predictable. Or at least she'd always thought he was. But David was a lie.

And Caleb was here, making her feel things she'd never felt before. Feelings she'd gone thirty-eight years without. Could she handle this kind of attraction with a man like Caleb?

June busied herself clearing up the papers on the coffee table, scooping them back into the cardboard box. Caleb leaned in to help, careful now—it seemed—not to get too close. When they had most of the papers back in the box, he paused with an article in his hand, holding it up to look more closely. June peered over his shoulder and saw it was about the harvest party.

"Jasper spent a lot of time looking at this one," Caleb said, smoothing it out on the coffee table.

Funny Caleb should pick that one to focus on. June had vivid memories of that day—a fundraiser the fraternity had hosted at a local farm for a charity she knew none of the guys cared about. But it looked good to do community service. Guests paid exorbitant amounts of money—or at least it seemed exorbitant at the time—to go apple picking, drink spiked cider, and dance to a country band.

In the article's main photo, David and his friends posed for the camera with drinks in their hands and their arms around a couple of girls from a nearby sorority. But in a smaller photo at the bottom of the page, the editors had printed a candid photo of June standing alone in a grove of apple trees, reaching up to pick one from a hanging branch.

It had been her freshman year, a few weeks after she'd met David. Looking at the photo years later, all the emotions of that day came rushing back. Excitement at hanging out with her new boyfriend's friends. Nervousness over whether they liked her. But she also remembered feeling out of place. Lonely. David had known everyone, had wanted to make the rounds, slap guys on the back and laugh at inside jokes. But he hadn't been so great about sharing stories with her, or making sure she felt included. That day, she'd wandered off into the apple grove so it wouldn't be so obvious she didn't have anyone to talk to.

June traced her hand across the faded photograph and something hollow opened up inside of her. Had nothing changed since that day? She still felt lonely and out of place so much of the time. More often than not, David expressed annoyance that she wasn't better at being social; at schmoozing clients and charming their spouses, drinking cocktails with other wives at the country club, or being on committees with the "right" parents at the girls' private school. None of it had ever come naturally to her.

When will I stop trying to be the girl in the photo, and just be me?

"Jasper talked about how solitary you seemed out there in the orchard." Caleb cut into her memories, dispersing them like leaves blowing in an autumn wind. "I remember thinking that if you were with me at a party, I'd never leave you all alone."

June's head jerked up from the page and her heart thudded at the sight of him there, leaning casually against the cushions. His faded T-shirt clung to his muscular torso and a lock of his hair teased his cheek.

"And with your talent, I'd never, *ever* have let you give up painting. Not without a fight." Caleb cocked his head, looking her up and down, and she felt—

Seen.

Seen in a way she hadn't been in years. Maybe not since she was a pink-haired girl who dreamed of being an artist.

June leaned across the couch then, grabbed hold of his T-shirt and pressed her mouth against his. Caleb wrapped his arms around her and kissed her back without hesitation, as if he'd been waiting for this since the day they'd met.

Maybe they'd both been waiting for this.

The heat between them burned brighter and more intense with each moment, like a bonfire they'd stacked with every look, and word, and gesture since their first fiery interaction. June slid onto his lap without breaking the kiss and pushed him back against the cushions. He filled her senses—his nutty scent, the taste of his mouth, the solidness of him against her. June pulled away for a second to shift her body so it was pressed against his, but he stilled, gently stopping her with his hands on her shoulders.

"June."

She blinked, momentarily disoriented.

Caleb sat up, breathing hard. "We should stop." He cursed under his breath. "Believe me, it's not because I want to."

June wrung the hem of her T-shirt in her hands. It was the first time they'd even kissed, and she'd practically attacked him. She tried to muster up shame or remorse, but she couldn't manage more than a faint blush. It had been amazing, and she wasn't sorry. But it was the middle of the day, they were facing a wall of windows, and her sisters and the girls could walk by at any moment.

"I know. You're right." June slid off his lap.

She watched with regret as he pulled his bunched-up T-shirt down over the brown skin of his muscled abs. Someone forgot to give Caleb the memo that artists were supposed to be pale and skinny.

"So… now what?" It had been so long since she'd made out with a man. The few obligatory before-bed quickies she and David sometimes managed hardly counted. She had no idea how to navigate this. Did they pretend this never happened? Make a plan to do it again?

I pick option B.

"You've had a really intense day," Caleb said, rubbing a hand across his face. "That bombshell from Raven, and now Jasper. I don't want to take advantage of that."

It *had* been an intense day, and intense month, really. But while most of it had left her feeling as tossed around and wrung out as clothes in the spin cycle, she was clear on one thing. "Caleb, nothing happened I didn't want to happen."

"Yeah?" Something hopeful moved across his expression, and he reached out and weaved his fingers through hers.

June scooted closer to him on the couch. "Yes."

"Good," he murmured, his gaze drifting from her face to her neck as if he were imagining kissing her there. "Because I've wanted to do that since the first day I found you standing here in the studio."

"Me, too," she whispered, closing the distance between them again. And for one gorgeous moment, all the intensity of the day... the week... the month... faded into the background and only this, only Caleb, came into sharp focus. June relaxed into him, shutting out everything but the warm pressure of his mouth against hers and the rhythmic beat of his heart.

When they finally pulled apart, June let out a half-laugh, half-sigh. "What was that you said about stopping?"

"That was temporary insanity." He flashed her a grin, and that unbridled smile was so rare, and so beautiful on his face, that her heart slid right up into her throat. This was more than just physical attraction to a good-looking guy. This was... feelings. And feelings could be complicated, given she'd be leaving at the end of the summer.

She should put a stop to it right now.

Except, thirty seconds later, when he suggested they meet back at Jasper's studio after Emma and Izzy went to bed, she didn't say no.

She said yes.

CHAPTER EIGHTEEN

"Mommy, you won't believe what we saw today from the boat!" Emma greeted June at the door, jumping up and down. "We saw *killer whales*!"

Raven appeared in the hallway behind the girls. "It was really cool. I got some great shots of the girls. I'll show you later."

June looked her sister up and down, noting with relief her smile looked relaxed and her cheeks pink and healthy. No evidence of the panic attack from earlier. "How are you?" she murmured to Raven as she eased past the girls into the house.

"I'm good. Everything is *fine*." Raven shot her a pointed look. "And I told Sierra what happened while the girls were helping the captain drive the boat. So, we can stop talking about it now."

June held up her hands in surrender. "Okay, okay. I'll stop asking."

"How was the studio?" Raven asked. "Anything interesting?"

June knew Raven was asking about the paintings, but her face heated at the memory of Caleb. "Actually, we didn't get too far with the paintings. Caleb had some pretty interesting information to share about Jasper."

"Really?" Raven's eyebrows shot up. "Like what?"

"Mommy, can we watch TV?" Emma's voice cut in.

June dragged her focus away from the studio and back to the girls. They needed a snack, and a bath, and she should probably think about starting dinner. Her body sagged with exhaustion. What she really wanted to do was run a bath for herself and go over the whole afternoon in her mind, until she could make all these new developments fit into her carefully constructed view of the world.

"Come on, girls," Raven said, ushering the girls toward the staircase. "I'll let you play on my iPad while Mommy and Aunt Sierra and I talk." She glanced up at June. "Okay with you?"

June nodded, grateful for her sisters' help. She hadn't completely faced the realities of being a full-time single mother, but it was probably time to start getting used to the idea.

While Raven got the girls settled, June made her way to the kitchen, where Sierra sat at the island, frowning at her laptop. She slammed it shut when June entered, looking up with a smile that appeared strained.

June walked towards Sierra and put an arm around her shoulder. "How are you holding up?"

Confusion crossed Sierra's face as her blue eyes darted from her laptop to June and back again. "Why? What do you mean?"

"I can't believe Raven didn't tell us right away," June prompted.

"Oh." Sierra's shoulders relaxed. "Yes. I know. I can't believe it, either."

June squinted at her sister as two pink splotches appeared on her pale cheeks. "Is something going on? You haven't told us much about your book."

"Oh, there's nothing to tell." She shrugged a slender shoulder, giving the laptop a shove and hopping off the stool to peer into the refrigerator.

June watched her sister dig through its contents and then close it again without taking anything out. Sierra had always been quieter than Raven, but this felt different. She was hiding something.

"Sierra, what's going on?"

Sierra let out a heavy sigh. "The truth is, my *book* isn't going. I have writer's block. I've entirely missed my deadline, and my editor is threatening to terminate my contract."

"Why do you think you're struggling? Did something happen?" June's mind immediately flashed to Raven's bombshell earlier that day.

"No, nothing like that. It's just—part of the process. I'll get past it." Sierra waved off her concern. "So, how was the studio?"

At that moment, Raven returned and settled on a bar stool. Sierra poured some wine and they all sat around the kitchen island, while June relayed the story Caleb had shared earlier about Jasper's bipolar disorder diagnosis, his accidental death, and the boxes of memorabilia.

As June finished speaking, Raven sank back into her bar stool. "Wow. That's a lot on Caleb's shoulders. No wonder he's been so aloof."

A weight settled on June's chest when she thought about his vague response to her question about Jasper's panic attacks. Why did she have the feeling there was more to the story? But maybe Raven was right. Caleb had been through a lot, and it was understandable that he didn't want to rehash every detail. He'd been open about the things that mattered.

"There's a box of photos and articles for each of you in the studio," June told her sisters. "You should look through them."

"I'd always imagined Jasper was a deadbeat dad who had no interest in us," Raven said. "It's almost sadder he collected all this stuff and still never got in touch."

"I keep thinking, what if we'd grown up knowing him?" June twisted her wineglass in her hand. "Who would we be right now?"

"I don't know." Raven wrinkled her forehead. "It might have been nice to know him but would you really want things to be different? We all have great careers and have achieved success on our own, not because our dad was some famous artist. And you have the girls, and I know you'd never change that, right?"

"No, of course not." June took a gulp from her glass. "But don't you ever wonder what might've happened if you'd taken a different path? What would you do if you could do anything in the entire world?"

Raven and Sierra went silent, exchanging a glance with each other. Raven opened her mouth and closed it again, and Sierra scrubbed briefly at a spot on the counter with her thumb.

Then Sierra reached out and put a hand on her arm. "Junie, is there some way you wish your life had been different?"

You want to be an artist, so be an artist.

"Sometimes I think about"—June took a deep breath and looked up at her sisters—"painting again."

"You do?" Raven nearly knocked her off her stool with a hug. "That's so exciting!"

Sierra smiled. "I remember how much you loved painting in high school. When you switched to accounting in college, I always wondered why you gave it up."

Caleb's voice echoed again, reminding June her sisters had no idea about the sacrifices she'd made for them. She couldn't tell them the truth. "I've been doing a little bit of drawing since I came to Wishing Cove, and I'm thinking of getting back into it."

The tension in her body eased with that small admission. "I showed a few of my drawings to Caleb, and he's been really encouraging. We're going to meet later." June's cheeks turned warm. "To talk about art," she quickly added. "That is, as long as you guys don't mind keeping an eye on the girls after bedtime."

Raven was still clutching her arm, and with that statement, she squeezed it tighter. "Of course, we don't mind."

"Not at all," Sierra chimed in. "Now, should we go upstairs and figure out what you're going to wear when you meet Caleb"—she held up her fingers in air quotes and shot her sisters a knowing grin—"*to talk about art?*"

A flush moved from June's face down to the rest of her body, and she was all set to deny this evening would be anything more than two friends chatting about a shared interest. But she remembered the kiss on the couch. "I haven't been on a date in almost twenty years."

"So, you've done it? You've left David for good?" Raven drew her words out, cautious almost.

Something about that statement had June's spine straightening. She'd put fifteen years into her marriage and had done everything right, supporting her husband and raising their children. David was the one who'd left their marriage. He'd walked away. That distinction was important to her.

"No." June looked back and forth between her sisters. "My marriage was over when David started sleeping with his assistant. He made the choice to end it; I'm just making the choice to move on with my life."

"Good for you, June." Sierra squeezed her arm.

"One hundred per cent," Raven agreed. "Now let's get you ready for your date. I'm here for moral support. And I'm *definitely* here for you moving on with your life by coaxing sexy, brooding Caleb out of his shell." She paused and flashed a grin. "And his pants."

"This is going to be so much fun," Sierra said, tugging June off the barstool. And with that, the three of them raced upstairs to dig through June's closet and dump the contents of her make-up bag all over the bed.

Just like old times, June thought, as Raven found a nineties playlist on her phone and they danced around the room. For the first time in as long as she could remember, June felt like she was on the verge of finding herself—her *real* self—instead of the person she needed to be for everyone else.

Just like old times, only better.

*

June stepped out onto the front porch as the sun made its slow descent toward the ocean. She paused, watching the blue and pink of the sky bleed into yellow and orange near the horizon. A soft breeze teased the hair around her face, bringing with it the heady scent of lilac, more potent in the evening.

June smiled to herself as she walked down the gravel path. Her body wasn't totally relaxed, but for once it had nothing to do with the anxiety of her life in Greenwich. Connecticut was worlds away. Now, her body hummed and her synapses fired with a thousand tiny explosions of excitement and anticipation.

What does Caleb have in mind for this evening?

When he'd asked her to come that night, the look in his eyes and the edge in his voice had suggested he didn't intend for them to sort through Jasper's paintings. But he also didn't seem like the kind of guy who'd expect to get right down to business on the couch in the studio. No, Caleb was too thoughtful. He'd try to romance her a little. Maybe a walk on the beach with a bottle of wine.

It had been a long time since anyone had tried to romance her.

Through the back window of the studio, June could see a light through the curtain, which meant Caleb was already there. She rounded the corner and pushed the door open.

Oh, my goodness.

She stopped short, blinking to adjust to the light glaring from every corner of the room. Caleb had turned on all the lamps in the studio. After watching the sun sink behind the horizon and walking down the hill in the growing dusk, June felt like she'd stumbled onto a movie set. Not exactly the moody, romantic setting she'd been expecting.

Once her eyes adjusted, she found Caleb standing in the middle of the room near Jasper's easel. He wore the same clothes from earlier that day and held a canvas under one arm. Maybe she'd gotten it totally wrong. Oh God, maybe he really meant for them to keep sorting paintings. Suddenly she felt silly in her maxi dress and denim jacket, and even sillier for having tried on every outfit in her closet, and most of Sierra's closet, before settling on this one.

"Hi." Caleb's eyes slid down to her feet and back up again. He cleared his throat. "You look beautiful."

She could have sworn he seemed nervous, which was even more embarrassing. He realized she'd dressed up for him, and clearly hadn't done the same. "Thank you." June smoothed an imaginary wrinkle from her skirt and looked around the room, mostly to avoid eye contact. Along the far wall, she spotted the outline of Jasper's paintings draped with drop cloths.

Why would he cover the paintings if they were going to look through them?

Caleb shifted the canvas under his arm and placed it on the easel. June blinked for a moment at the expanse of pure white that seemed almost to glow in the glare of the lamplight.

"Come here," he said, holding out a hand in her direction.

She took a few tentative steps forward as her mind whirled with a thought even worse than the idea she'd gotten this whole thing wrong. *Please don't let him suggest he paint me naked as if this is some kind of cheesy* Titanic *seduction scene.* Because that was a hard no, especially in all this harsh lighting. "What are we doing?"

He walked to where she stood and took her by the wrist, gently tugging her the last few feet toward the easel. "Don't be mad," he began, and suddenly June wanted to laugh. How had this evening gone from romantic walks on the beach to *Don't be mad?*

"Why would I be mad?" she asked, slowly.

"Because this is for you."

"What's for me?"

He moved behind her and took her by the shoulders, gently turning her body until she faced the easel. "This. It's a brand-new canvas. I stretched it after you left today. And I ran to the art store in town and bought you these." He gestured to the table where, earlier that day, Jasper's half-used tubes of paint, a smudged jar of linseed oil, and a handful of brushes and pallet knives had been scattered. All of it was gone now, replaced by perfect rows of new paintbrushes and untouched oil paint tubes organized by color. Behind it sat a pallet and a pristine white artist's smock.

June's mouth dropped open and she spun around to face him.

He ran a nervous hand through his hair. "Look, before you say anything, I want you to know I looked at your other sketches after you left. And I was *overwhelmed* by how beautiful they are. And I know it's your decision, but I had to at least try to get you to see you need to be doing this..."

"Caleb?" She cut him off.

"Yeah?"

She smiled. "Thank you."

His head jerked back as if he'd been expecting her to take a swing at him. "Really?"

She nodded.

"Okay." Caleb blew out a breath and took her by her good shoulder to plant a kiss on her cheek. "I'm leaving you now." He turned to go but stopped short, flashing her a grin. Then he leaned in for another kiss, this one on her mouth, before he backed up again. "All right, I'm really going." He paused again. "*Have fun.*"

And he was gone.

June turned back to the canvas and stared at the expanse of white space until she lost focus. Pressing on her temples to clear her head, she turned to the art supplies on the table, uncapped a couple of tubes of paint and took a minute to pull the smock on over her dress.

She tilted her head left and right and shook out her arms, ignoring the slight jab of pain from her broken collar bone. A few deep breaths in and out, savoring the nutty scent of linseed oil. She closed her eyes and tried to clear her mind; to stop thinking so damn much, and let the feelings come.

Finally, June opened her eyes and, before she could lose her nerve, she squeezed a few colors of paint onto the pallet and picked up a brush. She dabbed it into Cobalt Green, the color of the hemlocks clambering up the hillside through a steely rain. Cadmium Yellow and Silver for the spaces where the light broke through. Burnt Umber and Van Dyke Brown for the trunks of the trees.

And Venetian Red for the dress of the woman standing in the foreground, with Alizarin Crimson patches where the rain soaked the fabric and pressed it to her skin.

With each brush stroke, a tiny spark of joy ignited inside her, and June felt freer and more alive than she had in as long as she could remember. Her body moved automatically, effortlessly, as all the pieces of her she thought were lost forever took shape on the canvas.

Hours passed, or maybe it was minutes—she had no way of knowing for sure—until her shoulders began to ache and the hand clutching her paintbrush stiffened, slowing her movements. The only indication that time had passed was that the sky was no longer streaked with color; it was now an inky black, illuminated by the moon floating above the water.

June surveyed her painting. She could see Jasper's influence in her work's figurative style, but while Jasper's subjects were concealed and camouflaged, hers stood unobscured, staring down the viewer with raw emotion. She looked into the eyes on the canvas, silver-blue like her own, and shivered at the tension and anticipation she saw in their depths.

I did that, she thought, fighting a sudden urge to pirouette like Emma or Izzy.

With a deep sense of satisfaction from the weight of her arms and ache in her back, June carefully packed up her paints and cleaned her brushes. But although her body was bone-tired, she knew her mind was too charged to sleep. She stepped outside into the cool night and looked over to Caleb's cottage, where the porch light shone through the misty darkness. And then it occurred to her.

Caleb *was* romancing her.

Her feet moved before her mind could make the decision and, in a minute, June stood at his front door. She knocked tentatively and, a moment later, Caleb stood there in a pair of dark gray cotton jogging pants and a T-shirt, with damp hair framing his face. He held a glass of amber liquid in one hand and had a book tucked under his arm. At the sight of him, June's heart slid up into her throat.

"I was hoping you'd come," he said, quietly.

With that, she stepped into the house and pressed her body against his, standing up on her tiptoes to wrap her arms around his neck. The book slid out from under his elbow and hit the floor with a bang. He pulled her into the hallway with one arm and with his other, reached out blindly to set his drink on a side table. The woodsy scent of his shampoo mingled with linseed oil, and as his lips found hers, she tasted whiskey.

Caleb tugged off her denim jacket and pressed her back against the wall while she yanked his T-shirt over his head. "I guess your night went well," he murmured against her hair.

"My night is going extremely well," she whispered, tilting her head back to give his mouth access to her neck.

His let out a laugh against her throat. "I meant the painting."

She paused now, reaching up to take his face in her hands. "Painting was incredible, Caleb. And you…" She gazed into his eyes. "You're amazing."

Her lips parted as his mouth found hers again. And right there in Caleb's hallway, and later in his bedroom, he showed her just how amazing he really was.

CHAPTER NINETEEN

Caleb woke to a pair of perfect lips grazing his temple. He opened his eyes and found June leaning over him, her wild curly hair brushing his cheek as she pressed a soft kiss to his face.

Before she could pull away, he snaked one arm around her waist and tugged her down on the bed. She landed with a squeak.

"Ah, I didn't hurt you, did I?" Caleb rolled onto his forearms so he could lean above her and look for signs she was in pain. He'd noticed the yellowing stripe across her clavicle the night before—the fading mark from where the seatbelt had bruised her—and remembered she'd recently been in an accident. But she'd stopped wearing the sling on her arm a couple of days before, and seemed to charge ahead like nothing had happened.

He had a feeling she did that a lot.

"No, I'm okay. But you have to let me up because I have to go."

Caleb squinted at the clock. *5:13 a.m.* "It's the middle of the night. Stay a little longer." He pressed a kiss under her jaw.

June shook her head. "I can't. The girls will be up in just over an hour. I can't have them seeing me do the walk of shame. They'd have a thousand questions."

Caleb pushed himself back so he could roll away. "The walk of shame is usually reserved for random hook-ups. Is that how we're thinking of last night?"

There was no denying this was complicated. He'd known it yesterday in Jasper's studio. But then she'd shown up last night on his doorstep with that wild, euphoric look in her eyes, like she'd jumped out of an airplane and wanted to do it again. He'd never met anyone who made him want to take a leap like June did.

But there were things she didn't know about him, things he'd never shared with any woman because he'd always kept his distance. If he told her the whole story, she'd probably be gone before he could blink. Women like June, women who wanted stability and security, didn't end up with men like him.

"Look, Caleb. Everything is happening really fast—coming to Wishing Cove, painting again, and *you*." She reached out and gently touched his forearm. "I have a whole life on the other side of the country... And I'm going back there in a couple of months. But for now, I'm here. Let's enjoy each other's company." She gave him a wry smile. "For once in my life, I'd like to just *be*, and not overanalyze everything to death."

He sat back and took in the sight of her in the sliver of pre-dawn light sneaking through the window. She was more beautiful than ever in a wrinkled dress, with her wild hair cascading past her shoulders and her freckles standing out against her pale skin. His stomach clenched at the thought of her going back to Connecticut at the end of the summer. Would she go back to that asshole cheating ex-husband, too?

He shoved the thought out of his head and focused on the woman in front of him now. She was offering him exactly what he always wanted in relationships: no strings, no demands, no getting too attached. The women he'd dated in the past would say they were okay with it, but inevitably, they'd started asking for more, complaining he was closed off. Eventually, they always ended up wanting his time, his past, his secrets.

Things he'd never, ever be able to give.

"Sure," he said, raising her hand to his lips and pushing aside the lingering unease. June would be taking off at the end of the summer, and there'd be no complications. It was an ideal situation. "Let's just enjoy each other's company." Caleb stood up and tugged her to her feet. "Come on. I'll walk you home."

With June holding his hand, the walk across the meadow to her front porch was way too short. They stopped in front of the steps and she turned to face him. "Caleb, come over tonight."

"Here? To the house?"

"Yeah. Just a—friendly dinner. With all of us."

Friendly, huh? Maybe her definition of enjoying each other's company was different from his. But seeing her in a room full of chaperones was better than not seeing her at all. "Yeah, why not?"

June leaned up to kiss him on the cheek. "Good. I'll see you at six."

The next thing Caleb knew, she disappeared into the house, and he was left standing out in the yard watching the gray light of morning dawn over the mountains to the east. He walked back across the meadow to eat some breakfast and maybe finally get some work done.

*

Caleb stood in his studio, brush in hand, and stared at the canvas in front of him, willing inspiration to hit. Instead, half-formed thoughts rushed at him like the crowds of pedestrians in his painting, one after another in an endless stream. June, from the night before, her wild hair cascading over one shoulder as she leaned down and—damn it, if he didn't get a grip, this painting would never be ready for the show in the fall—but had he eaten breakfast? Toast. He'd had toast. Except was that yesterday, or today? That song he'd heard in the car yesterday was stuck in his head. He needed to get this painting done.

Caleb sat down on the floor of his studio and pressed his hands to his temples, taking deep, sucking breaths. In. Out. In. Out.

After about five minutes, he was able to settle his mind enough to focus on his present situation. These racing thoughts weren't a good sign. He should call Emily, his therapist, and see if she had any openings. But he was sick of Emily, sick of talking about what was wrong with him, sick of Jasper's death pulling him down like quicksand. He was sick of being sick.

Last night with June was the best night he could remember in a long time, and maybe ever, if he was honest about it. For once in his life, he wanted to just be a normal guy, enjoying the company of a beautiful woman, and not worry that he would eventually mess it all up. And if June was the first person since Kaitlyn to unearth these feelings in him, well, he didn't want to think about that either. Not every relationship ended in tragedy, even if it felt that way sometimes. June would be gone at the end of the summer, and then he'd have the rest of his life to talk to Emily. He could handle this on his own until then.

With that, Caleb packed up his paint brushes and headed back to his house to eat something and quiet his thoughts with an eight-mile run.

At precisely 6 p.m., Caleb stood on June's front porch in a button-down shirt and a pair of dark jeans—the nicest outfit he owned aside from the suit he wore to gallery openings. Caleb had checked his appearance in the mirror three times—about three times more than he usually did—before leaving the house.

To say social events were not his thing was putting it mildly. The thought of making small talk and trying to charm people generally made him want to break out in hives. Will was the twin who excelled at that kind of thing, while Caleb thrived on a quiet space with a paintbrush and blank canvas for company. He managed to muddle through gallery openings because his art was vital to him, but he couldn't remember the last time he'd been to a dinner party.

He knocked on the door and, a moment later, June stood in front of him in a blue sundress that matched her eyes. At the sight of her, his pulse picked up speed.

"Hi," Caleb said, handing her a mason jar of wildflowers he'd picked from the hillside earlier. "This is for you." For a second, he'd wondered if he should run into town to buy a fancy bouquet of roses, but had decided her artist's eye would appreciate the playful combination of red columbine, rust-colored tiger lilies, and sunny yellow evergreen violets. Her smile told him it had been the right call.

June glanced over her shoulder into the house, then quickly stepped out onto the porch and closed the door behind her. She leaned in and gave him a kiss that vibrated all the way down to his toes. When they finally broke apart, she looked as flustered as he felt.

"I've been thinking about doing that all day," she murmured, against his mouth.

"Me, too." Caleb tightened his arms around her and leaned in.

"Oh, *hello*," a familiar voice cut in.

June stumbled backward, her cheeks turning as crimson as the columbines in her hand.

Caleb spun around to find his brother standing on the path with a grin on his face. Caleb cursed under his breath. "What are you doing here?"

"I was invited to dinner." Will strolled up the steps. "Hi, June. Sorry to interrupt."

"Hi, Will." June smoothed her dress. "Thanks for coming."

"I wouldn't have missed it." Will adjusted the bouquet of roses in his arms. "I see my brother has flowers covered, so if you don't mind, I'll save these for your sister."

"Sure." June fumbled with the door handle. "Come on in, both of you." She opened the door and bolted into the house.

"After you," Will said breezily, waving for Caleb to go first.

Caleb hadn't punched his brother since high school, but the temptation was strong. Lucky for Will, he'd spent a lot of time ironing his shirt. It would be a pity to get blood on it now. "Stop looking at me like that."

"Okay, okay." Will smoothed his face into a neutral expression. "I just wasn't expecting that."

Caleb ran a hand through his hair. "You and me both."

"I thought she was married." Will crossed his arms over his pristine white oxford shirt.

"Her husband is cheating. That's part of the reason she came out here." Caleb took an angry breath.

Will's eyebrows shot up. "I didn't take you as a rebound guy for vulnerable divorcées."

It bugged Caleb more than it should to hear his brother reduce his connection with June to something so meaningless. "June isn't some desperate housewife and I'm not some random pool boy," he growled. "We like hanging out, and we have a lot in…" He trailed off when he spotted the knowing smile stretched across his brother's face. "What the hell is that look you're giving me?"

"You're into her. I haven't seen you get worked up about a woman since—"

"*Stop it.*" Damn it, he didn't want to talk about Kaitlyn right now. Not when he was actually feeling something bordering on happy.

"Are you going to tell June about—"

"No."

"*No?* Don't you think you should?"

Why hadn't he ended this conversation already? Caleb was beyond tired of his brother's meddling. "She goes back east at the end of the summer. There's no reason to get into it, not that it's any of your business. Back off, okay? I don't need a babysitter."

"Babysitter?" A dark cloud drifted across Will's face. "Excuse me if I worry about you. I think I have a right to be concerned." He shook his head. "I guess I shouldn't expect you to understand what it's like to think about someone besides yourself."

Before Caleb could respond, Will stalked toward the front door. But then he suddenly stopped short. "Oh, hey, June."

Caleb whirled around to find June standing in the doorway of the house.

"I was just checking on you guys. Everything okay?"

Shit, how loud had they been talking, and what had she heard?

Will flashed her that charming grin he was so good at. "Oh, yeah, we're great. Just catching up."

June smiled. "Okay, well come inside. The appetizers are ready, and the girls are dying to tell you about their whale-watching adventure yesterday." She turned back into the house and headed down the hall.

Caleb relaxed. If she'd overheard them, she wouldn't be smiling, would she?

They entered the house and made their way toward the voices in the kitchen. Sometime over the past few days, Caleb had begun to think of the house as June's, instead of Jasper's.

He needed to remember this was all temporary.

But that sentiment lasted a whole thirty seconds, until he walked into the kitchen and saw her standing by the stove, laughing at something Raven had said. Her hair was twisted on top of her head in a bun, and the steam from a pot boiling on the stove had released several tendrils to curl around her face. She looked up, their eyes met, and a truck slammed him right in the solar plexus.

I'm screwed.

"Guess what, Mr. Caleb," Emma bellowed from across the room. "You shouldn't go in the ocean because killer whales live there, and they could *eat you*."

A small hand tugged on the bottom of his shirt. "They're not really killer whales," Izzy whispered. "They're called *orcas*. And they eat fish, not people."

"Whew, that's a relief. Thanks for letting me know," Caleb whispered back, giving Izzy a wink. She giggled, revealing an adorable gap-tooth smile, and an unfamiliar sensation settled over him.

The past few weeks hanging around Emma and Izzy were probably the most time he'd ever spent with the under-ten crowd. He'd never wanted kids. Never even thought about it, really. Jasper's history with his own children had illustrated why people like them were better off alone. A family and kids weren't in the cards. There was too much at stake, too much volatility.

Too much to lose.

So why was he having these ridiculous thoughts that maybe someday…

Caleb shifted his focus to the adults in the room, and exchanged greetings with Raven and Sierra, who sat on stools around the island. June bustled around them, stirring a pot on the stove, filling up the flower jar with water, and offering everyone some wine.

"I can do that," Caleb said, taking the bottle from her and peeling off the foil. She flashed him a grateful smile and went back to checking on the delicious-smelling thing she had roasting in the oven.

As Caleb topped off everyone's glasses, Will held out the bouquet of roses to Raven. Caleb noticed his brother actually looked a little nervous.

"What?" Raven said, reaching for them cautiously, as if she expected them to be full of thorns. "You brought me flowers?"

"I saw them, and I thought of you."

Caleb rolled his eyes. To her credit, Raven didn't seem to be buying it, but she didn't look completely uninterested either. Maybe something would work out between them, and then Will would get off his back for once. But as soon as that thought crossed Caleb's mind, he felt bad about it. Will had earned the right to meddle in Caleb's life.

His attention was drawn back to June as she set an appetizer tray on the island, complete with several different kinds of cheeses, dips, freshly roasted vegetables, and what looked to be homemade bread.

"June, this is amazing," Will said, snagging an asparagus spear from the tray.

The girls hopped up on stools next to their aunts, and everyone dived in.

Caleb watched June stir a pot on the stove again. Though he didn't know what she was making, it looked elaborate and smelled amazing. Had she spent the entire day cooking? Had she even sat down today? She moved back to the refrigerator and began unloading vegetables for a salad. Caleb slid off his chair and stepped up behind her, gently taking the knife out of her hand. "Let me make the salad. Here." He handed her his glass of wine. "Sit for a minute."

From the way she blinked, he had a feeling she wasn't used to the people in her life—and maybe one man in particular—offering to take over so she could relax. David was probably that guy who worked the same number of hours as his wife, but expected her to do all the household chores when they got home.

But then Caleb looked at June's sisters enjoying their appetizers. Maybe he wasn't being totally fair. More likely, June would take over with her usual efficiency, and everyone had been going along for so long it never occurred to them to do things differently.

"Emma and Izzy," Caleb said. "Do you want to be my helpers?"

"Okay!" The girls jumped off their stools and crowded around him.

"Go wash your hands and you can set the table." He gestured to a set of drawers. "Silverware here, and napkins in the cabinet over there." He'd spent so much time in Jasper's kitchen over the years, he probably knew it better than anyone else. "Sierra, would you mind getting the heavy dishes from above?"

"Sure." She grabbed a stack of dishes from the cabinet and headed for the dining room.

"I'll get the glasses," Raven offered.

Caleb glanced at June. He found her looking at him with a slightly bemused smile on her face. She took a sip of her wine, and something swelled in his heart as he watched the tension leave her shoulders.

Twenty minutes later, they all sat down at the table to eat.

"So, Caleb," Sierra said, handing him a basket of bread. "Tell us how you came to work here with Jasper."

"Mommy, who's Jasper?" Emma leaned over and whispered.

"Remember I told you about the man who gave us this house? He was my daddy, but I didn't know him."

"Yeah, Grandpa Jasper," Izzy said, in a voice of authority.

Once again, Caleb ached for the loss of his old friend who would never get to experience being *Grandpa Jasper*. "I met Jasper at one of his gallery openings." Caleb swallowed hard over the sandpaper scraping the back of his throat. "I was living in LA, trying to sell my paintings to tourists in Venice Beach. I'd read an article about Jasper's show. It was invitation-only, of course. Jasper was really starting to hit the big time right around then. But I snuck in the back door with the catering staff."

"Oh, I love it," Raven said.

"I was this long-haired, scruffy kid," Caleb said, with a rueful smile.

"Not much has changed since then," Will chimed in with a good-natured laugh.

Caleb shrugged. "I was trying to blend in with all these wealthy art buyers but Jasper spotted me right away. I thought he was going to kick me out, but instead he came over and asked what I thought of the painting in front of us."

"What did you say?" June asked.

"I was so terrified, I blurted out the truth before I could stop to think."

"What was that?"

"I said the subject was a guy who was lying to everyone, including himself. That his face looked confident but didn't quite mask the doubts in his eyes." Caleb paused, looking around the table. "It was one of his self-portraits."

"Ooof," Raven gasped, clutching her chest. "How did he take it?"

Caleb rubbed his hand over his eyes, remembering the day like it was yesterday. The moment of stunned silence that followed, the way his heart had thudded like the bass vibrating from a car cruising down Ventura Boulevard. And then—

"Jasper laughed." Caleb smiled at the memory. "He took me over to the bar and ordered two glasses of whiskey. He spent the next half-hour talking to me and ignoring the 'real' art crowd. He asked me about my work, what kind of training I'd had, what my plans were. And then he offered me a job."

Sierra turned to Will. "What did you and your family think about Caleb going from selling paintings on Venice Beach to being the great Jasper Luc's apprentice?"

Will shook his head slowly. "It was a very happy surprise."

Caleb took a gulp of his wine. "Let's just say I'd been a little directionless before Jasper came along."

"How old were you?" Raven asked.

"Nineteen."

She shrugged. "It seems pretty natural to be directionless at nineteen."

Caleb exchanged a glance with Will. If only he'd been going through the normal exploration of a kid finding himself. It left him lightheaded to think of what he'd put his parents—and Will—through when he took off for LA the night before high school graduation. How he'd moved in with Kaitlyn and disappeared without so much as a call to let them know he was okay. How it had all gone south from there.

Will cleared his throat. "We're all proud of Caleb's success. He was lucky to fall in with Jasper, but his talent got him where he is today."

Damn it. His brother's words left an unexpected warmth in Caleb's chest. He should really apologize for the things he'd said to Will earlier.

Raven grabbed the water pitcher and topped off her glass. "Caleb, I saw on your website you recently had solo exhibits at galleries in New York and Chicago. That's pretty prestigious."

Will raised his eyebrows. "You've been googling my brother?"

"Maybe." Raven stared at him over her glass. "Why? Jealous?"

Caleb laughed. "Come on, you two. Get a room."

Both Raven and Will flushed pink and took a sudden interest in the food on their plates.

"What does that mean?" Izzy asked Caleb quietly. "You said Aunt Raven and Mr. Will should get a room. What room?"

Caleb rubbed a hand across his forehead. He was horrible at this. "Oh, um… It means they should stop bickering in front of us and go someplace else."

Emma nodded. "Like the way Mommy and Daddy shout in their bedroom and think we can't hear them."

A silence settled around the table, and Caleb's embarrassment for June weighed so heavy, he couldn't meet her eyes.

"Nice one, bro," Will muttered under his breath.

Eventually, Sierra plunked her glass down and gave an exaggerated smile. "So, anyway. What about you, Will? How did you end up in Wishing Cove?"

Caleb finally mustered up the nerve to peek at June, and instead of the mortified expression he was expecting, her lips were pressed together. She looked like she was trying not to laugh.

I'm sorry, he mouthed at her.

She glanced around to make sure nobody was watching and winked at him. And with that small gesture, the door to his heart crashed open and slammed against his ribcage. All he wanted to do was pull her up out of her chair and run somewhere they could be alone.

But damn it, for the foreseeable future, they were stuck in a room full of chaperones. He cleared his throat and did his best to focus on his brother's story.

"After law school I worked for a firm in New York for a few years," Will continued. "I came here for one of Caleb's art shows and met an attorney who was retiring and looking to transition her practice to someone younger. It worked out perfectly and, of course, I got to live closer to my brother."

Caleb was grateful his brother didn't go into any more detail about why he wanted to live near him.

They made it through the rest of dinner without any major gaffes on his part. Even though June's food was delicious, Caleb could barely choke it down. He was too distracted by the little, private smiles she directed at him when nobody was looking.

When the meal was over, June stood up from her chair, and he got up to help her clear the dishes. She waved a hand at him, indicating he should put down the platter he was holding.

"Caleb, I need to get the paint you bought for me in town today."

"The—" He hadn't gone into town that day.

"Yes. *The oils I asked you to pick up for me.*" She gave him a bug-eyed look.

Right. "Yeah, um… they're in my studio."

June looked around the table at her sisters. "You can handle the dishes, right?"

Caleb bit his lip to keep from grinning. He had a feeling she rarely left messes for other people to clean up.

"Of course. You guys go ahead," Sierra said, standing up and stacking the dirty plates. "We can't wait to see the painting you're working on."

June made her way around the table. "Girls, give me a hug. Aunt Raven is going to put you to bed tonight."

Raven broke the eye contact she seemed to be locked in with Will. "I am? Okay, sure."

The girls huddled around June to give hugs and demand she peek in on them when she returned. Then they turned to Caleb and threw their little arms around him. He hugged them back, swallowing hard to extinguish the unexpected twinge in the back of his throat.

Caleb and June headed out the door and walked in silence to the studio through the cool night air. When they arrived at Caleb's studio, June reached for the light switch, but he took her hand and pulled her in close, wrapping his other arm around her back. He leaned into her, pressing a kiss against her mouth that was hard, hot, and hungry.

He pulled away only long enough to tug her dress over her head and then she was back against him. His hand roved across her bare skin, finding the strap of her lace bra and releasing the clasp. He dropped it on the floor as she worked the buttons on his shirt and slid it off his shoulders. Pulling her against his bare chest, he backed up into the room until his calves hit the couch against the wall. He fell backward, and she tumbled on top of him.

CHAPTER TWENTY

Just like that, June's world turned as vibrant and beautiful as the colors she was applying to her canvases. She couldn't believe a few short weeks ago, she used to dread getting up in the morning, and had to drag herself out of bed with two alarms. Now, she woke before dawn to sit on the front porch, drinking coffee and watching the sky turn from black to gray to pink. Every day, she waved to Caleb as he left his cottage and headed to his studio, pretending she hadn't crawled out of his bed a few hours earlier.

She ate breakfast with Emma and Izzy, taking the time to fry up omelets with potatoes, or make pancakes from scratch with wild blackberries from the hill behind Caleb's house. Then she'd take the girls to the art summer camp in town and head to Jasper's studio, which she'd begun to tentatively, cautiously, think of as *hers*.

Often, she'd find notes that Caleb had left her, messages of encouragement or compliments about the colors or shading in her latest painting. To make her smile, he'd add little doodles to the bottom of the pages that she'd tack up around the studio.

Once June started painting again, it was impossible for her to understand how she ever stopped. *And for more than fifteen years.* Art was as essential to her as breathing. She woke up in the morning with her latest painting swirling in her head, and it stayed there, constantly in the back of her mind until she was able to get back to the studio. And time seemed to fly by. She could work for hours without looking up from the canvas.

Caleb was meticulous about stopping for breaks and food—he'd learned to follow a routine over the years—and he came by every day to drag her away long enough to eat lunch with him. On sunny days, they took their sandwiches down to the beach to sit on the sand and talk about art. On rainy days, they stayed inside, huddled on the couch in his studio, unable to keep their hands off each other.

June knew the summer couldn't last forever—her collarbone no longer throbbed, her headaches were subsiding, and David continued to press her for a date she'd be returning to Connecticut with the girls. Soon she'd have to face the reality of going home, returning to work, and cleaning up the wreckage of her marriage.

But not right now.

For now, June planned to soak up every minute because once she was back to the real world, she didn't know if she'd ever be this happy again.

*

"Oh, come on, Junie. I'm going to trip and break my arm." Raven took baby steps into the studio with one hand pressed over her eyes and the other waving wildly in front of her. "Can I look now?"

"No. Wait for Sierra." June put a hand under Sierra's elbow and guided her to the center of the room next to Raven. "Okay. Ready?"

"*Yes!*" her sisters exclaimed in unison.

June clutched one sweaty palm with the other. "Open up."

Raven and Sierra pulled their hands from their faces. Both of their mouths dropped open as they each took a slow turn in the center of the room.

"Oh, June," Sierra breathed.

"Holy shit," Raven chimed in.

After weeks of Raven's pestering, and Sierra's subtle comments that they'd love to see her work whenever she was ready, June had finally agreed to let them come down to the studio. She'd carefully propped her paintings on chairs arranged in a wide circle, shifting one a little to the left, another to the right, switching two and switching them back.

Now she stood in the center of it all, about as nervous and proud as she'd been when she had been a new mom who'd just given birth.

Raven and Sierra spun again, taking it all in. The woman in the red dress in the rain. The girls playing on the beach. Close-up portraits of each of her sisters, staring out at the viewer, Sierra's gaze muted and slightly wary, Raven's intense and defiant. And finally, Caleb, sitting on the beach, elbows resting on his knees.

"June, these are *amazing*." Raven grabbed her arm. "I can't even believe you had it in you all this time and we had no idea."

"Speak for yourself," came a voice from behind them. June and her sisters turned around to find Caleb standing at the studio entrance leaning casually against the doorframe. He gave June a smile that made her heart stutter. "*I* knew she had it in her."

"You did," June agreed.

"We're eternally grateful," Sierra added. "June told us you've been really encouraging. Thanks for giving her the little push she needed."

"Speaking of little pushes. I saw this in the art shop in town." Caleb pulled a flyer from his back pocket and handed it to June. "The Starlake Arts Center is organizing a show to raise money for their new studio space and is calling for work from local artists."

Raven peered over her shoulder as June unfolded the paper. "Junie, you should enter! You could help out the art center, show your artwork, and maybe even sell your first piece!"

Caleb nodded. "Starlake is well-respected around here. Gallery owners will probably come up from Seattle. It could be a great way to get your name out there, at least regionally. That's the first step."

June twisted the flyer in her hands. "Oh, I don't know. I mean, there will probably be people entering who've been doing this their whole lives. Like you. I couldn't go up next to your work."

"Sure you could," Caleb said without hesitation.

"Your work is really powerful, June," Sierra chimed in.

June's first instinct was to pick apart her paintings. To hunt down the places where she hadn't gotten the light and shadows quite right, where she'd struggled with color and brushstrokes. But the longer she looked, the more the paintings drew her in. That expression in Sierra's eyes, mysterious and cautious. Raven's face, still strong and determined, even after the tragedy she'd lived through. And Caleb.

He'd once told her it didn't matter if her work was technically perfect; it mattered how her paintings made people feel. She'd poured every emotion into capturing the open and unrestrained smile he reserved only for her, on the face she was growing so attached to. If she'd put so much of her heart into her work, was it possible other people would feel it and respond to it?

She'd never know if she didn't give it a shot.

June took a deep breath and looked from Caleb to her sisters. "Okay. I'll do it. I'll enter a painting."

*

A few days later, June headed out the front door, a set of new paintbrushes in hand. She passed by her laptop sitting on the entry table, and guilt elbowed her. She should check her work email. Keith, her assistant, had written to ask if he could take a stab at the CitiTech projections, but he wasn't ready. CitiTech was one of Westwood Management and Consulting's biggest accounts, and she should be handling it personally.

Except she wasn't handling it. She was thoroughly ignoring CitiTech in favor of adventures with Emma and Izzy when they weren't at camp, and painting in her studio when they were. June couldn't remember having so much unstructured time when she wasn't worrying over meetings, spreadsheets, or the girls' latest after-school activities.

When she'd looked in the mirror before her last shower, June had hardly recognized herself. It wasn't just the wild hair whose curls hadn't seen the light of day since college. Her cheeks glowed pink and her shoulders were tanned from all the sunshine and outdoor activity. Without even trying, she'd finally lost the ten pounds she'd been trying to diet away since the girls were born. And her eyes glowed with excitement and hope.

But all that only increased her guilt over leaving work and her other commitments in a state of neglect. Hikes in the woods and painting in the studio weren't real life, and while it was nice to pretend for a while, it was only going to be harder to go back to Connecticut when the time came. Although she was on medical leave, she couldn't help worrying David might push her out of the company if she didn't keep up with her biggest accounts.

And there was the nagging fear. The one that showed up, usually late at night, to whisper she was a single mother, now. Sure, she'd inherited Jasper's estate and paintings. But she'd be splitting any assets three ways with her sisters, and if they kept the house and land, they'd require a lot of maintenance. The property was beautiful but, apparently, Jasper hadn't always kept up with repairs. Playing at being a painter like she was a teenager again was nothing short of irresponsible when she had two kids to think about.

June sighed and dropped the paintbrushes on the table, picking up her laptop instead. She settled on the couch and opened up her email. Along with three new messages from Keith was a note from David about the date of the first day of school. It was still almost two months away. Did he really think she didn't know when school started? She was the one who kept track of those things, meticulously adding important dates to the shared family calendar, shopping for school supplies in early August, before all the lunchboxes and backpacks were picked over.

No, more likely the reminder was David's passive-aggressive way of saying her stay in Wishing Cove had a clock that was slowly ticking. Was he using the girls to try to control her?

June shuddered and quickly clicked back to Keith's emails. She'd finally managed to focus on the CitiTech file when Emma and Izzy burst into the room, followed more slowly by Raven.

"Mommy, look what we found on the beach!" Emma thrust a pile of smooth, round stones into June's hand. "They're called wishing rocks."

"Beautiful," June murmured, running a finger over the white vein bisecting a gray pebble. But more beautiful than the stone was the excitement on the faces of her two girls. June wasn't the only one having the best summer of her life in Wishing Cove. Emma and Izzy were thriving, with beaches and woods to roam, and the attention of adults who weren't stressed out all the time.

Back in Connecticut, Izzy always seemed to have tummy aches. The pediatrician had handed June a brochure about food allergies and suggested a gluten-free diet. But now, June wondered if Izzy's ailments had actually been the result of stress from their scheduled days and the tension projected by her overworked parents. Izzy hadn't complained about tummy aches since her many school activities had been replaced by running in the meadow and throwing stones in the ocean.

Both girls jumped out of bed each morning and were waiting by the door with backpacks in hand on the days they went to art camp. June was impressed with the talent she saw in the paintings and drawings they brought home. Izzy strived for hyperrealism, and it was clear she'd spent hours on the careful lines of one sketch of a horse, while Emma dashed off piles of drawings of people with exaggerated facial features and long skinny limbs that reminded June of Expressionism.

"Mommy, Aunt Raven says we can go into town for ice cream." Emma bounced on the arm of the couch. "Want to come with us?"

"I really should get some work done." June scrolled through the page in front of her until the lines of numbers began to blur. She'd been an accountant for fifteen years. Why did one spreadsheet feel like a pile of rocks sitting in her stomach?

"Oh, come on, Junie," Raven argued. "You're on leave from work, aren't you?"

Emma heaved a sigh. "Mommy *always* has to work."

June looked up, ready to protest the unfairness of the statement. She didn't *always* have to work, but she did have a job she took seriously. The girls should thank their lucky stars they had it so good. Would they prefer it if she acted like her mother—unreliable, always flitting off on her latest whim, someone they could never depend on?

The muscles in her shoulders tightened, and with that, the wishing rock weighed heavy in her hands. June squeezed, and the smoothness of the stone grounded her. She abruptly closed her mouth.

What was the harm in going for one ice cream cone? She had the rest of her life to follow the safe, responsible path. In another six weeks, she'd be back in Connecticut, back at work, and back to the old routine. This time with the girls and her sisters in Wishing Cove was fleeting. David's email couldn't have been clearer, and she knew on some level it was better not to get too attached to a life three thousand miles away from home. But right now, she was going to enjoy every moment.

June slammed her laptop shut. "Let's go."

"Yay!" the girls chorused, jumping up and down.

Raven held out her hand and, with only a moment of hesitation, June tossed aside her computer and grabbed hold.

*

Later that afternoon, June found Caleb on the beach, sitting cross-legged in the sand, stacking rocks on top of each other. She paused on the last step down, watching his brows knit together with such concentration that he didn't even notice her standing there. He placed a smooth, gray stone on the top of the pile, balancing it on a tiny bump protruding from the rock beneath it, and then held his hands on either side to make sure it wouldn't fall.

"Impressive," June said, stepping down into the sand.

Caleb jumped and knocked the top rock, sending the whole pile toppling.

"Oh, no, I'm sorry!"

"No big deal." Caleb shrugged.

June walked closer. "So, you're the one who made these rock piles all over the beach."

"They're called cairns," he said, standing up and brushing sand from his pants.

"I didn't know you also had a thing for sculpture as well as a painting."

"I don't make them for art. I make them to relax. It's meditative."

June thought back to her short-lived yoga class and shuddered. "So, you just come out here and pile up rocks for fun?"

"It's not just *piling up rocks*," he said wryly, making air quotes with his fingers. "There's concentration and balance involved." Caleb's eyes roamed over what she guessed was a skeptical expression on her face because his lips curled into a grin. "You can't imagine calmly sitting here and doing something like this, can you?"

She really couldn't. Just the idea of sitting in the sand meditating with some rocks made her twitchy. Her to-do list would be playing in her head on repeat the whole time. Still, she wasn't going to give him the satisfaction of admitting she didn't have the patience to make a pile of stones on the beach. Especially when he had that challenging grin on his face. "I'm sure I could do it."

He waved a hand at the toppled pile with a raise of his eyebrows.

June took Caleb's place in the sand, lifting the largest rock and turning it over until she had it angled as flat as possible. Then, she placed the next largest on top, and more after that. The task was fairly simple until the rocks grew smaller and the pile grew taller, and soon she found herself holding her breath as she slowly balanced stone after stone on top of the tower, hoping they wouldn't fall. With each addition that held, her chest swelled with satisfaction.

Placing the last rock on the pile, June finally looked up and found Caleb sitting a few feet away, watching her. "See?" She waved triumphantly at her sculpture. "Easy."

Caleb grinned, glancing at his watch. "That took you a half an hour."

June scrambled to her feet. "Really?" The time flew by.

"Told you it's meditative."

June stepped back to take in her creation and, at that moment, a wave came rushing into shore: the afternoon tide coming in. It foamed around her sneakers and hit her rock tower squarely in the center, knocking it over. "*Damn it.*" She turned back to Caleb, surprisingly disappointed over some toppled rocks. "Why would you build it here if the tide is just going to come in and ruin it!"

From his perch on a piece of driftwood, out of the path of the rising tides, Caleb's shoulders shook with laughter. "It's about the journey, not the destination."

She shot him an exaggerated glare, pulling her wet feet out of the suction of sand just as another wave came rushing in, soaking her up to the ankle. Caleb laughed harder.

"I'm glad one of us is having fun," June said, unwinding a slimy piece of seaweed from around her sock. Caleb's laughter had him bending at the waist, so June took the only logical next step and flung the seaweed at him. To her satisfaction, it landed directly on his head. He sat up, and in one swift motion, stood in front of her. The next thing June knew, he'd swept her up in his arms and carried her out until he was knee-deep in the water. Of course, he was barefoot and wore shorts so he didn't have to worry about saturated shoes and pant-legs like she did.

June flung her arms around his neck, clinging to him. "Caleb, that water is freezing."

"Maybe you should have thought of that before you threw seaweed at me," he said, with a chuckle.

"Caleb. Take me to shore."

"Admit you found the rocks meditative."

"Never."

"Last chance," he said, loosening his arms until she felt herself slipping.

June tightened her grip on his neck. "Caleb, that water is sixty degrees!"

"Fifty."

"Okay, okay, I admit the rocks *were* meditative. Now, put me down," she said, laughing as hard as he was now. He dropped one arm, lowering her feet to the ground just as another freezing wave rose up, sloshing her all the way up to mid-thigh. She gasped at the cold seeping into her jeans. "I didn't mean *here. In the water.*"

"You'll need to be more specific next time."

Another wave rolled toward them. Spotting an opportunity, June shoved her shoe between Caleb's legs, tangling her foot up with his and sending him off-balance. Just like her rock creation, he toppled backward. Only at the last moment, he reached out and snaked an arm around her waist, tugging her with him. And, laughing harder than she had in years, June fell into Caleb's arms in the cold, frothy sea.

CHAPTER TWENTY-ONE

A week later, June opened her email to find the name *Starlake Arts Center* highlighted at the top of the screen. Across from it, in the subject line: *Your submission.*

Her pulse doubled in speed.

June had sent in her entry the night Caleb brought the flyer, wanting to get it over with before she could talk herself out of it. She'd chosen her first painting—the woman in the rain—because it represented so much about this new creative journey she'd embarked on. Raven had taken photos of the canvas and helped her put together a submission package she was proud of. But now she was second-guessing. Maybe she should've painted something new. Maybe she shouldn't have entered at all. Maybe she should've waited a year or two—or twenty—before she put herself out there.

The committee had gotten back to her awfully quickly. That probably meant rejection. June stared at the screen in front of her.

It will be okay. I'm new at this. It doesn't say anything about my talent.

But she didn't believe it for a second.

With a shaking hand, she hovered the mouse over the email. And clicked.

She scanned the words on the page.

Dear Ms. Westwood,

Thank you for your submission to the Starlake Arts Center's benefit showcase. Our committee reviewed your materials and we are happy to inform you your painting has been accepted. Please watch for another email from our committee chair with further details about the show.

June clapped her hand over her mouth. *Oh. My. God.* She jumped up from the chair and raced downstairs to find her sisters. The kitchen and living room were empty, but she could hear yelling outside. Raven and the girls were playing soccer in the yard.

June flung the front door open and found Sierra standing on the porch. "Sierra, I did it!" She ran over and grabbed her sister's arm. "My painting was accepted into the show!" Too late, June realized she'd interrupted her sister talking to a tall, blond man. Will's friend, Sam Grayson, the contractor who'd fixed the broken gutter a few weeks earlier. She'd forgotten he was coming back to talk about some other house repairs.

"Oh, gosh, I'm sorry to butt in. I'm"—June gave Sam a rueful smile—"I'm a little excited."

He flashed her a set of straight, white teeth. "No problem. Whatever you're excited about—congratulations."

"Junie, this is wonderful." Sierra threw her arms around her. "I'm so happy for you!"

Over Sierra's shoulder, June saw Raven drop the soccer ball in the grass and approach the porch. "What'd I miss? What's going on?"

"June's painting was accepted into the show!"

Raven charged up the porch and nearly knocked the two of them over with a hug. "Of course it was!" She turned out toward the yard. "Girls, Mommy's painting is going to be in an art show! We need to celebrate! Who wants cake?"

"Me! Me!" Emma and Izzy jumped up and down, clapping their little hands. June wasn't sure how much they understood about the importance of this event, but the girls would never say no to a celebration, or cake.

"Did you tell Caleb?" Sierra asked.

"Not yet. I just found out. I think he ran into town and was going to stop by Will's."

Raven pulled out her phone. "I'll text Will and tell him they need to get their butts back here right now."

June raised an eyebrow. "Since when do you text Will?"

Raven shrugged. "Since... whenever. I don't know." She avoided June's eyes, tilting her head toward her phone, but June didn't miss the hint of a smile there. "Anyway, I'll see if they can pick up some champagne and cake on the way."

Sierra turned to Sam. "Would you like to join us for an impromptu celebration? My sister's painting was accepted into the Starlake Arts Center showcase, and this is a big deal."

"Starlake *is* a big deal." Sam nodded in appreciation. "Congratulations again."

June couldn't stop smiling. "Thank you."

Forty-five minutes later, Will and Caleb showed up with pizza, a box from a local bakery, and a bag from the wine shop. Caleb dropped his packages on the porch steps and gave a quick glance around at the occupants of the porch before he lifted June off her feet in a hug. "You did it. I'm so proud of you." He put her back down and backed away as the front door swung open and the girls came outside to inspect the treats.

June felt like someone had switched a light on inside her, and she glowed from the inside out. Raven gave a toast with the champagne before they dove into the pizza. It turned out Caleb liked pineapple on his, something she had to tease him about mercilessly, and Will was more than willing to join in. Then Sierra passed around slices of cake covered with a corny depiction of a paintbrush, pallet, and the words *Congratulations June!* in multicolored script. For some reason, the idea of aloof, brooding

Caleb asking the bakery to decorate this silly cake just to make her happy had her heart doing a little somersault in her chest.

The girls had a million questions about the show, including if they would be allowed to go and whether there would be cookies served. Finally, Will insisted June stand up and give a speech, which she had trouble getting through because everyone was slightly tipsy and kept cracking up. All the while, *we are happy to inform you your painting has been accepted* played in the back of her mind on repeat.

As the afternoon drifted toward evening, June settled into a chair on the porch and marveled at her surroundings. If someone had told her two months ago she'd be living in Jasper Luc's house, painting every day, and having her work accepted into an art show, she never would have believed it. And even more unbelievable, she found herself surrounded by a wonderful, supportive group who encouraged her and accepted her for exactly who she was.

June smiled as she watched the girls, hopped up on too much sugar, chase Caleb and Raven back and forth across the yard while they pretended to be monsters. Will had gone into the house, insisting she wasn't allowed to clean up the kitchen on her big day. And Sierra sat on the porch steps talking to Sam Grayson, who turned out to not only be good-looking and great at fixing stuff, but a nice guy, too.

By the way Sam couldn't seem to stop grinning, it was clear to June he was enamored with her sister. And every once in a while, she noticed Sierra's cheeks flush pink at something Sam said. June couldn't help but smile. Maybe Sierra's next book would be a romance. There certainly seemed to be something in the water here in Wishing Cove.

The sun dipped toward the horizon, slanting its rays in June's direction and warming her bare shoulders. This would be one of those rare, flawless moments she'd hold on to for as long as she lived. Someday, she'd be back at work or rushing to get the kids to school on time, and she'd pull out this sepia-toned day, flip through each perfect memory—the girls laughing in the meadow, the salty sea air mingled with pine and cedar, the tiny glimmer of hope flickering in her heart.

The front door opened, and Will stepped outside. June looked up and smiled as he approached the seat across from her. "Mind if I sit?"

She waved at the chair, struck again by how similar his features were to Caleb's, yet they formed such a different picture. "Please."

Will settled back into his chair and took a long drink from the beer in his hand. "You know, if you'd told me to imagine what my brother would look like a month or two after Jasper's death…" Will waved his hand at Caleb, who was tossing a soccer ball over the girls' heads. "This wouldn't have been it."

June cocked her head and squinted at Will. "I'm picturing the scruffy, unkempt man demanding to know what I was doing in Jasper's studio the first time I met him."

Will laughed. "Nailed it." He looked out in the yard again and turned to June, his face more serious. "Caleb and I grew up knowing our parents loved us equally, but they were never really sure what to make of Caleb and his art. He was always so intense, so troubled. But then Jasper came along and understood him in a way that, honestly, none of us did."

Will leaned in, and his coppery-brown eyes seemed to cut right to her core. "You understand him the way Jasper did."

June bit her lip. "We understand each other."

Will took another swig of his beer. "In my experience, that's pretty rare."

June didn't say it, but it was rare in her experience, too. She'd grown up watching her mother flit from one man to another, enamored by their talent and the attention they paid her, with little connection or substance to hold the relationship together.

While she and David had shared an attraction in their younger days, in the past few years their marriage had felt more like a business transaction than a relationship. Even in their most passionate moments, June couldn't say David *understood* her.

"You know," Will said, setting his empty bottle on the table and standing up. "Just because your life was always headed in one direction, it doesn't mean you can't take a turn." Before June could respond, Will trotted down the porch steps and tried to steal the soccer ball from Raven, who didn't seem to mind his hip bumping against hers or his arm sliding around her shoulder.

June understood what Will was saying, she really did. Caleb had suffered a huge loss, and Will didn't want to see his brother hurt again. She'd feel the same way if they were talking about Raven or Sierra. But Will didn't know she and Caleb had agreed to keep things casual, and she had a whole life to go back to at the end of the summer. Caleb was such a loner, it was probably an arrangement that suited him perfectly.

But Will's words—*it doesn't mean you can't take a turn*—stayed with her: as she got up from her chair and went to join the game in the yard; as they stopped playing to watch the sun drop behind the horizon, leaving behind a firework sky; and later—after she'd put the girls to bed—as she said goodbye to Caleb in front of the house, lingering until he tugged her into a grove of trees behind the house and down into a bed of leaves that shimmered with moonlight.

CHAPTER TWENTY-TWO

On Saturday morning, Caleb stopped by as June and the girls were finishing breakfast on the front porch. June had to smile at the sight of him grinning at her like they hadn't seen each other in weeks, instead of a few hours earlier. Of course, she hadn't been able to see him well—it had been dark then. Her gaze roved over him; he was ridiculously appealing in a pair of camo shorts and a fitted black T-shirt, and it was all she could do not to fling herself off the porch into his arms. By the way his eyes grew soft at the sight of her, it was clear he wanted to do the same.

The girls had none of the same caution holding them back, and they jumped down the stairs and swarmed Caleb.

"Look, Caleb!" Izzy opened her mouth like a seal waiting for a fish. "I lost another tooth!"

"Nice job, kid," Caleb said, holding out his hand for Izzy to slap.

"Caleb! Caleb!" Emma tugged at his arm. "Look what I drew for you!"

Caleb examined the pastel drawing Emma thrust into his hand. "Wow. I've been wanting a unicorn picture to add to my art collection. Thank you." Caleb turned his attention from the girls and squinted up at June. "I came by to see if you and the girls wanted to go on a hike."

"Can we, Mommy?" Emma asked.

"There are some really nice trails up the road." Caleb patted the backpack he carried over one shoulder. "I have water and snacks. All you need are walking shoes."

The day was warm, and they didn't have other plans. And she'd never pass up an adventure with Caleb. He'd become sort of an unofficial tour guide, taking her and the girls on a ferry ride to the San Juan Islands, for a picnic on a secret beach outside of town, and one day last week, they'd driven into Seattle for lunch and a visit to the aquarium. He said she and the girls should experience the Pacific Northwest while they had the chance. A little part of her wondered if maybe he had an ulterior motive. Was he trying to make her fall in love with Wishing Cove so she wouldn't want to leave?

As they crossed Pinecrest Drive and followed a path winding up the hill under a canopy of hemlock and pines, June had to admit she could see the appeal of living in a place like this. Everything in Connecticut was so tidy and manicured. To go outside in nature, you had to pack up the car and drive to a state park, or one of the meticulously combed beaches. Here in Wishing Cove nature surrounded you, whether you were driving up the coast along the rocky cliffs hanging over the water, heading east through the dense evergreen forests, or just stepping outside the house.

Although the girls skipped ahead on the trail, progress was slow because they had to pause and examine every caterpillar, mushroom, and wildflower in their path. Caleb brought up the rear and seemed to take their constant stops and starts in his stride, getting into the spirit by pointing out any bugs they might have missed.

At home in Connecticut, Saturdays were reserved for lessons they couldn't fit in during the week: dance classes and soccer in the morning, and swimming at the country club in the afternoon. Neither she nor David had much patience for the girls' attempts to stray from the schedule. There were too many activities they had to squeeze in to stop and watch a swarm of ants on the sidewalk.

Maybe now they would rethink the schedule and cut back. Just because the neighborhood kids took ballet, played a sport, and learned the piano didn't mean Emma and Izzy had to do everything too. She'd have to talk to David about it.

But nothing about that plan reassured June the way she expected, and a heavy feeling settled in her heart.

Eventually, she, Caleb, and the girls made it to the top of the hill. The trees thinned out to reveal a gentle slope covered in scrubby brush and moss-covered granite. Caleb led them up the path, and they climbed until they were above the tree line. Beneath them, the fuzzy pine-covered hillside stretched downward until it touched the ocean in the distance.

Caleb sat down on a rock and opened his backpack. "It's beautiful up here, huh?" He handed out granola bars and water, and they sat on the rocks, looking out across the bay. Caleb pointed out a ferry gliding by, like the one they'd taken last week around the San Juan Islands; an airplane in the distance he told the girls was probably headed for SeaTac airport; and a bald eagle swooping in circles above the treetops. They asked questions— "How does the ferry driver know where to park the boat? How does an airplane stay in the air? Why is it called a bald eagle if it has feathers?"—and he patiently answered each.

The girls couldn't sit still for long, though, and soon they got up and began clambering around on the rock. The incline was gentle enough that June felt comfortable letting them explore as long as they stayed within eyesight.

"Mommy!" Emma exclaimed, standing on the highest point and waving her arms. "Can you take a picture of me for Daddy?"

"Sure, honey." June pulled her phone from her jacket pocket and snapped a few photos.

"Now I'll take one of you and Mr. Caleb, so Daddy can see our new friend."

The phone slipped from June's hand, but she caught it on her lap right before it could slide to the ground. "Oh, no. That's okay. Daddy will just want to see his girls."

The girls skittered off, distracted by a hole in an old tree perfect for building a fairy house. June shot a glance at Caleb. His face was inscrutable.

"So…" Caleb seemed to find his backpack absolutely fascinating. He slid the zipper open slowly and stared inside. "How *is* David?"

"He's—" June had no idea. They hadn't had a real conversation in months. Maybe even in years. And that was probably part of their problem. "He's expecting me to bring the girls home at the end of the summer."

Caleb abandoned whatever he'd been pretending to dig out of his backpack. "Is that what you want?"

"The thing is, when you have kids, it's not always about what you want. The girls and I have a whole life there. School. My job. I'm the treasurer for the PTA, plus I'm on the board of a local non-profit." Caleb didn't have the kind of responsibilities she did. He didn't know what it was like to have all those people counting on him.

"So, you're going home." His voice was flat, emotionless. Almost like he didn't care one way or the other. But the muscle tightening in his jaw told her otherwise.

Moving back to Connecticut had always been the plan. But now June tried to imagine the reality of it. Renting a house in the gated, sterile neighborhood David liked so much so the girls could easily go back and forth. Rushing between work meetings and the girls' school activities. Gulping black coffee as she ran out the door, the constant ping of email on her phone, the persistent buzz of her pulse racing.

Sort of like it was racing now.

How was it possible she'd lived that life for fifteen years, and now it felt like it belonged to someone else?

"I don't know."

"What about painting? Are you going to have time for that between PTA and non-profit meetings?"

It was like he'd knocked the wind out of her. "*I don't know, Caleb.*" The words came out more harshly than she'd intended. June took a deep breath and blew it out slowly. "I don't know." She stood. "I'm going to check on the fairy house."

She left him sitting there on the rock.

On the walk back down the hill, June hung back, letting Caleb go ahead with the girls and field their constant questions. Every few minutes, he glanced back at her, but didn't say anything. She knew she was being childish, especially because she wasn't even mad at him, really.

Since the day she'd admitted to Caleb that David was cheating on her, neither of them had mentioned her husband. It was as if he, and her life back in Connecticut, didn't exist. And if they didn't talk about it, June could keep living this alternate life Jasper had given her: painting in his studio, living in his house, and—*oh God*—falling for his protégé, like the summer would never come to an end.

June wrapped her arms around herself and shivered. Her entire life—her *real* life—was three thousand miles away. As much as she'd been pretending this summer, she wasn't a kid without responsibilities. So many people counted on her—employees at work, all the committees she ran—plus there was David. He was still the father of her children, even if their marriage was over. He'd humored her by letting her take the girls for an extended vacation, but there was no way he'd sit by quietly if she proposed keeping them in Wishing Cove forever.

No, she wasn't mad at Caleb.

She was heartbroken.

When they arrived back home, the girls ran inside and left her alone with Caleb outside.

He approached her cautiously. "June, I'm sorry." He reached his hand out, but dropped it by his side before he touched her. "I don't mean to push you."

June shook her head. "No, I'm the one who should be sorry. I'm defensive because you're right. I have absolutely no idea how I'll make it all work. It's so much more complicated than saying I'll quit my job or drop out of committees and paint instead. I've made commitments."

"I know." Caleb set his mouth in a grim line. "And I know you're the kind of person who always honors your commitments. But—" He hesitated, as if he were weighing his next words carefully. "When will you stop taking care of everybody else, and make a commitment to yourself?"

Caleb had lived his life as a loner; he couldn't possibly understand none of this was as simple as he was suggesting. June had grown up with a mother who'd chosen the selfish path every time, and look where it had gotten her. June could never do that to Emma and Izzy. They deserved all the security and stability she'd never had.

Suddenly, all the late nights of painting—and the even later nights with Caleb—caught up with her. Her body sagged with exhaustion and her head began to throb. "You don't get it." She pushed past him and headed for the porch. "I can't talk to you about this."

June made it all the way to the front door before Caleb called out to her from the lawn below. "Fine, June. But if you want to talk about commitments, then what about me?"

"What?" June spun around. "What about you?"

Caleb stood with his feet set apart and arms crossed over his chest, almost as if he were silently challenging her. "What about a commitment to me?"

She put her hands on her hips. "I never made a commitment to you. It was just for the summer, remember? No over-thinking?"

"What if I want to change our deal?" Caleb dropped his hands to his sides as something naked and vulnerable flashed across his face. "What if—" He shoved his hands into his back pockets. "What if I'm in love with you?"

June froze, staring at Caleb's face as tears slowly pricked the back of her eyes. "Oh, Caleb."

She took a step toward him, then another, and her heart slowly folded in on itself. Until this moment, at least she'd had the comfort of believing this was only a fling, and they were better off ending it sooner rather than later. Of thinking a relationship could never really work out between them. But now... now she knew, without a doubt, that she loved him. That what she'd felt for David, even in their best moments, had never come close to touching this beautiful, agonizing fist of longing that gripped her heart. In another time, another place, back when she was still that pink-haired girl who believed in art and love and possibility, she and Caleb, they could have been... everything. But even back then, that idealistic girl knew in her heart that art and love were about as stable as the girls' fairy house up on the mountain. This was summer love, and soon a cold, autumn gale would scatter the pieces to the wind.

June made it across the porch before her legs gave out, and she sank down on the steps. She cradled her face in her hands until the heat of Caleb's body slid up next to her.

"Damn it, June. I'm sorry. I didn't mean to say it like this."

June lifted her head and turned to face him, her gaze roaming over his dark eyes, golden skin, that perpetual stubble that dotted his jawline. Searing every angle into her mind for when she was home in Connecticut, all alone with her memories. "I think I might be in love with you, too."

His eyes widened a tiny fraction, but before his lips could fully curve into a smile that would only tear off another piece of her heart, she said, "But I don't see how this could ever work."

Caleb's face smoothed into a more neutral expression, but she could still see the hint of a grin in the lines around his eyes. "Okay, so it's not ideal." He took her hand and weaved his fingers with hers. "But we can work this out. I've been coming to New York for work four or five times a year anyway, and Greenwich is only a train ride from there. I can extend my visits and stay for longer periods of time. Hell, I can probably rent a studio space and work in New York. You can figure out the PTA and your committees, back off slowly, and find some wiggle room so you can paint. Maybe next summer, you and the girls could come back here to Wishing Cove. And we could go from there."

His hand—strong and a little bit rough—wrapped around hers as his words slowly sank in.

Was it possible?

He made it sound so simple. She didn't have to yank the foundation out from under everything she'd ever known in order to build the life she wanted. She could work it all out the way she worked everything out—carefully and thoughtfully. Caleb understood her need to take things slowly and come up with a plan.

June peeked at him from under her lashes. "Would you really be willing to work from the East Coast for extended periods of time?" She'd grown so attached to this land these past few weeks. The meadow, his clapboard cottage, the blue-green sea beyond. He'd been staring at that horizon for almost two decades. Could he really leave it all to work in New York? "I know how much this place means to you."

"I want to be where you are. I can work from anywhere."

At that moment, the front door to the house swung open, and Caleb jumped away from her. It was something else she appreciated about him—he was always careful around the girls. June would tell them eventually, but not yet.

"Mommy, we need your help," Emma called. "We tried to make cereal but Izzy dropped the milk."

"It's not my fault!" Izzy yelled from inside the house.

"Okay, okay." June stood up and shot at glance at Caleb. He said he wanted to be with her, well, this was her life. It wasn't always adorable kids chattering delightedly about wildlife.

But Caleb grinned. "You need help?"

"No. Thank you, though." She sighed. "Come on, Emma. You're helping me."

Emma spun on her heel and went back into the house, letting the screen door slam behind her. From down the hall, June could hear the girls bickering.

She looked at Caleb. "I want to believe we can make this work."

"We can." The confidence in his tone almost had her convinced it really was simple. "Come over tonight after the girls go to bed and we'll talk more."

"Okay."

Caleb glanced at the door, probably making sure there were no little faces peering out, and pressed a quick kiss to her cheek before heading out across the meadow toward his house. Halfway there, he turned around to wave and nearly tripped over his own feet.

June laughed out loud, a sound that had been scarce over the past few years, but was becoming more familiar again. She went into the house and found the girls surrounded by paper towels scattered across a sopping kitchen floor. A hint of apprehension flashed across their faces as she approached, and June realized they were expecting her to snap at them for making a mess. It was what she would've done a couple of months ago.

Back home, she'd been so obsessed with being the perfect wife to David, mother to Emma and Izzy, and team-player in the company, it had been impossible to do a good job of any of it. Nobody could live up to the expectations she'd set for everything to run smoothly, and when things went wrong—as they often did—she'd reacted by becoming stressed out and angry.

June took a deep breath now, surveying the milk and waiting for her usual anxiety over the spill and chaos to bubble up in her chest like fizz in a soda can. But instead, she found herself shrugging at the girls.

As the saying went, it was only a little spilled milk. Accidents happened. June grabbed the paper towels and blotted at the milk on the floor, humming under her breath.

CHAPTER TWENTY-THREE

When June knocked on his door at 8:30 that night, Caleb was so tightly wound, he couldn't sit still. Since their conversation that afternoon, he'd gone for a run, cleaned his entire house, and forced himself to eat a sandwich despite the protests from his stomach.

He couldn't believe he'd blurted out he loved her. Yeah, it was something he'd been thinking for a couple of weeks now, and he'd known for sure the day her painting was accepted to the Starlake show. Until that day, Caleb hadn't realized how much he'd wanted that win for her, how much her happiness mattered to him. But he'd planned to say it—*if* he was going to say it at all—when they were alone, maybe after the show.

But she'd started talking about David wanting her home, and going on about her committees and work and the *goddamn PTA* and he couldn't believe she couldn't see how wrong it was. The next thing he knew, the words were flying out of his mouth, edged in frustration, though he meant every word.

But it wasn't admitting his feelings for her that had him pacing around his kitchen. If anything, saying the words—and unbelievably, hearing them back—had quieted his nervous energy. No, he wasn't wearing a groove in his wood floor because he had doubts about being in love with June.

It was because he didn't know if love would be enough once he told her the truth about himself.

Caleb swung the door open. She stood there in a long dress with her hair curling around her face, and his heart knocked against his sternum.

"Hi," she murmured, clutching her left hand with her right and spinning a nonexistent ring around her finger. He'd noticed her doing it ever since she'd ditched her wedding band. Usually when she was nervous.

"Hi," he parroted in return. *Nice one. Real creative.* What was it about the act of admitting their feelings that somehow transported them back to those uncertain, early days where neither of them was quite sure how to behave?

Oh, screw it.

He reached out and took her by the shoulders, pulling her to him for a kiss that left both of them breathless. *There, that's more like it.*

When they finally broke apart, June breathed out a laugh. "I guess that answers my question about whether you spent the afternoon regretting what you said to me earlier."

"For the record—no. Not even close."

"Good. Me, neither." Her shoulders relaxed. "I've been thinking about what my next steps need to be. Talk to David first, obviously. He's traveling this week for work, but I need to get on his schedule and have a really frank conversation with him. And I have to look into renting a place in Greenwich for me and the girls. David can have the awful house. I don't want it."

"June—" he cut in, but she was apparently deep in planning mode, because she kept talking.

"I could look for a house with a space for a studio, maybe a converted garage or guest house—"

Caleb was learning this was June. She took charge, made plans, and forged ahead. Aside from the fact that this had probably landed her on every goddamn committee in Connecticut, he admired her energy and was happy to see her using it to focus on herself for a change. But before she made too many plans, she needed to know what she was getting herself into.

"—I'll find an intern from the local university to take over the PTA's accounting while I supervise—"

"*June.* Hold up, okay?"

Her head jerked up. "I'm getting ahead of myself, aren't I? I know I do that."

"No… it's great. It really is. I just have to tell you something." He cleared his throat and fixed his eyes on the wall behind her. "Something that might affect all of this. Something you need to know before you make any decisions about being with me long-term."

"Okay." She twirled her invisible ring again.

Caleb took June's hand and pulled her into his kitchen. On top of the farmhouse table sat a small basket of pill bottles. He'd taken the basket out of the cupboard earlier that day, when it was time to take his meds. But instead of stashing it back up on the top shelf, he'd left it there. Every time he'd walked past the kitchen, that basket had seemed to grow in size until it loomed and mocked him. Over and over, he'd resisted the urge to hide it away, knowing what he really wanted to hide wasn't the pills, but the reason he needed to take them. Now, he led June over and seated her in front of them.

"What?" she asked, as he slid into the chair next to her. "More pills?" She picked up one and read the label. "Lithium again? Caleb, you showed me this."

"Yeah, but this time it's not Jasper's name on the bottle."

June's wide blue eyes flew back to the container in her hand and then to his face. "These are yours?"

"Yeah."

"So, this means you…" She trailed off.

Was she afraid to say it?

"I have bipolar disorder."

Just like that, it was out there in the room, a physical presence taking up too much space, crowding him in the small kitchen. The secret he'd never told anyone outside of doctors, his family, and Jasper.

June picked through the basket, reading the rest of the labels. "What are the rest of these for?"

He waved his hand in the general direction of the bottles. "Depression, anxiety, a couple of them are supplements."

"And you take them every day?"

"Yes. Some a couple of times a day."

She carefully placed the bottles back in the basket and slid it toward him. "Okay."

He opened his mouth and snapped it shut. Finally, he sputtered, "What do you mean, *okay?*"

"I mean, thank you for telling me. What part is going to affect my decision to be with you long-term?"

"That *is* the part. All of this." He sat back in his chair with a huff. "I have bipolar disorder. Do you understand what I'm telling you?"

She leaned in and pressed her forearms on the table. "I don't think I do. What *are* you telling me?"

"I'm telling you I have a serious mental illness." Did he have to spell it out? Even after everything he'd told her about Jasper? "I take handfuls of drugs every day, I have a psychiatrist and a therapist and whole regimen of coping techniques, and deviating from any of it could lead to serious episodes of mania or depression. For the rest of my life, that's never going to change." Caleb stared at the wood grain on the table, tracing the lines with his finger. "I may be stable now, but when it goes south, it's ugly, and people can get hurt."

"Who have you hurt?"

Who *hadn't* he hurt? "My family. My parents. Will." He paused, and then, "Some... other people."

She reached over, grasped his hand, and squeezed. "You can tell me."

Something about the small gesture, and the fact that she moved toward him instead of away, had him taking a deep breath, and starting at the beginning.

He'd always been a lot quieter and more introverted than Will. While Will was homecoming king and captain of the debate team, Caleb was the weird, long-haired kid producing angsty paintings in the art room. But it was mostly normal teenage angst, at least until he turned sixteen. Until his family moved again, this time to a small town in Ohio.

"I *hated it.* It was so much harder to move at sixteen than when I was younger. Harder to make friends. Our school was in this little Podunk town that had no art curriculum, and I'm sure the raging teenage hormones didn't help. Will handled it a lot better than I did, and it only grew worse. I started hiding out in my room, barely eating, and skipping school to go home and sleep. My parents thought I was suicidal. I probably *was* suicidal."

Caleb shifted in his chair, remembering those dark days. They took him to Cleveland, to the best psychiatric hospital in the state, where doctors diagnosed him with depression and prescribed antidepressants.

"Six weeks later, I had a manic episode."

"What was that like?" June asked, eyes widening.

"To be honest, it was fantastic." His mouth pulled into a grim smile. "When I was depressed, I lost all interest in art and spent most of my time in bed, but with the mania, I could sleep for two hours a night and jump out of bed feeling rested. I was more sociable than I'd ever been, and for the first time in my life I didn't feel so out of place and awkward all the time. But the best part was my art. I became absolutely obsessed with painting, and would stay up all night producing canvas after canvas."

"So, it was like a light switch, all of a sudden?"

Caleb shook his head. "It didn't happen overnight, but it happened fast enough that it was notable."

At first his parents were thrilled he was showing so much improvement, but their happiness quickly morphed into concern over his erratic behavior. "One night, when I was up working at all hours, I got it in my head I needed to go to the beach. I had to see the waves and smell the salt air, and I couldn't finish my painting unless I did."

June blinked. "The beach? I thought you said you lived in Ohio."

"I wasn't going to let a little detail like that stop me. So, I stole my dad's car. It was parked right outside the house, keys by the door. I headed east, figuring I'd end up on the Jersey shore by morning. My parents didn't even know I was gone until they got the call from a Pennsylvania state trooper telling them I'd been in an accident."

June gasped. "Were you hurt? Was anyone else hurt?"

"Thank God it was four in the morning and there weren't any other vehicles on the road. I totaled the car, but I got off lucky and walked away with nothing more than a bunch of bruises and a broken arm. My parents came to get me from the hospital in Hershey and took me directly back to Cleveland, where I got the official diagnosis of bipolar disorder. They stopped the antidepressants, suspecting it had trigged the manic episode, and started a new combination of drugs."

"Is that the combination you're on now?"

Caleb ran his hand through his hair, shaking his head. Remembering how, all of a sudden, he'd been an alien in his own body. "Hell, no. The side effects of some of those early drugs were horrible. I gained weight, was dizzy, and had blurred vision. One of the drugs—an antipsychotic—had sexual side effects. For a seventeen-year-old boy, not being able to get it up is about as bad as it gets."

June bit her lip, her expression sympathetic.

"The doctors were willing to tweak things, but for the most part, I felt like everyone wanted me to suck it up and deal with it. Especially my parents. In their minds, a few side effects weren't as bad as the alternative. As an adult, I can absolutely see their point, but at seventeen years old, it felt like a death sentence." It was hard to explain just how desperate he'd felt in those days, with his body and mind out of control, and his parents making all the decisions.

"My senior year of high school turned into an all-out battle with my parents over my meds and my art and just about everything else. And it definitely didn't help that my carbon copy was there at every turn, applying to colleges and taking popular girls to dances and generally being the perfect golden boy.

"On the night before graduation my senior year, when everyone was at an end-of-school celebration in town, I packed a bag, left my meds on the front table where everyone would see them as soon as they walked in—basically a giant *fuck you* to my family—and got on a bus to LA."

"So that's how you ended up living in Venice Beach?" June asked, and Caleb remembered how he'd candy-coated this part at dinner a while ago. He wished he could gloss over it again now. But he'd gotten this far, and there was no turning back.

"At first, I moved in with a woman I met online, on a message board for artists with bipolar. Kaitlyn was six years older than me and had her own apartment in LA. We had this immediate connection, and I was in love with her before I even met her in person. We got married after we'd known each other for a week."

Caleb turned to gauge June's reaction. Her face had drained of color, but she looked back at him, unflinching, and reached out to squeeze his hand again.

In LA, for once in his life, Caleb had felt superior to Will, who was off having his lame college experience at Northwestern, while

Caleb was living as an artist in one of the most exciting cities in the world. Not that he'd kept in touch with Will, or with any of his family. "I cut off contact entirely, and they had no idea where I was. At that point, I didn't give a damn about any of them. But as my meds wore off, I became increasingly manic. I wasn't sleeping, barely eating, and I spent all my time painting, convinced I was a genius and that the world just needed to discover it. I was too wrapped up in my work to notice that Kaitlyn wasn't in a good place." Caleb pressed his fingers to his temples. He couldn't even look at June. "Looking back, all the signs were there. But at the time, I thought she was jealous. I was producing a new painting every week, while she could barely get out of bed."

"She was depressed," June offered.

"Yeah. Major depression. That's what the medical examiner said. After—" He hadn't talked about this in twenty years. Not even to Emily. Definitely not to Will, although his brother tried to bring it up every once in a while. Caleb's heart pounded in his ears, and he could barely hear his own voice forming the words. "After she committed suicide."

"Oh, Caleb." June stared at him with her hand pressed to her mouth, and he could finally see the ugly reality of his past sinking in. A tear trickled down her cheek and he wanted so badly to reach out and wipe it away. But he couldn't touch her now, and maybe he'd never be able to again.

"That's when I started sleeping on the beach, sneaking into empty motel rooms to shower when it got to be too dire, and eating only when I was able to sell a ten-dollar painting to a tourist…" Caleb trailed off. There was nothing he hated more than the offhand comments he'd hear now and then about how the homeless weren't motivated to find a job. Because it had nothing to do with motivation, and everything to do with mental illness. There were so many people like him out there with untreated bipolar disorder or schizophrenia.

"When I met Jasper, I was truly at my worst. If he hadn't invited me to come and work for him here in Wishing Cove, I really believe I'd be dead right now."

June swallowed hard. "Did Jasper know you had bipolar disorder?"

"I didn't tell him right away, but I think from the beginning he recognized it. I know he saw a lot of himself in me, and there's something about a person's energy when they're bipolar that other people who have it can pick up on. Eventually, Jasper helped me find a good doctor who figured out an effective combination of meds without too many side effects."

He gave the basket of pill bottles a little shove. "I have a therapist named Emily who works with me on something called 'social rhythms therapy'. It's all about following regular routines and monitoring my moods. I have a lot of support from my parents, and Will came around eventually." Caleb's stomach clenched at the realization he could no longer add Jasper's name to the list of people who supported him.

"What do you mean?" June asked. "That Will came around eventually?"

"When I eventually reconnected with my family, my parents were angry, but mostly relieved I was okay. But Will didn't speak to me for two years."

"*Two years?*" June gasped, and Caleb could see her struggling to imagine cutting off her sisters for two years. Maybe she'd feel differently if Raven or Sierra had behaved like he had. "Why?"

Caleb's mouth twisted into a wry smile. "Because he's a really good grudge holder." He shook his head, shaking off the lame excuse for a joke. "But I get it. We were so close our entire lives, and then I took off without a word for almost a year. My family thought I was dead. If I'd been in Will's position, the minute I found out he was alive, I probably would've killed him."

His parents flew out to Wishing Cove as soon as they got his call, but Will had refused to go. "I tried for almost two years to reach out to Will, only to have my calls blocked and my letters returned. I finally went home for Christmas, and as soon as my brother walked in the door, he punched me right in the face."

Caleb rubbed his jaw at the memory, knowing he'd deserved Will's right hook and more. They stayed up late that night, finally having it out, and it was one of the only times he'd ever remembered seeing his brother cry. The image of Will with his head in his hands, sobbing that he thought he'd never see his brother again, would torment Caleb until his dying day. "I try not to get irritated when he acts like an overbearing babysitter because I know he gave up a great job in New York to come out here a few years after law school and look out for me. And I know what I put him through."

June bit her lip and he could see her weighing her next words. "Since that time when you were a kid, before you had the right meds, have you ever relapsed?"

"All the time," he answered, without hesitation.

"Oh." Her head jerked back slightly, as if he'd come at her with his hand, instead of with the answer to her question. He could tell she'd put a positive spin on it in her head, talked herself into a happy ending. But there was no end to bipolar disorder. Not unless you went the way of Jasper.

"I haven't had any major episodes since then, but it's a constant juggling act. Even finding the right meds doesn't mean everything is stable. There are tons of things that can trigger a relapse—stress, illness, caffeine, alcohol, not getting enough sleep. I've gotten pretty good at recognizing the signs, watching out if I start to feel really irritated over things that don't usually annoy me, or if I'm getting a buzzy feeling in my head."

He fixed his eyes on her, unblinking. This was the important part. This was what she needed to understand before they moved another step forward. "But I will always have bipolar disorder, and unless the drug companies have a major pharmaceutical breakthrough, I will probably always have relapses. But I'm committed to treatment and I'm not going off my meds. And I have Will and Emily and my psychiatrist for support."

"And me."

"You?"

"Now you have *me* for support." June tilted her head to one side. "If you want me."

If I want her. Somehow this summer, she'd become as vital to him as his art, and as much a part of his home as the cliffs hanging over Everett Bay.

He sat back in his chair and blew out a breath, more physically exhausted than he'd felt after his ten-mile run earlier. "After all that, are you really sure you don't want to think this through a little? Think about what you're getting into?"

"Caleb, I'm coming into this relationship with baggage, too. None of this is going to be easy, but we'll handle it together."

Caleb's eyes roamed over her: curly hair, ice-blue eyes; down to her hand reaching across the table. She was still here, still holding on to him, even after everything he'd told her.

He tugged her across the sliver of space between them and pulled her into his lap.

June took his face in her hands and gazed into his eyes. "I see how sweet and patient you are with the girls. How thoughtful and supportive you are to me. How you put so much of your heart into your work. Everything you overcame in your past is what made you the man you are today." She paused now, a breath away. "The man I'm madly in love with," she whispered, right before she pressed her lips to his.

Caleb slid one hand behind her head, tangling them in her wild hair. The other hand roamed across her back, pulling her closer and holding her more firmly against him. And although he'd kissed her a hundred times before, maybe a thousand times at this point, this kiss felt different.

This kiss felt like a beginning.

*

The next morning, Caleb rolled over in his bed and grabbed the pillow next to him, inhaling the faint smell of vanilla lingering on his sheets. He'd walked her home late last night after they'd talked, tumbled into bed, and then talked some more. Planning their future together.

It was a concept he'd never let himself entertain before. Partly because he'd never met the right woman, but mostly because he'd been too closed off. Too afraid to let someone in and then hurt them. Too afraid to get hurt when they saw him for who he really was. But he'd laid it all out on the table for June, and she'd stuck around.

Caleb smiled at the memory of the night before as he hauled himself out of bed and went into the kitchen to make breakfast. The basket of pill bottles still perched in the middle of the table, where he'd left it the night before. For the first time, he didn't have to hide it away. He took his meds with a cup of tea, and set to work finding something to eat.

He had got as far as putting a pan on the stove when someone pounded on his front door. June's show was that evening, and in a moment of weakness, he'd agreed to go shopping with Will for something to new to wear. They were the same size; he didn't know why Will couldn't just bring something over. But Will had insisted, arguing Caleb would probably hate everything he picked. Will was probably right.

Caleb yanked open the front door for his brother. "It's barely past eight. Aren't stores closed until at least ten or eleven?"

"What are you talking about?" Will ran a hand through his usually styled hair, leaving the side sticking up.

Caleb squinted at his brother. Was it possible he'd forgotten they were going shopping? "Clothing stores, remember? They won't be open at eight-thirty. Aren't we looking for something for me to wear tonight?"

"Oh, shit. I forgot." As Will pushed past Caleb and headed down the hall, Caleb noticed he'd left the house without shaving. He followed his brother into the kitchen, and found him opening and closing the cabinets. "You don't have any coffee in here, do you?" Will muttered.

"Nope. Black tea?"

"Whatever."

Caleb switched on the kettle. "If you're not here for shopping, what *are* you doing here?"

Will ran his hand through his hair again and flopped into a chair. "Listen, Caleb. I have some news about Jasper."

Caleb slowly lowered the canister of tea to the counter. "What kind of news?"

"The police chief stopped by early this morning. She knows I'm Jasper's attorney, and she wanted to tell me in person. It's about Jasper's death."

Caleb stared, taking in Will's messy hair, five o'clock shadow, and rumpled T-shirt. He never left the house looking like that. Caleb strode over to the table and sank into a chair across from his brother. "Tell me."

"Caleb, Jasper's death wasn't an accident. They're ruling it a suicide."

CHAPTER TWENTY-FOUR

Caleb had been in Chicago for a gallery show when he answered a phone call from an acquaintance at the Museum of Modern Art. Jasper had no-showed for an event in his honor, she'd said, and the museum couldn't get hold of him. The person knew Caleb lived on the same property as Jasper and might know what was going on. Since Caleb was out of town, and Jasper wasn't answering his calls either, he finally reached out to the local police and asked them to do a welfare check.

The police found Jasper in his bed, where it appeared he'd gone to sleep the night before. On the counter in the bathroom were his bipolar meds and a bottle of sleeping pills with three pills missing. Jasper wasn't breathing.

The coroner at the scene estimated Jasper had died the night before, and the preliminary report suggested an accidental reaction from the mix of bipolar meds and sleeping pills. But now they were saying—

"*Suicide?*" Every part of Caleb rejected it. He'd known Jasper for half his life and had supported him through relapses and bouts of depression. He'd seen what depression that led to suicide looked like when he was nineteen years old. He'd promised himself he'd never, ever miss those signs again. Jasper had been tired from the pneumonia those last few weeks, but he hadn't been depressed or manic. "I would've known if Jasper was suicidal."

"That's what I told the police chief." Will picked up a napkin off the table and began tearing it into pieces. "She said sometimes when severely depressed people finally make a plan to commit suicide, they hide it from everyone. If they've been struggling for a long time, they might suddenly become more upbeat, knowing their pain has an expiration date."

For about the hundredth time since Jasper's death, Caleb thought back to the time leading up to that final day. Jasper had been sick and exhausted during his bout with pneumonia. But he'd seemed to have turned a corner—his color came back, he started painting again, and one night he'd even insisted Caleb come to dinner. They'd had a nice time laughing over the early days when Caleb had been an eager kid apprenticing for him. Could Jasper have been planning to commit suicide the whole time?

No, it didn't make any sense. Caleb's head wagged back and forth. "How could they conclude suicide from—what—three sleeping pills? If Jasper had been trying to kill himself, why didn't he take the whole bottle?"

The lines around Will's eyes deepened. "Jasper did take the whole bottle, Caleb. He took two bottles. Apparently, Jasper had been stocking up on sleeping pills for a couple of months. The police became suspicious when they noticed the address on the bottle was for a drug store in Port Hood, not Wishing Cove. Why would Jasper drive a half an hour north to fill a prescription when he had a regular pharmacy here in town? One where the pharmacist knew him?"

Caleb struggled to wrap his brain around this news. Every instinct screamed at him to deny what his brother was saying, to leave the room, to stand up and punch Will in the face.

Will kept talking. "They did some digging, and found out the sleeping pills were prescribed by some shady doc who works out of a strip mall in Port Hood. After the police started putting it together, they ran tests and found six hundred milligrams of the sleeping pill in Jasper's system." Will's voice turned softer and—to Caleb's ears—pitying. "Caleb, that's the equivalent of thirty sleeping pills."

A flock of birds took up residence in Caleb's head, flapping their wings and screeching. His hands were shaking and his brother was still talking, but Caleb couldn't hear a word. He reached blindly for the basket in the center of the table, grabbed his bottle of emergency anxiety meds, and shook two into his hand. Before Will could share his opinion on whether or not it was a good idea, Caleb tossed the pills back with the dregs of his now-cold tea. The medicine hit the back of his throat, scraping as it went down, and the tea tasted like dirt, but he swallowed another gulp.

Will stood and paced across the small kitchen. "Listen, Caleb, I know this is a shock, but—"

Caleb cut him off. "Can I be alone for a while?"

"I don't think that's a good idea." Will ground to a halt. "We were going to hang out today. Let's ditch shopping, I know you hate that. But we could go out to breakfast, or maybe for a run or something."

"No." Caleb shook his head. Suddenly, Will's presence overwhelmed him in the small kitchen, filling too much space and sucking up all the air. He needed his brother to get out of there. He needed to be alone. *Right now.*

Caleb summoned the part of his rational brain that knew Will would never leave if he appeared to be upset. He weighed his next words carefully. "No, but thanks, bro. It's a shock, but I'm okay—honestly. I think I want to get to my studio and work for a while."

Will studied him with uncertainty masking his face. Finally, he nodded. "Okay. Why don't I call June to come over?"

"*No.*" Caleb cleared his throat. "No. Tonight is June's big night. You can't break this kind of news today. Look"—making his way over to the counter, he focused on cleaning up the tea he'd abandoned earlier— "I need to paint for a few hours. You know that's the best thing for me." The sponge emitted a loud squeak as he rubbed it hard on the counter. Caleb tossed it in the sink and turned around. "Honestly. I'm fine. Come by later and bring me a shirt to wear tonight, okay?"

Will nodded slowly. "Sure. I'll pick out something for you."

"Thanks. Nothing too hipster, okay?" With that, Caleb could see the relief settle on Will's face, like he knew it would. He was acting just like his old self. Everything was normal. All he had to do was keep it up for two more minutes.

Caleb walked over and put a hand on Will's shoulder, gently guiding him out of the kitchen. "Thanks for coming by to let me know. I really appreciate it."

"Of course."

They made it to the front door. One more minute now. "Call when you're headed over later, okay?"

"Sure." Will hesitated, then moved forward a fraction of an inch as if he were going to lean in and hug him.

Caleb took a quick step back and gave the door a push. "Okay, thanks. See you."

When the door was securely in its frame, he turned the lock, just in case. Caleb trudged back into the kitchen, annoyed that it had taken so long for his brother to leave him the hell alone and, at the same time, irrationally pissed off that Will had left. Didn't his brother know him better than to believe he was okay right now?

Jasper had committed suicide. And Caleb—who'd known him better than anyone, who'd been like a son to him, who'd been well acquainted with the kind of pain Jasper must have been experiencing—had completely, utterly missed it. What kind of friend, *what kind of person*, overlooked their best friend sinking straight to the bottom of the sea?

His mug of cold tea still sat where he'd left it on the table. Caleb picked it up and stared inside at the brown liquid and bits of tea leaves settling at the bottom, as if they contained some clue as to what Jasper had been thinking.

What made him do this?

And what was Caleb supposed to do now?

He closed his eyes and the images came fast. A woman lying in bed, her head on a pillow and the blanket pulled over her shoulders. Caleb called her name. Pulled the sheets back. Reached out and shook her arm.

Cold.

Her arm felt cold.

Three orange medicine bottles lay tipped over on a table by the bed, white and pink pills spilling out across the wooden surface.

Caleb called her name again.

Kaitlyn.

Jasper.

The rage came like a fire sweeping across a drought-ridden prairie, scorching everything in its path. Didn't Jasper know this would destroy him?

Caleb's hands shook, splashing leftover tea against the side of the mug. In the next moment, he'd spun around and hurled the mug at the wall, where it shattered into a hundred pieces. They rained down on the floor like bullets. Tea dripped from the gash in the drywall down to a puddle on the tile.

Caleb stared at the mess he'd made of the kitchen as reality began to sink in. How could he blame Jasper? Caleb knew how deep and suffocating that darkness could be, and he should have been there to toss in a rope and help Jasper find a way out. But he'd been busy, wrapped up in his work, preoccupied with his own success. And he'd missed the signs. Again. No, it wasn't Jasper's fault that he'd wanted to end the pain any more than it was Kaitlyn's.

But there was one common denominator here. One person who managed to let down everyone who needed him the most. Himself. He was like some kind of curse.

Caleb sprawled on the damp floor, relishing the sharpness of pottery digging into his back. The physical pain soothed him, releasing the anger and self-loathing and leaving a blessed numbness in its place.

Caleb had no idea how long he stayed there draped on the cold, wet tile, when suddenly there was a knock on the door. For a moment, he ignored it and continued staring up at the ceiling, hoping whoever it was would leave. But another knock echoed from down the hall—this one more insistent than the last.

Goddamn it. Had Will come back?

Caleb pushed himself to a seated position and sliced his palm on a piece of broken mug. *Good.* The physical pain was good: numbing the ache in his chest and quieting the buzzing in his head. Caleb grabbed a paper towel and folded it against the cut as he made his way down the hall.

He swung the door open, expecting his brother, and gave a start when he found June standing there. The smile she directed at him—innocent, happy, carefree—would have cracked his heart right open if he didn't feel as crumpled and empty as a beer can lying in the street. He held the door half-closed with his injured hand, hiding the cut on his palm behind the knob. "Oh, hey."

"Hi." June looked him up and down, clearly waiting for something. She took a baby step forward. The silence stretched between them until, finally, June cleared her throat. "Um, are you okay?"

Caleb shook his head to try to clear it. *Get your shit together.* "Yeah, sorry, I have a headache. I'm not feeling well."

June's face instantly changed to concern as she reached up and—in the ultimate mom-gesture—tried to feel his forehead. "Are you getting sick?"

He brushed her hand away. "No, I'm not sick. I just get migraines sometimes. I need to lie down and I'll be fine in an hour."

"Can I get you anything? I could make some tea?" She took another step forward and jolted to a stop when Caleb slammed his shoulder against the doorframe, blocking her entrance.

"No," he said. "I already had some tea. All I need is sleep."

"If you're sure…" She bit her lip, and he knew she didn't completely believe him.

How could he tell her the truth? How could he tell her that her father's downslide had gone far beyond what even he'd imagined? Or that she'd shackled herself to a man hounded by the same darkness?

Caleb fixed his gaze on her creased forehead and blue eyes shuttered with concern. And there it was—a tiny flicker of fear.

Would this be her reality from now on? Worrying over his every statement, gesture, and expression? Wondering if everything slightly off-kilter was in the range of normal, or if he were having another episode?

She has no idea what she's signed up for.

There was a reason Jasper had stayed alone and avoided sucking people into relationships. Because people got hurt.

People always got hurt.

"I'm sure," Caleb said, pulling the door closed another inch. "I'll see you this evening, okay?"

"Okay." She grasped her ring finger with her right hand and stepped back. "Feel better."

"Thanks." He eased the door shut, fighting the same contrasting emotions he'd felt toward Will: simultaneous anger that June stuck around asking questions, and irritation that she'd left without calling his bluff. But there was no way for her to win when it came to his bipolar disorder. No way for anyone who cared about him to win. They were better off without him.

He went to clean up the mess in his kitchen.

As Caleb swept up bits of pottery and scrubbed tea stains from his wall, he replayed his conversation with June from the night before. He'd convinced himself he'd been honest with her—he'd laid it all bare. But now he could pick out a hundred holes in his story. Lies of omission.

He'd said he had a great therapist and was committed to treatment when, in reality, he hadn't returned any of Emily's calls after Jasper died because he didn't want to talk about it. He hadn't told June the whole truth about the time he'd lived in LA, either. Like the time he'd been arrested for stealing when he was homeless.

His past was a series of exploding landmines, just like Jasper's had been, and if June got involved with him, there was a good chance she'd end up abandoned by an artist with bipolar disorder for the second time in her life. How could he ask her to give up the safety and security she'd craved since childhood to take a risk on a guy like him?

As Caleb stood to unloaded the dustpan into the garbage can, the vague lightness in his head and loosening of his muscles told him his anxiety meds had kicked in. He rarely took them, because a benzo addiction on top of everything else was the last thing he needed. But right now, he welcomed the haze settling around the edges of his consciousness.

Caleb leaned the broom against the wall and headed upstairs. The covers on his bed were still tossed to one side from when he'd climbed out of it an hour ago, so he crawled right back in and pulled the sheet over his head. Moments later, he escaped into a dark, dreamless sleep.

CHAPTER TWENTY-FIVE

June paused at the top of the steps and took one more look in the mirror before she made her way downstairs to leave for the show. She had to admit that, somehow, she'd managed to pull off artist-chic. Raven had watched the girls that afternoon while Sierra took her shopping in Seattle. They'd hit the boutiques in the Ballard and Fremont neighborhoods, where Sierra had talked her into buying a mod black and orange shift dress and a pair of black boots. It was an outfit she never would have glanced at on her own, but once she'd pulled it on in the fitting room, she hadn't wanted to take it off again.

At the hair salon, June had insisted on wearing her hair curly, and it had been the right choice. Caleb liked it that way, and the pin-straight style reminded her too much of the old, accountant June.

She tucked a curl behind her ear. Yes, at least on the outside she looked every bit the up-and-coming painter off to her first show. But on the inside, a thousand tiny breakdancers turned headspins in her stomach. Was it ludicrous to think she could pull this off? Wishing Cove and the surrounding coastal towns housed dozens of talented artists—*real* artists—like Jasper and Caleb. Her last art show had been in the smelly gym of her Philadelphia high school.

Caleb believed she was good enough. He'd recognized she was talented before anything romantic had happened between them, so she believed him... to a degree. Maybe it would take time to build the confidence of an artist who'd been doing this for a lifetime.

At the bottom of the stairs, June found a crowd waiting for her in the living room. Sierra was sitting on the couch with Raven, who for once wore a dress instead of her usual army pants and cotton button-up. Will sat in the chair across from them, sneaking glances at Raven when she wasn't looking. The girls took up the center of the room doing spins to show off their swirly skirts.

June spotted Caleb in the opposite doorway, and her heart sputtered in her chest. He stood with one shoulder propped against the frame, looking movie-star handsome in a pair of slim-cut black trousers, an Oxford shirt, and black boots. When he saw her, he took an audible breath as his eyes widened.

"Damn, June, you look beautiful," Will said, standing up as she entered the room.

Raven nodded. "You really do. Nobody's even going to look at the paintings!"

"I seriously doubt it," June said. "But thank you." She glanced at Caleb, who stood frozen in the doorway, now looking a bit pale. He'd said he had a migraine earlier; maybe he *was* getting sick. She wished she could go over, put her arms around him, and ask how he was feeling. But the girls fluttered around her, so she'd have to wait until later to check in on him.

Will and Caleb had offered to drive to the show, and somehow June ended up in Will's car with Sierra, and the girls and Raven rode with Caleb.

June grew jittery as the wood and glass structure of the Starlake Arts Center came into view, glowing from the headlights of cars pulling into the parking lot and the solar lamps marking the path to the entrance. June wished she'd gone with Caleb, as she could have used a reassuring smile or hand squeeze at that moment. Instead, they hopped out of the car and all met by the entrance to the building. He barely looked at her as he held the door open.

Before June could pull Caleb aside, Moira, Starlake's executive director, approached them. They'd met previously when June had come to drop off the painting, and she'd found they had a lot in common. They were both working moms juggling little kids, activities, and committees.

"June, it's lovely to see you," Moira said, holding out her hand. "Your painting looks wonderful in the Andersen gallery. I'd love to show you after I say hello to your friends and family." She gave June a wink. "Of course, I already know Caleb Valencia. He's a bit of a local celebrity around here. Thank you again for donating a painting, Caleb. I imagine the sale of it will go a long way toward building the new studio."

June turned to Caleb. "I didn't know you donated a painting."

He shrugged it off. "Starlake does great work for arts education. I'm happy to help."

Moira put her manicured hand on June's arm and leaned in. "I'm always trying to convince Caleb to teach a class here but, so far, I haven't been successful," she faux-whispered. "Maybe you can talk him into it."

Caleb cleared his throat and looked uncomfortable. "Oh, I don't think I could fill a classroom."

June doubted that. She'd had hours of interesting conversation with him about painting, and had experienced his ability to critique artwork in a way that was encouraging but productive. Will's thoughts must have gone in the same direction as hers, because June saw him roll his eyes and give a shake of his head as Caleb continued to give non-committal responses to Moira's attempts to change his mind about teaching.

Finally, Moira sighed. "The offer is always open." She smiled and shook her head. "You remind me so much of Jasper. I could never get him to consider teaching, either."

For the briefest second, June thought she saw Caleb flinch at the mention of Jasper's name, but it was gone before she could be sure. Was that what was bothering him? That people would undoubtedly bring up Jasper tonight?

He'd seemed so much more comfortable discussing Jasper these past few weeks, talking openly about him to her and her sisters, and responding graciously when someone in town offered their condolences. Again, June thought about pulling him aside, but he gave Moira a lopsided smile and a shrug, so maybe she'd imagined his discomfort.

"June," Moira said. "Come and see where we put your painting. I've already had several people express interest in making a bid. One of them wants to meet you."

June looked around for the girls, but Sierra waved her away. "Go! Meet your fans! We'll keep an eye on the girls."

June's gaze darted to Caleb, but he stared past her into the growing darkness outside the windows. Before she knew what to think about that, Moira tugged on her arm and whisked her into the Andersen gallery.

The next two hours were a whirlwind of conversations with other artists and locals who'd come to support the arts center. Several people mentioned they planned to place a bid on her painting, and a gallery owner from Seattle asked her to send him a portfolio. Emma and Izzy came and went with Sierra and Raven, sampling the refreshments when they weren't exploring the artwork. Will made the rounds, chatting and shaking hands with just about everyone, and occasionally bringing someone by to meet her.

June had always dreaded these kinds of events at home because, generally, they centered around David's business. All the schmoozing and backslapping and making the same small talk over and over left her exhausted. But here at the arts center, June found herself energized by the engaging conversation and genuine love of art reflected by the guests at the show. It would have been an amazing night—if she hadn't spent half of it looking over her shoulder for Caleb.

Every couple of minutes, June glanced around the gallery, trying to catch sight of Caleb, but she had no idea where he was. June knew he was an introvert and these kinds of social situations weren't his thing, but he'd been in the art scene in Wishing Cove long enough that the people here weren't exactly strangers, even though he wasn't involved with local events the way Will seemed to be. When she'd pictured this night, she'd imagined he'd be right there next to her, showing the pride in her accomplishments he'd been professing for weeks.

June excused herself from a conversation with a couple of local business owners, and went looking for him. Finally, she spotted him in a corner, talking to an older man in a fedora. Or more accurately, listening to the older man talk, June realized, as she stepped closer. The man waved his hands and barely stopped to take a breath as a lecture spilled from his mouth, with Jasper's name on repeat. Caleb stood with his back pressed to the wall, face pale, as the man droned on.

"One could argue," the man intoned, "that from a legacy perspective, dying at the height of his career served Jasper well. Adding to his fame, it puts him on a par with the greats such as Andy Warhol and—"

"Excuse me," Caleb said, when he spotted her, pushing past the man. He took June's arm, tugging her away from the corner. "June, I'm leaving."

"What?"

"I need to get the fuck out of here."

June flinched at the curse word, but Caleb didn't seem to notice. His eyes darted around the room and he shifted his weight back and forth.

He's just upset. What a callous thing for that man to say. June squeezed his forearm. "Caleb, don't listen to that guy. He's clearly an ass, and he doesn't know the first thing about Jasper—" Abruptly, she stopped talking as he yanked his arm from her grasp.

"Stop." Caleb pressed his hands to his temples.

"Stop what—?"

"I can't talk about Jasper." His voice rose, and a couple of other guests turned to look at them with interest.

June took a step back as a little slice of alarm cut into her. Caleb was acting—strange. "Caleb, can we go somewhere quiet and talk about what's going—"

"There's nothing to talk about." He looked at her now, but she got the sense he wasn't really seeing her. "I'm just—I've got to go."

And with that, he turned away from her and headed out of the gallery into the main hallway. For a moment, June stood there, stunned. Caleb had been acting strangely all day, and it couldn't be a migraine. He was clearly upset about something. She'd never seen him like this. Had something happened? Was it related to his bipolar disorder?

June whirled around, intent on following him, when she heard Moira call her name. "June! Over here!" Moira stood across the room and waved to June. "I want you to meet the mayor of Wishing Cove."

Moira and an attractive middle-aged woman made their way over to her. "Mayor Alvarez was raving about your painting, and she wanted to meet you." Moira introduced her to the mayor, and June did her best to politely engage in a conversation about figurative art. As soon as she could find a window, June excused herself, citing the girls' bedtime, and hurried into the main room where she found Sierra sitting on a bench talking to Sam Grayson.

"Sierra, did you see Caleb go by?"

Sierra looked up from her conversation. "Oh, yeah, he left about ten minutes ago."

He probably ran out of there. June's shoulders slumped. "Would you mind if we found Raven and the girls and asked Will to drive us home? I'm exhausted."

"Oh—sure, we can go," Sierra said, standing up and brushing off her skirt. "But Caleb took Raven and the girls with him."

"He—what?" June's heart thudded. Caleb had been upset. Irrational, even. She didn't like the idea of him driving in that state, and now he had the girls in the car, too. "Why did they go with him?" June heard the wobble in her voice and, apparently, so did Sierra, because she gave her a sideways look.

"Raven asked him to. The girls were tired, and Caleb had their booster seats in his car. We wouldn't have all fit in Will's car anyway, so she figured she'd put them to bed and let you enjoy the party. Is that okay?"

"Yes. Yes, of course." June squared her shoulders. It was only a couple of miles to get home. "But if it's okay with you," she said, "I'd love to go now too. Can we find Will?"

Sam reached into his pocket and pulled out a car key. "I can drive you."

June gave him a smile, grateful not to have to waste time looking for Will, and they headed out.

As Sam turned the car onto Pinecrest Drive and coasted down the first hill, June's shoulders began to relax. She'd put the girls to bed and then go over to Caleb's house. Maybe by then he would have calmed down and they could talk. Maybe everything had just been blown out of proportion.

Whatever "everything" was.

But as they rounded the next curve on the winding road, June sat up in her seat, heart thudding.

Ahead, on the crest of the next hill, were flashing red lights cutting through the darkness. She could make out the outline of a fire truck and two police cars blocking the road.

"Looks like an accident," Sam said, from some echoing, faraway place, flipping on his hazard lights and slowing the car to a crawl.

"Oh my God," June whispered. Because, suddenly, she knew. Mothers have an instinct for when their kids are in trouble, and *she knew*. Her girls were up there, somewhere, maybe hurt, maybe crying for her. Maybe they were—

Blood roared in her ears, drowning out the sirens.

No. No. No. She couldn't think that way.

Before Sam could bring the car to a full stop in front of the traffic flares blocking the road, June had flung the door open and jumped out.

"*June!*" she heard Sierra scream. "Wait!"

But June kept running.

CHAPTER TWENTY-SIX

June swerved around the fire truck blocking the road and skidded to a stop, panting and shaking in horror. Caleb's Jeep sat at an angle in the middle of the road with the front end hanging out over the center line and the hood crumpled. On the back end, both taillights were shattered and the bumper smashed. Behind the Jeep sat a sports car with the hood folded like a piece of paper and, in the other lane, sat an SUV with smoke billowing from its engine.

June spun around wildly, searching the crowd of bystanders and first responders for any sign of the girls. The night was cloudy, moonless, and there were no streetlamps on this stretch of road. The red lights of the fire truck were more disorienting than helpful, flashing on and off, shining through the smoke and against the shifting shapes of the rescue personnel's reflective clothing.

"Miss!" A police officer ran up behind June and grabbed her by the elbow. "I'm sorry, but you can't be here. You'll need to stand behind the traffic flares over there."

June gripped the police officer's arm. "My daughters. They were in that Jeep. They're only six and seven. Please—" she gasped.

"June!" Raven's voice cut through the din. "June, over here!"

June whirled around to find Raven standing on the side of the road, holding an ice pack to her forehead. Next to Raven stood Caleb and—

"*My babies.*"

"Mommy!"

June ran over and fell to her knees in front of them, grabbing the girls and clutching them to her chest, breathing in the lavender scent of their no-tears shampoo. "Thank God you're okay." She sat back on her heels, her gaze roaming over each girl, looking for signs of injury. "Are you hurt?"

"No, but that was scary, Mommy," Izzy whimpered, fat tears welling up in her eyes.

"I know, baby, I know," June said, pulling the girls back toward her.

Sierra and Sam ran up and skidded to a halt, panting hard. "Is everyone okay?" Sierra gasped.

"We're all fine," Raven said, shifting the ice pack on her head and revealing a purple bruise the size of a quarter.

"Raven, your head." June clambered to her feet.

Raven waved her off. "Just a little bump. I'll be okay."

At that moment, a loud *whoosh* came from the direction of the cars in the road. The SUV that had been smoking earlier suddenly burst into flames, and fire flickered out from under the hood. June grabbed the girls, yanking them safely away from the burning vehicle as a cacophony of voices rose from the rescue workers. June stared as the fire grew larger, its red and orange glow lighting up the darkness as black smoke billowed into the sky.

And then from somewhere in the far reaches of her consciousness, she saw another fire.

A pot on an avocado-colored stove bursting into flames, lapping at the curtains and leaving black scorch marks on the wall. The flames grow bigger, and June reaches for the pot, tossing it into the sink and flinging on the water faucet. Hot oil sputters, landing on her arm and burning her wrist. The fire in the pot fizzles out, but the curtains have already ignited.

"Mommy! Daddy!" she screams.

But Mommy isn't home, and Daddy is out in the garage painting, where he's been for days without stopping to sleep or eat. How many hours ago did he leave this pot on the stove?

A second curtain catches fire, and the wooden frame around the window begins to smolder.

Sierra and Raven are napping upstairs. How will she get them out of the house? She'll never be able to lift the baby out of the crib. She'll need to put out the fire.

Baking soda. The fireman that came to her first-grade class said to use baking soda. June grabs the box from the fridge and a chair from the corner, dragging both back to the stove. She climbs up on the chair and dumps the baking soda on the curtains, shaking it to get every last bit out of the box.

Smoke rises in the kitchen as the flames peter out.

A loud hiss brought June back to the present, and she looked up as fire fighters sprayed a thick white fire retardant on the hood of the car.

"He left a pot on the stove," June murmured.

Sierra reached out and grabbed her hand. "What, honey?"

"Jasper. He left a pot on the stove. There was a fire. Raven was a baby. I didn't know how I'd get you both out." For the first time, June looked at Caleb, and he stared back at her with regret slashed across his features. "He could have killed us."

And suddenly, all the terror of the past few minutes turned as red and hot as the fire that still burned in her mind. She turned on Caleb, grabbing him by the arm and shaking hard. "What were you thinking? What *the hell* were you thinking? You were in no mind to be driving my children anywhere. *You could have killed them.*"

"Whoa, June…" Raven began, tugging on her shoulder. "The accident wasn't Caleb's fault. That guy in the black sports car came zooming up behind us, and—"

June shrugged her off, turning back to Caleb. "Is this a manic episode? Just like the last accident?" He flinched, and for just a second, her heart ached at the hurt in his eyes. But she swatted the regret away. This wasn't only about her. He'd put the girls in danger. "How could you allow my children to be in the car with you?" She dropped his arm. "How can I ever trust you?"

There was a long pause, and then Caleb took her by the shoulders so she had to face him. "June, listen to me." He swallowed. "God knows I've screwed up a lot in my life, but that last accident was *over twenty years ago*. I was a stupid kid. I would never, *ever* let anyone get in the car with me if I thought I couldn't drive safely. Especially the girls."

June looked up to find Emma and Izzy staring at her, wide-eyed, with tears streaked across their cheeks. She wrapped her arms around herself and walked away from Caleb. The memory of Jasper and the fire still burned in her mind; the girls needed her, and she couldn't do this right now.

Sierra came up beside her, putting an arm around her shoulder. "Are you okay?"

June shook her head. "Let's get the girls home."

Sam stepped up, his tall frame towering over them. "I'm sure the police will want to take Caleb's statement. I'll stay with him and call Will to pick us up." He held his car keys out to Sierra. "Take my car and I'll get it from you later."

With one last accusing glance at Caleb, June took the girls' hands and followed her sisters back to Sam's car.

With the accident blocking Pinecrest Drive, the ride home took an extra twenty minutes since they had to backtrack through town. They mostly drove in silence, and both of the girls nodded off, a fact that June was grateful for. She'd have to apologize for her outburst and explain it—as best as she could—because they'd have a lot of questions in the morning. But at least they'd sleep tonight.

When they arrived at the house, June picked up a dozing Izzy, and Sierra took Emma. June felt another rush of gratitude to have both her sisters with her all summer. They'd been such a huge help with the girls and, right now, their quiet presence was a comfort.

They turned down the path, and June glanced in the direction of Caleb's cottage, crouching there in the darkness. All she wanted to do was get the girls down and then climb into her own bed. She had a lot to discuss with Caleb, but she had no idea what she'd say to him. Maybe another driver had technically been at fault. But she'd seen how he'd been acting strangely all day and then tore out of the gallery without an explanation. How could she be sure he'd been driving safely and watching the road?

As they approached the house, June noticed movement on the porch. She squinted through the shadows and made out the outline of someone sitting in one of the wicker chairs. Her heart stuttered. Could it be Caleb? Was it possible he, Sam, and Will had gotten past the accident site and made it home before them?

June shifted Izzy's weight, and the person on the porch stood up. June gasped and stumbled to a stop so abruptly Sierra nearly crashed into her.

"June," Sierra whispered. "Keep moving. Emma's getting heavy."

But June stood frozen to the spot, staring up at the porch.

Raven came up beside her, carrying the girls' jackets. "Is that Caleb?" she asked, craning her neck to see.

"No." June's voice shook. "It's David."

CHAPTER TWENTY-SEVEN

June took slow, deliberate steps as she descended the stairs and turned the corner to where David sat in Jasper's living room. She'd told him to wait there while she put the girls to bed, partly because she didn't want them to wake up and see him or they'd never go back to sleep, but mostly because she needed a few minutes to get her thoughts together.

The abrupt transition from her art show, to the accident, her revelation about Jasper, and David standing in Jasper's house, made her head spin.

David stood when she entered the room. "You look different," he remarked.

She opened her mouth to say something defensive but realized he was smiling, and she abruptly closed it.

"Kind of like the girl I met in college." He cocked his head to the side and if June didn't know better, she would have said he looked almost sentimental. "I haven't seen you wear your hair curly in forever."

"You don't like it curly," she reminded him, sinking into the chair on the opposite side of the room.

"I wouldn't say that. It's more professional when it's straight. But it's pretty like this."

Why were they talking about her hair? "David, what are you doing here? I sent you the itinerary of when we'd be returning to Connecticut."

He sat down on the couch opposite her and leaned forward, resting his elbows on his knees. "I got the itinerary. When I realized it would still be a few weeks before I saw you and the girls, well—" He looked down at his hands. "I missed you."

"Yeah?" she asked, her voice flat. "What does Priya think of you being here?"

"I don't know. I didn't tell her." David met her eyes. "I ended things with Priya."

June raised her eyebrows. "Why?"

"Why? Because you're my wife, and I want us to be a family again." He stood up and paced to the fireplace. It was as disorienting to see David standing in front of Caleb's painting as it was to hear the words coming out of his mouth. This was not the direction she'd expected this conversation to go.

Did he think it was that simple? "David, just because the affair is over doesn't erase the fact that it happened."

"I know." He hung his head. "I'm so sorry. If you come back, things will be different."

She shook her head slowly. "It's too late."

"It can't be too late. It was one mistake."

One very big, very hurtful mistake. But it wasn't even about the affair anymore, or about David. It was about her. She'd changed. She wanted different things. And then there was Caleb.

Her stomach clenched at the thought of Caleb.

David's voice cut into her thoughts. "Things will be different, June. I swear. We'll go to counseling. On dates again. We'll save our marriage—" He kept talking, listing all the ways he planned to make changes.

In her heart, June knew there wasn't much to their relationship worth saving. But a tiny, rational part of herself held back from cutting David off completely. She'd expected him to argue with her, maybe try to suggest the end of their marriage was her fault. But to come here with a plan to fix it? He'd clearly thought this through, and—counseling? David was willing to go to counseling?

"June, this isn't just about us. What about Emma and Izzy? Think about what a struggle it was for you growing up in a broken home." He blew out a sigh and leaned a shoulder against the fireplace mantle. "I don't want that for the girls, do you?"

Of course she didn't. She'd worked her entire life to make sure nobody she loved—not Raven or Sierra, and not the girls—ever experienced that kind of stress and uncertainty. She'd sacrificed so much to give them the security she'd never had.

"Think of what it will be like for the girls to go through a divorce," he continued. "To shuttle back and forth between houses and trade off holidays, to never know where they're staying next."

June gazed up at David as he stood there with his hands tucked into the pockets of his navy chinos. He projected the quiet elegance that came with a life of always having enough. David had never had to worry over the cost of rent or groceries or a medical bill, and it showed in the way he moved with self-assurance and ease. From the moment she'd met him, he'd represented everything she'd never had as a child. Everything she'd wished for her daughters.

It wasn't about the money. It was about the girls growing up knowing where they belonged, with two parents they could count on. Two parents who never flaked on them, took off, acted erratically.

Or put them in danger.

David paced back across the room again. "Come home and let's work this out." His blue eyes pleaded with her. "Please, June?"

June pressed her hands to her temples. The last twenty-four hours lapped at her like the waves on the beach outside. It was all too much. She hauled herself out of the chair and moved away from David to the other side of the room. Avoiding his eyes, she stumbled around, pulling throw pillows off the couch and taking a blanket from a trunk in the corner. Then she shook it out and spread it on the couch. "You can sleep here tonight."

"Is that my answer?" he asked, his voice hoarse.

She stood up straight and finally looked at him. "We'll talk about this tomorrow."

Before David could say anything else, June fled from the room. Upstairs, she crawled into bed, not even bothering to take off her dress. She stared up at the ceiling, her gaze tracing the shapes of moonlight streaming in through the window as she tried to lull herself to sleep. But although she was exhausted, the events of the day zipped through her mind on repeat. Finally, June gave up on sleep, and reached over to grab her phone off the bedside table.

She hit a number, and her mother answered on the third ring. "June?" Esther slurred, sounding half-asleep.

"Oh, I woke you. I'm sorry." It must have been close to midnight, and three hours later on the East Coast. "I forgot how late it is."

Through the phone, June heard a click of what was probably a bedside lamp.

"Is something wrong?" Esther asked, her voice clear of sleep now. "Is it the girls?"

"No, the girls are fine." June shoved the image of them standing on the side of the road next to a smoldering heap of crumpled metal out of her head. "I—uh." Why *was* she calling her mother? They hadn't talked in weeks. "How's Wolf?"

"Oh, he's fine, thanks for asking."

"Mom, do you ever wonder what your life would have been like if Jasper had stuck around?"

"Oh, June." The sound of Esther shuffling around in bed drifted through the phone. "There was no danger of that. Jasper was never going to stick around. Men like that—the really talented ones—have too many demons. It's not in their DNA to stick around."

"I remember the fire. In the kitchen. When I was little."

"Oh, yes, the fire." Esther sighed. "Jasper was always going through these dark phases where he'd become single-minded, hiding out in the studio painting day and night. You couldn't reach him in that state. He'd put a pot on the stove or leave the car running and then become so immersed he'd forget to come back to it. The fire was the worst incident, but then again, it was also the last."

"Is that why he left?"

"The fire was the catalyst. Once he came out of it and realized what he'd done, he had terrible guilt that he'd put you girls in danger. But no—Jasper would have left one way or another. They all do."

June traced the pattern on the quilt draped over her knees. "If that's true, then why do you keep dating artists? Why do you keep putting yourself in that position?"

"Because men like that are exciting. They have an energy. A *passion*—"

June thought back to all those days with Caleb in the studio. The intensity in his eyes when they talked about art… and when they tangled up together on the couch…

"At least until things go bad. And they always go bad." Esther's voice dropped in pitch, and she sounded almost sad. "I guess I'm a glutton for punishment."

There was that little tug of compassion again. June had always seen things in black and white, but this summer had shown her so many shades of gray. "No, you're not. You're just… an optimist."

"Well, sometimes I wish I were more like you."

"Me?" June sat up higher. "Why?"

"I know I give you a hard time about your life, but maybe it's because I'm jealous. You were smart to choose a man like David.

He may not have that fire in him, but you always know what you're getting. There's something to that."

June was silent for a minute, processing her mother's words. It was hard to imagine Esther dating a man like David. She would have grown bored in ten minutes. Drama was in Esther's DNA.

People couldn't change who they were, deep down.

"Maybe you're right." June finally said. "Thanks, Mom. I'm sorry I woke you up."

"It's fine. Have a good night."

"You too."

June switched off her phone and put it on the side table. As she shifted in the darkness, pulling the covers higher and fluffing up her pillow, the acrid scent of smoke rose up around her. It had seeped into her clothes, her hair.

Her memories.

She squeezed her eyes shut, trying to block them out, but the images still came, one after the other, all the way back to childhood. And with them came the fear, the doubt, the intense desire to hold on to something safe and stable and predictable.

David had flown all the way out to Wishing Cove to tell her she could have her old life back if she wanted, the life she'd spent more than fifteen years gripping so tightly. He was willing to go to counseling, to listen, to make space for her needs.

David loved the girls, and—June hesitated here. Okay, so she couldn't say for sure he loved her. But he was here. He was trying.

Maybe that was enough.

CHAPTER TWENTY-EIGHT

Caleb left his studio as the darkness began to fade and a watery, silvery light peeked out over June's house on the hill. He tore his gaze from the window he knew was hers, tempted to use the key Jasper had given him ages ago and sneak up the stairs to her room. Maybe if he begged, she'd forgive him for everything that had happened yesterday.

Caleb's stomach clenched at the reminder of the accident, and what led up to it. Running out on June had been a terrible thing to do on her big night but, all of a sudden, he hadn't been able to take it anymore. Those people coming at him from all directions, wanting to process what a tragedy Jasper's death had been, what a loss to the art community, how Jasper was *gone too soon.*

Maybe June was right, and he shouldn't have allowed Raven and the girls to get in the car with him. He was sure he'd been driving safely, and he never would have put them in danger. But maybe Jasper had thought the same thing, right before he'd almost burned the house down with his children inside. In manic states, you didn't always know *what* you were doing. Living with bipolar disorder was like walking on the edge of a cliff. A gust in the wrong direction could blow him off balance. Anyone who loved him would go over too, and end up broken on the rocks below. Which was why he'd never taken chances. Until June, anyway.

Caleb locked his studio door and turned toward the path to his cottage. He'd barely taken a step when a deep, male voice called out, "*Hello?*"

Caleb spun around to find a blond man about his age striding toward him. The man looked harmless in khakis, a navy sweater, and brown loafers, but Caleb instinctively set his feet apart and curled his hand into a fist. "Who are you?"

The blond man's arm extended toward him, and Caleb's muscles tensed until he realized this guy was holding his hand out to shake. "David Westwood."

As the name sank in, Caleb shoved his fists in his pockets to tamp down the urge to put one through the man's face. David stood there stupidly, his hand in mid-air, until he eventually dropped it to his side.

"You must be the other artist living on the property," David said, probably to fill the silence because Caleb wasn't about to help him out. "June mentioned you were a friend of her father's—?"

Caleb nodded.

"Sorry to sneak up on you," David continued. "I'm still on East Coast time—it's 9 a.m. for me. Couldn't sleep anymore, so I thought I'd take a little walk around. Beautiful property." He looked out at the view of the islands in the distance, nodding his head. "I have to admit, I didn't expect all this when June told me her father was an artist." David paused, and then seemed to realized what he'd implied. "No offense."

Caleb stared at him flatly. "Does June know you're here?"

"Yeah, I saw her last night."

Caleb recoiled slightly at that news. So, June and David had hung out last night. Caleb had a feeling David would be acting decidedly less friendly toward him if she'd mentioned the accident. He'd probably be less friendly if he knew Caleb and June were involved, too. So, what *had* they talked about?

"You're here to visit the girls?"

David nodded. "June, the girls, and I are heading out tonight."

Caleb's pulse pounded in his ears. "You're leaving tonight? All of you?"

"Yes."

Caleb looked David up and down. The guy seemed so normal. So clean-cut All-American business owner and dad. He probably had the neighbors over for barbecue on the weekend. Drank two light beers and stopped because he was driving. Balanced his checkbook.

David looked exactly like the kind of stable, predictable guy a woman who'd grown up with an erratic childhood should end up with. It didn't change the fact that what he had done to June was terrible, but maybe he was sorry. Maybe he'd traveled all the way to Wishing Cove to beg for June's forgiveness and ask her to come home.

If that was the case, what right did Caleb have to stop her?

At the thought of June going back with David, Caleb's knees almost buckled. But the only thing he had to offer June was uncertainty and heartache, and she deserved better. Emma and Izzy deserved better. He'd let them into his life without thinking about the consequences.

If he really loved them, he'd let them go.

Caleb turned away from David, unable to look at him anymore. "Have a good trip," he muttered, and took off up the hill.

*

When Caleb got to his cottage, he found his brother lounging on the deck with a to-go cup of coffee in his hand. Goddamn it, Will's timing couldn't be worse. The last thing he needed was more criticism about the night before.

Caleb gave a curt nod in greeting. "What do you want?"

"Is that any way to talk to your own flesh and blood?" Will took a sip of coffee, obviously not too worked up about it. "Who's the blond guy down by the studio?"

Caleb sucked in a breath. "June's husband."

"What's *he* doing here?" Will asked, peering at the spot where David had disappeared down the steps toward the beach. And then—"Wait." His eyebrows shot up. "Don't you mean *ex*-husband?"

Caleb shrugged, the casual gesture belying the acid churning in his gut. "He says June and the girls are leaving with him tonight."

"Yeah?" Will took a sip of coffee and regarded him over the plastic lid. "What does June say?"

Caleb shrugged again, and Will slammed the cup down on the table. "Jesus, Caleb, you haven't talked to her, have you? Are you just going to let her go?"

Caleb had never wanted to be an only child so much in his life. He'd give anything for Will to disappear so he could be alone. "You need to back off." He turned abruptly and went into the house before he said or did something he'd regret.

Unfazed, Will followed him into the kitchen. "So, are you going to hide behind bipolar forever? Use it to push everyone away?"

Caleb ignored him, switching on the kettle and grabbing the tea from the cabinet. He wasn't *using* his bipolar disorder like it was a convenient excuse because he was one of those guys who couldn't commit. He was protecting June from the inevitable fallout.

"I'm asking so I know what to expect." Will sank down into a kitchen chair, seemingly oblivious to the fact that this conversation was one-sided. "I know Mom and Dad would love to have grandkids someday. I'm wondering if that's all on me, because it looks like you're really leaning hard into this recluse persona. If that's the case, I want to suggest cats. Definitely more than one."

Caleb slammed the canister of tea down on the counter and spun around. "Would you please shut up." He waved a hand in his brother's direction. "You, of all people, should know how this thing could go. Remember when I completely disappeared from your life, destroying your freshman year of college because you thought I was dead? Is any of that ringing a bell?"

He yanked open a drawer, grabbed a spoon, and tossed it into his mug with a clatter. "You gave up a great career in New York and moved all the way out here, just to babysit me. June spent her life chasing the kind of security and stability Jasper's bipolar disorder took from her. What kind of asshole would I be if I asked her to give that up just to saddle her with my issues?"

"Are you serious?" Will shook his head. "First of all, Jasper's bipolar disorder didn't take anything from June. *Jasper* did, when he took off. I'm grateful you came here to work with Jasper, and you learned a lot from him. But the one thing I'm sorry about is how he taught you to blame everything on your bipolar disorder as if it's a terminal illness."

"In Jasper's case, it *was* terminal."

Will stood abruptly and knocked his cup over. Black coffee seeped out of the hole in the lid and pooled on the table. "Jesus, Caleb, it didn't have to be." He grabbed a pile of napkins and slapped them down on the puddle. "Has it ever occurred to you maybe Jasper would still be here if he had let people in once in a while? Yeah, he screwed up when June and her sisters were young. But you know what, it was one mistake, and nobody was hurt. Is everyone supposed to keep paying the price forever?"

Will swept the coffee-soaked napkins into a pile. "What if Jasper had stayed connected with his kids, instead of disappearing on them? He might've had three daughters checking in on him to make sure he was okay, supporting him going to therapy and taking his meds. And those two freaking adorable little granddaughters might've given him something to stick around for."

Caleb hesitated, remembering all the times this summer he'd regretted Jasper missing out on Emma and Izzy. How much he'd wished Jasper were there to know those little girls, and June and her sisters, too. Was it possible that if Jasper had let them in, he might still be alive?

Caleb's therapist was always going on and on about the research showing people with more social support had fewer relapses. Emily's favorite refrain was pushing him to make friends and to consider more than casual dating relationships. But it would have required opening up to people, so he'd pretty much tuned her out when she started in on him about it.

"I see you doing exactly what Jasper did." Will crossed his arms over his chest. "This town genuinely admires you and your work. People in the art community want to connect with you, but you're always pushing everyone away. Why *don't* you teach a class at Starlake? Why are you always saying no?"

Caleb had spent his whole life being Will's difficult twin brother, the problem child who kept his parents up at night worrying over how to fix him. Letting people in meant opening up to them about all his issues. It had always been easier to close himself off and not take the risk.

Will tossed the napkins in the trash along with his cup. "And what's this about me giving up a job in New York to babysit you? How long have you been telling yourself this story?"

Caleb dropped a teabag in his mug and poured hot water over it. "Why else would a young, single guy give up a loft in Williamsburg and a high-paid corporate job to move to small-town in Washington and write wills and trusts for old people?"

His brother looked at him sideways. "So, first of all, fuck you. That's not all I do." Will walked over to where Caleb stood at the counter and grabbed the mug of tea he'd been making for himself.

"*Hey.*"

"Second of all," Will dropped back in the chair he'd vacated earlier. "Thanks for thinking I'm that selfless, but I'm really not. I had the same childhood as you did, asshole. You think I liked moving every couple of years? Maybe I handled it better than you did, but it sucked for me to always have to adjust to a new place and make new friends, too."

Will took a sip of Caleb's tea and made a face. "When I was offered the chance to settle down in Wishing Cove, run my own business, and be a part of a community, I jumped at it. I worked ninety hours a week in New York. I barely even saw my fancy loft, and I definitely didn't have a social life outside of eating crappy take-out in a conference room with the other overworked associates."

Caleb stared at his brother. "So, you *wanted* to move to Wishing Cove?"

"I would not be here if I didn't," Will said in a flat voice.

"Why didn't you tell me any of this?"

"I thought I did." Will gave the mug of tea a shove to the middle of the table. "But is it possible you only heard what you wanted to hear?"

Was it possible? Caleb had been carrying around so much guilt when it came to his brother, maybe his entire view of the situation had been colored by it. He'd only been able to see another sacrifice someone he loved was forced to make on his behalf. Another way he'd screwed up, and someone else paid the price. But Caleb couldn't deny Will was thriving in Wishing Cove. It wasn't only his long list of clients at the law firm; his brother couldn't go anywhere in town without people stopping to engage him in conversation.

Caleb swore under his breath and turned to his brother. "I don't know what to think anymore."

"Maybe that's your problem. Stop thinking so much. Stop doubting yourself. You're not the same kid whose body and brain were out of control. But it's like you still see yourself that way and blame yourself for mistakes you made half a lifetime ago." Will leaned back in his chair and propped a foot on his opposite leg. "Wake up and take a good look at yourself. Aside from being

lucky to share my excellent genetic material"—he smirked—
"you're talented, successful, and the fact that you managed to
convince a woman like June to fall for you says an awful lot."

Caleb stared at his brother as the words sank in.

His parents used to tell him not to define himself by his
mental illness, and those kinds of platitudes had always annoyed
him. He'd been diagnosed at the exact time in life when people
start to figure out who they are, so how could it *not* define him?
Bipolar disorder was with him every moment of every day, and
it always would be.

But he *wasn't* that same confused, messed-up kid he was when
this all started. Now, he had a place to live, plenty to eat, a decent
relationship with his family, and he was making a living as an
artist. But even more importantly, he was managing his bipolar
disorder. It wasn't perfect, he'd certainly had his share of struggles
lately, but the fact that he'd lost Jasper and was still holding it
together was a huge victory.

He'd probably always define himself by his bipolar disorder.
But maybe, for once, it didn't have to be something that limited
him. Maybe it was time to stop building his life on the illness
part of mental illness. Because having anxiety, depression, and
manic episodes didn't mean he was *ill*. He'd been ill when he
didn't have any coping skills and ended up estranged from his
family and living on the beach. But he wasn't ill anymore, and
he hadn't been in years.

Will had argued Jasper might still be alive if he hadn't worked
so hard to isolate himself from his family. Were June and her
sisters really unsafe with Jasper when they were young, or was it
a story Jasper had told himself because it fit with the narrative
he was ill? If June's memory of the fire was accurate, Jasper had
messed up. But did that condemn him to live out the rest of his
life alone? Jasper had thrown it all away—the chance to know his
children and his grandchildren, the chance to have a real family.

Just like I'm throwing away my chance right now.

"Shit." Caleb pushed away from the counter. "I need to talk to June."

"Damn right you do."

Caleb made it to doorway of the kitchen before Will called out to him. He spun around to find his brother giving him a lopsided grin. "Maybe you want to shower first?"

Caleb ran a hand through his hair and looked down at his paint clothes. He'd been up all night and probably looked just as bad as he did on that first day he and June met in the studio. It wasn't exactly the impression of a man who had everything together. "Good thinking."

"Okay, I'm going." Will stood and took a few steps toward Caleb. "Good luck, brother."

"Thanks."

Before Caleb could react, Will gave him a hug. A real one, not a bro-hug. "I love you, dumbass."

Caleb gave his brother an extra slap on the back. "Love you, too."

*

An hour later, Caleb stepped out of the shower and heard a rap on his door. He quickly dried off and pulled on a pair of jeans, yanking his T-shirt over his head as he hurried down the hall. Caleb swung the door open and froze when he saw June standing there. "June," he said, breathless from running, or maybe from her presence there in front of him. "I was just coming to look for you."

"David's here," she blurted out. The dark circles under her eyes stood out against her pale cheeks.

Burnt Sienna blended with Cobalt Violet.

"I know." He moved back, swinging the door open wider. "Come in."

But she shook her head. "No, I can't. I have to get back."

Caleb stepped outside onto the narrow front porch, and June stumbled backward, away from him. His heart played a drum solo on his sternum. He took a deep breath, but before he could say a word, June cut in.

"I came to tell you we're leaving. We're going back. I—I'm going back. To Connecticut." Her eyes darted around the porch, settling everywhere but on him, and her voice shook. "With David."

Caleb's breath hitched. "*No.*" He stepped forward, taking her by the hand. "June, listen to me. I shut you out, and I'm so sorry. But don't do this. Don't go back to him. I know I have no right to ask, but I'm asking anyway. Please give me a chance to explain what happened yesterday." He'd tell her the whole story about Jasper's suicide and the pain of Kaitlyn's death. Maybe if he were honest, everything would be okay. Maybe she could forgive him. Maybe his guts would stop spilling out all over the ground.

But, at that moment, the front door to Jasper's house opened, and David stepped outside carrying a suitcase under each arm. June yanked her hand away from Caleb's grasp and tucked it into her pocket. "Caleb, it doesn't matter what happened. We both knew this couldn't last forever."

For a moment, Caleb could only stare as she stood there shrugging off their relationship, as if this hadn't been the best summer of his life. As if she actually believed the words coming out of her mouth. As if an avalanche wasn't burying his heart so deep, nobody would know where to find it.

Behind June, across the meadow, David made his way to June's rental car and opened the trunk. He set the suitcases inside and then took a few steps toward Caleb's house, stopping at the edge of the driveway. "You ready, June?" he called in their direction, a hint of impatience in his voice.

"Wait a minute," Caleb hissed. "You're leaving *now*? I thought you were going tonight."

June looked at her hands. "We're flying out of Seattle, so we're heading out early to beat the traffic and see some sights in the city."

She was running away.

He was surprised she even came to say goodbye at all.

June spun around then, leaning forward on the porch railing. "I'll be there in a minute," she called to David. "Can you tell the girls to go to the bathroom?" She gave a wave, and David nodded, heading back to the house. Didn't David see how forced the smile was on June's face? Didn't he hear her voice shake? Maybe the man didn't know her at all. Or maybe he only saw what he wanted to see.

How could June go back to him?

As soon as David disappeared into the house, Caleb took a step toward her. "You're wrong, June. We both knew this could last forever. *It still can.*"

June shook her head, over and over. "I have to go."

"June, don't do this." He could hear the tremor in his own voice. "Don't go back to David when the man you love is standing in front of you, begging you to stay."

Her sharp intake of breath was followed by an agonizing silence, and it took everything in him not to reach for her. Then her shoulders sagged, and she looked past him at the wall.

And that was it. That was the moment he knew it was over.

"I'm sorry." June stepped away from him, swiping at her eyes with the palm of her hand. "I wish it could have been different."

He wondered then, deep down, if what she really meant was *I wish* you *could have been different.*

With one more look, she turned and walked out of his life.

CHAPTER TWENTY-NINE

When June got back to the house, she found her sisters standing in the hallway, both still in their pajamas, worried looks straining their faces.

"June, what's going on?" Sierra twisted the end of her braid around her finger. "I came down to make coffee, and saw an awful lot of suitcases by the door."

"I hope those are David's, and you told him to get out," Raven chimed in.

June pressed her palms to her temples, suddenly desperate to put as many miles between herself and Wishing Cove as possible. What had she been thinking, coming here, playing at being an artist, at being Jasper Luc's daughter, at this relationship with Caleb? She'd been living in a dream world these past few months, and it had turned into a nightmare. Just like she'd always known it would.

"They're mine and the girls'. We're heading back to Connecticut tonight." June paused, knowing the next part wasn't going to go over well. "With David."

"You're not serious." Raven's head snapped back. "You're not going *back* to him—?"

"I really can't talk about this right now." June brushed past her sisters and headed down the hall to look for coffee. She'd barely slept last night and her eyes felt coated in sandpaper this morning.

June's sisters' feet padded behind her as she made her way to the coffee pot.

"June, are you sure?" Sierra asked, leaning on the counter next to her. "You're still upset from the accident yesterday, and you don't have to decide anything right now. Maybe you should ask David to leave, and tell him you'll call him in a week."

"June, listen." Raven reached for her arm. "Caleb wasn't driving erratically. I was there. I promise I'd tell you if he was."

June pulled away from her sister. No matter how hard she tried, she couldn't erase the image of Caleb's crumpled Jeep from her head. Her chest burning as she sprinted up the hill. The girls crying for Mommy. She sucked in a deep breath and grabbed a mug from the cabinet. "The accident showed me that I need to start paying more attention to my responsibilities. But it's not the reason I'm leaving."

"Well, it can't be because you really want to go back to that… asshole."

June spun around to face her sister. "Watch what you say, Raven." What if the girls overheard? June stomped over to the coffee pot and sloshed some into her cup. It splashed over the side, and she cursed as it burned her hand.

"Run it under here," Sierra told her, flipping on the faucet.

June shoved her hand under the flow of cold water and then wrapped it in a towel. "This isn't only about me. I have the girls to think about."

"But couldn't you work out a custody arrangement with David?" Sierra asked. "Do you have to go back to him?"

June picked up a sponge and scrubbed at the spilled coffee on the counter.

"What about Caleb?" Sierra continued to press.

June glanced down the hall. David was outside packing up the car. He could be back any minute. "I don't want to talk about Caleb."

"Okay, fine." Raven crossed her arms in front of her. "What about me and Sierra? We were so good, the three of us here together, like when we were kids. Did it ever occur to you that Sierra and I need you?"

And suddenly, it hit June all at once. Her body ached from the strain of holding it all together, holding everyone else together, and her heart cracked under the weight of three decades of grief, helplessness, and fear.

And then came the anger, rolling in with the force of a fighter jet.

But the one person she really wanted to scream at, to lash out at, to hurt the way he'd hurt her over and over again—he was gone forever. He'd checked out, run away, and *died* before she could punish him for the enormous hole he'd left behind. So, instead, she whirled on the two people standing right in front of her.

"Of *course* it's occurred to me that you need me," June yelled at her sister. "I've spent my entire life with that responsibility hanging over my head." June threw her coffee mug into the sink, not even caring when it hit the drain with a crack. "Have you ever stopped, even once, to think about me? No, you were too busy flitting off around the world taking photos. And you"—she waved an arm at Sierra— "you were busy hiding out writing your novels. I sacrificed *everything* for you both. So, don't you dare try to make me feel guilty now."

And with that, she stalked out of the kitchen, past the stunned faces of her sisters, and marched upstairs to find the girls and take them home.

*

A week later, June stepped off the elevator onto the fourteenth floor of the downtown New York City offices of Westwood Management and Consulting. Her black leather pumps clicked across the slate as she approached the curved mahogany counter where the receptionist sat.

"Good morning, Mrs. Westwood," Yvonne Peterson murmured with a muted smile. Yvonne had worked at the front desk ever since David started the business a decade ago, and June had always been secretly envious of the self-assurance and competence she projected. Never once in all those years had June seen Yvonne rush in to work a few minutes late with coffee sloshing on the lid of her cup or sweat beading on her brow. So unlike the frazzled way June felt most mornings.

Well, except this morning. June had sat up in bed with a gasp at 4 a.m., disoriented and confused about where she was. As soon as she'd recognized the master bedroom of her house in Greenwich, her heart rate had slowed, but the ache had set in.

Tiptoeing past the girls' room and the guest bedroom where David slept, June had headed downstairs in her newly dry-cleaned blouse and pencil skirt, ready for her first day back at work. She'd had plenty of time to straighten her hair and apply more make-up than she'd worn in the past two months. Eyeliner and shadow, blush and lipstick. June hardly recognized herself, but at least all the camouflage masked the dark circles under her eyes. Besides, there was a certain comfort in slipping back into this costume. If she put enough effort into resurrecting Accountant June, maybe her life would go back to normal.

June greeted Yvonne and headed down the hall to her office. Her assistant, Keith, sat at a desk outside her door. He stood as she approached.

"Mrs. Westwood, it's nice to have you back," he said, but his smile didn't quite reach his eyes. June couldn't blame him, really. A recent MBA grad, Keith was young and eager to prove himself. He'd been given a golden opportunity to take over her accounts when she went on leave, and he probably wasn't all that thrilled to hand them back over.

"Thank you. It's nice to be back," June said, because that's the sort of thing you're supposed to say. "Are the CitiTech files up to date? I'd like to take a look at them." She'd done a pitiful job of keeping up with Keith over the summer, and June had a feeling she'd be doing a lot of clean-up work to get her accounts back in order. She relished the challenge, though. Burying her head in budgets and spreadsheets might keep her busy enough to stop thinking about Wishing Cove.

Keith confirmed she'd find everything on the network, and June slipped into her office and sank into the chair behind her desk. Everything waited exactly where she'd left it—a dark leather journal and pen lined up by the phone for taking notes during conference calls; her gold and cream-colored mug, always rinsed immediately so the coffee didn't stain the bottom, next to the keyboard; a navy cardigan folded neatly over the back of her chair for when the air conditioning kicked in.

The familiarity of it all should've reassured her but, instead, she'd stumbled onto a movie set of her life, one where she followed her cues and recited her lines, but had somehow lost the thread of the story. Despite her best efforts, June's thoughts drifted to Wishing Cove. What were her sisters doing right now? And Caleb—was he—?

No. It didn't matter what Caleb was doing.

As if her sister had sensed the direction of her thoughts, Sierra's name popped up on June's phone.

"Sierra?" June said, cautiously. They hadn't talked since her blow-up in Wishing Cove.

"Hi, Junie. How are you?"

Just the sound of Sierra's voice brought tears to June's eyes. She missed seeing her sisters every day, missed their easy conversations over coffee and dinner. Despite the general racket and chaos the girls generated, the Westwood house felt very quiet lately. June longed to tell her sister about how strange it felt to be back here, and to have Sierra reassure her in her usual supportive tone that it would take a little time to settle back in.

But of course, June couldn't say any of that. Not after her big blow-up. "Oh, I'm okay," she said, doing her best imitation of cheerful. "Busy. Back at the office today."

"Well, I don't want to keep you. I know you have a lot to catch up on. But I wanted to call because I have some news. About Caleb, and the car accident—"

"I don't want to talk about Caleb," June cut in. She'd agreed to move back home, to go to counseling with David, and to work on her marriage. That meant letting go of Wishing Cove, and Caleb, once and for all.

Now, if only her stupid heart would get on board with the plan.

"June, listen, I know you're angry with him about the accident. But I think you should know the police arrested the guy who hit him that night."

"They—why?"

"The guy was drunk. He was speeding when he rear-ended the Jeep. It sent them into oncoming traffic and that's how they got hit by the second car. The one that caught fire."

June closed her eyes and saw the flames shooting out of the SUV's hood. Smelled the stinging scent of gasoline and smoke. Heard her voice screaming at Caleb for putting the girls in danger.

"So, the accident wasn't…" She trailed off.

"No," Sierra said, gently. "The accident wasn't Caleb's fault. Not at all."

Raven had insisted that Caleb had been driving safely. June felt the tears burn the back of her eyes again. Why did she suddenly seem to be on the verge of crying all the time? It was a relief to know that Caleb hadn't put anyone in danger. But even before the accident, he'd been acting strangely and wouldn't tell her why. He'd run out on her, hadn't been honest with her, had shown she couldn't trust him.

June propped her chin in her hand and pushed the pointed toe of her high-heeled shoe off the floor, nudging her office chair into a slow twirl. When she drifted back around to her desk, Keith was gazing at her through the doorway with his eyebrows knitted together. June sat up in her chair and started her computer, smoothing her face into the serious expression of a busy professional.

"Thanks for letting me know." Her voice sounded hollow and faraway, like she was talking into an aluminum can. "I should probably get back to work."

June was about to end the call when Sierra stopped her.

"June, wait…"

June paused with her finger hovering over the red hang-up button. "Yeah?"

"Listen, I'm not trying to change your mind about David or anything. But just so you know—you can always come back here if you want. The house is here if you ever need it. And so are Raven and I."

June hesitated, for one wild moment considering her sister's suggestion. But the barriers piled up around her. How could she just pack up and make a permanent move to Wishing Cove? It was easy for her sisters to pick up and go on a moment's notice when they only ever had to think about themselves. Life wasn't so black and white when you had kids to worry about. Even *if* she could dump her job and other responsibilities, *and* there was enough money from Jasper's estate to support them, *and* she could imagine living across the meadow from Caleb for the rest of her life… did Sierra really think David would just sit back while she moved the girls all the way across the country? That he wouldn't fight her for custody?

June sighed as the CitiTech file popped up on her screen, reminding her that her life was here in Connecticut. "Thanks, Sierra. I appreciate your support, but I have to get to work."

Through the phone, she heard Sierra heave an exasperated sigh. "Okay, I'll talk to you later."

*

An hour later, June sat around a gleaming mahogany conference table with Keith and the executive team, while David advanced through a PowerPoint detailing the company's second-quarter client acquisitions. He'd barely made it four slides in before June's vision began to blur. It was probably the lack of sleep combined with the fact that she wasn't used to concentrating for hours on numbers and calculations anymore.

June had chosen a chair along the inside wall of the conference room, and soon she found her attention drawn to the arched windows of the Art Deco building across the downtown New York City street outside. Her right hand twitched and, almost as if it had a mind of its own, her heavy silver pen began sketching those curved lines into her journal. Above the arched windows, sandstone bricks fanned out in even hatches, like sunbeams, and something about the contrast appealed to her. She was filling in the decorative grid on the window panes when, from somewhere in the background, she heard a voice say her name.

June looked up to find eight pairs of eyes staring at her.

"Care to answer Annette's question, June?" David asked, with an arch of his brow that matched the windows in her sketch.

"Uh." June looked down at her notes as if something scribbled on the page would unlock the mystery of what they were talking about. "Yes, of course." She flipped to a blank page and back again. "Um."

"June and I were discussing this earlier," Keith cut in. "We can write off the expenses using a provision in the tax code…" He continued talking, and his answer seemed to satisfy everyone in the room because the conversation moved on to something else. June shot Keith a grateful look, and he smiled in return. Maybe she'd underestimated him.

June sat up straight, determined to focus for the remainder of the meeting, but a moment later, her attention was drawn to the conference room door. Priya tiptoed into the room and slid into a seat at the far end of the table.

"Sorry, I'm late," she whispered.

June's body stiffened with shock, and her eyes swung to David. For a moment, David's voice faltered and he looked like he was going to throw up. June knew exactly how he felt. It would be illegal for David to fire Priya, but June hadn't prepared herself to see the younger woman sitting around the table at team meetings.

David turned to face the whiteboard and, a moment later, seemed to get a hold of himself because he continued his monologue about closing a deal with a client. If his voice sounded slightly more subdued, it was probably only June who noticed it.

She turned her eyes back to Priya, who sat with her head bent over a notebook. If the woman in question hadn't been having an affair with June's husband, June would've been very worried about her. Priya had the blanched, hollow-cheeked appearance of someone recovering from the flu. *Or of someone whose boyfriend just broke up with her.* Dark smudges underscored Priya's eyes, her mouth was set into a grim line, and she'd pulled her normally glossy black hair back into a simple ponytail.

Priya's appearance should've given June at least a small measure of satisfaction, especially today, when she'd gone out of her way to look her best. But all she could muster was pity.

David sped through the rest of the meeting and abruptly ended with an excuse about rushing off to lunch with a client. As soon as he dismissed everyone with a curt, "See you all next week," he picked up his laptop and left the room.

June took her time closing her leather journal, tucking her pen in her purse, and answering a text from the girls' nanny. But as soon as she looked up from the phone, she realized Priya had remained in her seat at the other end of the table. An awkward silence stretched across the otherwise empty room.

"Excuse me," June muttered, grabbing her things and heading for the exit. But before she made it to the door, Priya stood abruptly and blocked her path.

"Wait," Priya said, holding out a hand.

June stopped because her alternative was to give her a shove. And while she'd pictured doing just that in the early days of discovering the affair, June found it didn't hold the same appeal now. "Please excuse me. I really don't have anything to say to you."

Priya studied her hands before dragging her red-rimmed eyes to June's face. "But I have something I want to say to you."

"Look, I know we have to co-exist here at work, but I don't think this is a good idea—" June brushed past her and headed for the door.

"I wanted to tell you I'm sorry," Priya blurted out.

"You—what?" June stumbled to a stop.

"I'm sorry. You've always been so nice to me, and you didn't deserve any of this." Priya shook her head slowly. "I don't have an excuse for any of it, except I got caught up in my feelings for David. But what I did to you was unforgivable."

"Your feelings for David," June repeated. "What are those exactly?"

Priya stared at her shoes as a tear slowly leaked from her eye. "I'm in love with him. I'm so sorry," she whispered. "He's so brilliant, and... amazing. I guess you already know that."

Just like that, the rest of June's ire for the younger woman flew right out the fourteenth-floor window, and she was left with feelings of—oh God—*empathy*. She understood better than anyone what it was like to love someone who was completely unavailable and wrong for you, but who somehow fit better than anyone.

Had June ever thought of David as *brilliant* and *amazing*? No, those adjectives conjured up someone else entirely.

June dug a pack of tissues from her purse and held it out to Priya. Then she turned and left the conference room to head back to her office. Keith had already typed up the notes from the meeting, and he handed them to her as she walked by. Over his shoulder, June could see he was immersed in a report the director of marketing had requested. It looked like he had everything under control.

June gently closed her door and sank down in a chair, where she spent the rest of the afternoon staring out the window.

CHAPTER THIRTY

Caleb spent the next week in his studio, but he shouldn't have bothered. He didn't accomplish a damn thing. Instead, he paced from the couch that reminded him of June to the table that reminded him of June, occasionally stopping to slap some color on a canvas he'd eventually toss into a graveyard of abandoned paintings in the corner. On the fifth or sixth day—what did it matter, they all ran together anyway—he gave up entirely and left the studio. Maybe he'd see if Will wanted to meet in town for a run and lunch. He'd been making more of an effort to get together with his brother, and one evening that week he'd even met Will and Sam Grayson at a bar in town to watch the game.

But when he stepped out into the yard, something pulled him left on the path and he found himself unlocking the door to the other studio. Just like the house, at some point over the summer, the place had switched over in his heart from Jasper's to June's.

His heart seized when he walked inside and the mix of paint and a hint of June's vanilla scent invaded his senses; Caleb almost expected to turn around and find her standing there at the easel with a brush in her hand. Instead, a half-finished canvas sat next to a pile of paint tubes with various amounts of color squeezed out of them. Something about the chill permeating the room and the cold mist drizzling outside the window gave the place an air of abandonment, as if June had up and disappeared. Which, in a way, she had. One day, she'd probably expected to come back and finish the canvas, and the next, she was on a plane back to Connecticut.

June's finished paintings were lined up against the side wall. Why hadn't she taken any of them with her? Until that moment, he'd assumed June would keep painting in Connecticut. She'd talked about finding a house with a studio space to rent, but if she'd gone back to David, she wouldn't be renting a house. Apparently, David didn't like paint and mess in his house, so Caleb doubted he'd be very supportive. Would June give up painting again?

Caleb sank into the couch along the back wall of the studio and put his head in his hands. A landslide of regret crashed over him. After setting aside her dreams to care for everybody else, June had finally focused on doing something for herself. Her painting had been the talk of the art show, and Caleb wouldn't be surprised if gallery owners had taken notice. June had been an entirely different person—relaxed, happy—from the anxious, stressed-out woman he'd first met at the start of the summer.

Caleb lifted his head. In front of him sat the box of photos and articles Jasper had collected about June. Just like Jasper, it was all he had left of her. Caleb gave the cardboard a hard shove.

The box slid across the coffee table and toppled over, spilling papers out all over the floor. Swearing, Caleb hauled himself off the couch and crouched down to shove everything back in. The pictures drifted by, and the more June's deceptively perfect Connecticut life flashed before his eyes, the more the wrongness of her being there and not here taunted him. He gripped the black and white newspaper clipping about the fraternity harvest party. Was David still leaving June all alone while he drank beer with his friends?

Or his mistress, Caleb thought, as an ache throbbed in his chest.

Caleb focused on the image of June reaching up to grab an apple as the sleeve of her dress slid up her wrist, and it made him pause. He'd seen the photo of June all alone in the apple orchard a number of times, but something about it nagged at him now. Something… familiar. He propped the photo against the box and sat back to examine it.

All of a sudden, Caleb knew what it was.

Jasper had had no idea how rich and colorful his world might've been with his amazing daughters and granddaughters in it, and he'd walked away. Just like the viewer of his paintings, Jasper had existed behind barriers—windshields, and tangled tree branches—watching a smudged, half-visible version of life instead of participating in it. Now it was too late.

But, Caleb thought as he shot to his feet and groped around in his pocket for his phone. *It's not too late for me. Or for June.*

He hit the first number at the top. A second later, his brother's voice came through the phone. "Hey, what's up?"

"Will, listen," Caleb said. "I need you to do your lawyerly thing and help me with something."

Will choked out a laugh. "Are you serious?"

"Dead serious."

Caleb's next call went straight to voicemail. "Hey, Emily, it's Caleb Valencia. Listen, I know I went MIA on our therapy sessions this summer, but I'd love to come back if you have any openings. Leave me a message with the day and time and I'll be there."

Finally, he made a call to the Starlake Arts Center. This one took longer. He and Moira had a lot to discuss, details to work out, a list of other people she'd need to bring into the conversation. But she loved his idea and was committed to making it work.

Then Caleb hung up the phone, placed June's box back on the coffee table, and headed outside. As he stood on the edge of the cliff overlooking the bay, Caleb held his palms to the sky to catch the rain before it fell to the earth, turning his face upward to relish the cold droplets peppering his skin. By the time he got back to his own studio, bursting with newfound inspiration, his hoodie was soaked and he was shivering, but that was okay. It made him feel alive, and that was something he was grateful for.

CHAPTER THIRTY-ONE

June was back in the conference room, pressing her fingers to her temples and trying to massage away the sound of David's too-loud voice carrying across the mahogany table.

"Steve-o, my good man," David said heartily, slapping Steve Watson, the silver-haired CEO of Wellbuild Industries, on the back. "Let's close this deal now and we can be on the golf course before lunch."

Steve opened his mouth so wide his silver fillings were on display as he let out a vigorous laugh. "I already put in my lunch order for a filet mignon with your secretary here." Steve nodded at Priya. "So you might as well give me the dog-and-pony show."

"The country club makes an excellent steak, Mr. Watson," Priya chimed in with a wink. "Go ahead and close the deal. You can still have a filet mignon while you golf." Steve laughed even louder.

David chuckled along, as if this exchange was hilarious. June noticed nobody corrected Steve about Priya's job title. *She's an executive assistant, not a secretary, Steve-o.*

June's head throbbed even harder.

Increasingly, she found herself sitting in these work meetings and imagining turning one of the guest rooms at home into a studio space, but she pushed those thoughts from her head. When would she have time to paint anyway? At least, on the surface, she was the same busy working mom and wife she'd always been. As long as nobody looked too closely.

She and David had been tiptoeing around each other at home, grilling the girls about their day over dinner so it wouldn't be so obvious they had nothing to say to each other. June couldn't imagine him coming back to sleep in the master bedroom any time soon. She couldn't imagine any of this feeling normal any time soon.

She'd snapped at the girls that morning when they were taking too long to put on their shoes, dawdling because they wanted to stay home and draw instead of going for a day of activities with the nanny. The anxiety had started buzzing in June's chest when she realized she was about to miss her train into the city. In the end, it hadn't mattered: nobody had noticed her slip into the meeting five minutes late, but the guilt stayed with her all morning. Izzy had cried, and Emma had yelled that she hated it in Connecticut and wanted to go back to Wishing Cove.

June shook her head. She'd made all these choices because she thought she was doing what was best for the girls, and somehow, it was still all wrong.

While David talked, Priya brought lunch in, handing food containers and silverware around the table. June didn't have much of an appetite, but she made the motions of opening her salad along with everyone else. It was the same salad she always ordered from DiAntonia's: kale and sweet potato. June hadn't even glanced at the other options; she'd just circled the same old thing she always ordered. It wasn't very exciting, but it was safe.

As June stared into the same pile of chopped vegetables she'd eaten a hundred times before, something inside of her cracked open. Was she going to spend the rest of her life ordering the same salad and doodling in her notebook during boring meetings? Tiptoeing around at home and pretending she and David had anything to say to each other? Sitting across the room from David's ex-girlfriend and ignoring his longing glances in her direction?

June gave the salad a shove and stood up. "Excuse me," she said, her voice carrying across the room and cutting into David's review of a profit projection chart. He abruptly stopped talking, and everyone stared in awkward silence as she slung her purse over her shoulder and picked up her journal and pen without explanation. The chair clanged as she shoved it under the table, and her high heels tapped against the floor as she made her way to the door.

Out in the hall, June sucked in a shaky breath. It was such a relief to be out of that room. Her feet moved automatically, taking her back to her office, where Keith looked up from his computer as she walked by. "A package came for you. Well, it's more like a container than a package. I had the delivery guy put it in your office."

June glanced through the doorway and spotted a wooden box about four feet high by three feet wide sitting in front of her couch. "What is it?"

Keith shrugged.

June approached the box. There were no clues as to what it was or where it came from. Her name and office address, along with the word *FRAGILE,* were printed on a label stuck to the top. June ran her hands around the edges of the box, looking for a way to open it, but it appeared to be nailed shut.

June turned to Keith. "Did they say anything about who it's from?"

"Nothing." Keith shook his head. "Two guys rolled it in on a dolly. Want me to get the toolbox from the supply closet?"

"Please."

Keith returned a minute later with an orange tool box. He placed it on June's desk, selected a hammer, and then wedged it between the top and side slats of the box. After a few vigorous yanks, the wood began to pop up, and after a few more, June was staring into a box full of packaging material. She pushed some of it aside and her hand hit against a wide, flat object encased in bubble wrap.

"I'll get it." Keith reached inside and grabbed the object, pulling it out slowly. He propped it on the couch and poked at the bubble wrap. "It looks like a painting."

"It must be," June said, her mind spinning over whose it could be. Had her sisters had one of her paintings framed and sent to her? The one of the girls on the beach, maybe? June's heart gave a little flip of both joy and dread at the idea. She'd left Wishing Cove before giving much thought to her paintings in the studio, but since she'd been back east, they were on her mind constantly. Would it be painful to look at one of them every day?

June grabbed the scissors from her desk and got to work, carefully cutting the layers of wrapping around the painting. After slicing through the final sheet, she pulled it aside.

June rocked back on her heels. *Girl in the Trees* sat there on the couch in her office.

"Jesus. Is that a Jasper Luc?" Keith asked, and it occurred to June he knew nothing about her connection to Jasper. Nobody at work did.

"Yes."

"A *real* Jasper Luc?" Keith's voice came out sounding a bit choked.

"Yes."

"*Oh my God.*"

It was so strange. How did it get here? Had someone from one of the museums sent it to her by accident, instead of directing it to the storage facility where she and her sisters had agreed to keep the other paintings? She'd have to call Will to get to the bottom of it.

But as June made her way to her desk to grab her phone, it suddenly hit her. This wasn't one of the paintings Jasper had left her and her sisters. This was *Girl in the Trees*.

Girl in the Trees belonged to Caleb.

It was supposed to be at the Whitney until January. There had to be some mistake.

June rooted around in the packaging strewn across her floor, and unearthed an envelope with her name on it. Caleb used to leave notes in her studio, and she'd know that handwriting anywhere.

Heart pounding, she tore into it.

June,

For the past fifteen years, I've lived in one of the grayest, rainiest places on Earth. But for one summer with you, my world was filled with sunshine and the brightest, most vibrant hues. I've bought every tube of paint in town trying to recreate the rainbow of color you brought to this place. But nothing can compare with seeing you here, in your studio, where you belong.

You're the strongest woman I've ever met, and a brilliant artist. You don't need David, or his company, or anyone but yourself, for security. I'm in awe of you every day, and I am so sorry that I pushed you back to your old life, where you gave up painting, to become the girl in the trees.

June, with your talent, you could have everything you dreamed about when you were a kid. Don't give up painting. Don't give up the life you want for the one you think you're supposed to have.

Caleb

June stared at the slip of paper in her shaking hand as all the emotions she'd packed up and tucked away when she'd returned to Connecticut came raining down around her. The pain of loving him and then losing him. And that little spark of hope that had ignited in her chest and burned brighter with each word of his note.

And then June gave a start, her gaze flying back to the canvas. What could he mean by calling her the girl in the trees?

Keith shifted next to her, and June remembered her assistant was still standing there, his mouth hanging open. "Is there anything else in the box?" she asked, peering inside.

Keith bent down to pick up something off the floor.

"This fell out of the envelope," he said, holding out a crumpled newspaper article.

June turned it over in her hand and let out a gasp. *The harvest party.* Her eyes flew from the article to the painting and back again.

Viewing them side by side, there was no mistaking the resemblance between the photo of her standing in the orchard and the girl in Jasper's painting, reaching up to the sky. June could see how she'd missed it initially—though the photo was on black and white newsprint, she could recall the hues of pink and magenta streaked in her hair and that her dress had matched the blue of the sky. The picture was taken in early autumn, and in June's memory, the trees were still covered in leaves.

In contrast, Jasper had painted her hair a dark brown, similar to her natural color, and used shades of gold and umber for her dress, hiding most of her body in the background behind the browns and blacks of the barren tree branches criss-crossing in the foreground. But the shape of her posture was exactly the same with her arm curving upward, head tilted back. The sense that she was reaching for something she couldn't quite grasp was mirrored in the painting and photo.

I am the girl in the trees.

The emotion Jasper had captured in his painting brought the memories of that day back even more sharply. Or maybe it was because she'd felt that same sense of being out of place in the meeting earlier today. That loneliness had seeped into her entire life.

My entire life, June thought, pressing a cool hand to her flushed forehead, *except for one short summer on a small plot of land at the edge of a cliff overlooking the Pacific.* For that brief, fleeting time, all the pieces had slotted into place, exactly where they belonged.

"Oh, wow," Keith muttered, looking at the article over her shoulder. "Is that you?"

June blinked as Keith's words registered. *Is that you?*

"No," she whispered.

"It's not?" Keith squinted at the photo. "The painting looks an awful lot like the newspaper picture of—"

"*No.*" This time June said it with more conviction. "No. It's not me. Not anymore." With that, she turned and marched down the hall to her husband's office.

David was still having lunch with the Wellbuild group, so June slipped inside unnoticed and sat behind his sleek Lucite and chrome office desk. As she settled back into the leather chair to wait, she noticed David's cell phone sitting next to his keyboard in front of her. He'd probably left it there so the buzzing wouldn't distract him during his presentation. June was pretty sure she knew his password, and it occurred to her she could pick up the phone, flip it over, and read his texts again. She could see how things had gone down with Priya, and find out if the affair was really over.

But she didn't.

Because I don't care. Not anymore.

When David returned to his office a half-hour later, June was still sitting in the same spot, breathing deeply through her nose. In for three. Out for four. Maybe there really was something to this yoga breathing, because a sense of calm had settled over her. Or maybe she'd finally found clarity about what she wanted.

"Hey." David flashed a cocky grin when he saw her there. "We got the Wellbuild account. This is going to be a big one."

"Congratulations," June said, voice flat. "I want a divorce."

For a moment, David froze. Then his mouth opened, closed, and opened again, but no sound came out. Finally, he sank down into the chair across from her.

"You can't be happy with this," June said. "The tiptoeing around, acting like this marriage can work when it's obvious both our hearts aren't in it. And it can't be good for the girls, either. They're getting old enough to understand what an unhealthy relationship looks like. I want to be a model for them, and I know you do, too."

David's shoulders slumped, and he looked down at his hands.

"I want to take the girls and move to Wishing Cove," June continued. David's eyes widened, but before he could open his mouth to object, she forged ahead. "I know you love the girls. But most of the time you're gone before they wake up in the morning and you don't get home until after they go to bed at night."

June leaned forward in the chair, pressing against the cold plastic of the desk. She liked this position, seated higher than David. He'd purposely chosen those chairs so they forced the person sitting opposite to look up at him. "Let me take them to Wishing Cove. You can visit them on holidays, and I'll bring them back here whenever you want me to—school breaks, for a few weeks in the summer. You'll probably get more quality time with them that way than you do now."

David remained silent, pressed back into his low chair, and June could see him processing this. Part of her wondered if this proposal wasn't a little bit appealing to him. He'd seemed to enjoy his freedom and single lifestyle while they'd been gone all summer. Since they'd returned, David had seemed even more annoyed than usual about the noise and mess, and he'd made a few resentful comments about having to be home in time for dinner. June knew he loved the girls, but he'd never exactly been an involved day-to-day dad.

His business had always been his baby.

Bolstered by that thought, June went for in for the kill. "Listen, David. You don't want me hanging around here while we go through a divorce, and it's not like you can fire me. I helped you build this company up from nothing. I think fighting over it could get really ugly, and obviously would be bad for business."

She paused, letting that sink in. He'd always framed Westwood Management and Consulting as *his* business. *He* was the boss. And she'd gone along, never saying a word about her contribution and sacrifices. Well, she was finished with going along. What would a *judge* say about whose business it was? By the way David was looking a little green, it was obvious his thoughts were going in a similar direction.

"If you let me take the girls to Wishing Cove," she continued, "I'll be out of your hair, and we can do this amicably."

David rubbed his hand over his eyes. June stood up and moved around the desk to the chair next to him. She sat down in it and turned so they were at eye-level. "I think we're both going to be a lot happier if we put an end to this marriage. But I'm committed to co-parenting peacefully with you, and I promise I'll make sure you get as much time with the girls as you want."

David sighed and looked up. "Okay," he said, finally. "You can take them to Wishing Cove. They haven't been able to stop talking about it since they got home. But I want them back here for a visit over fall break. And maybe I can come out there for Thanksgiving."

June sank back in her chair as relief swept over her. "You're welcome to come whenever you want."

David leaned back and tapped his fingers on the arm of the chair. "So, what are you going to do in Wishing Cove? Become a painter?" He said it with more curiosity than contempt, but it was clear from the slant of his eyebrows that he'd never understand why she would give up the corporate life for a creative one.

June hesitated as Caleb's words echoed. *With your talent, you could have everything you dreamed about when you were a kid.*

Caleb understood. He'd always understood.

But this wasn't about Caleb, not entirely. Was there a chance for them? The ember of hope burned brightly. But she was going back because she'd finally found her voice in Wishing Cove. She was going back to build a life for herself and the girls where her happiness mattered. "Yes. I want to see if I can make a career of being a painter."

"I hope it works out for you," David said. "I remember you were talented."

June gave him her first real smile in a long time. "Thank you. I have a painting for you. I'll arrange to have it shipped when I get to Wishing Cove." She'd send him the painting of the girls on the beach. In a modern frame, it would look beautiful over the mantle in the living room.

For one last time, she gazed at the man she'd spent two decades of her life with. She couldn't look back and regret her marriage to David, or all the time she'd spent as an accountant. It had given her the security she'd badly needed, and most importantly, the girls. But this world had always fit her like the wrong-sized pants. It was time for her to stop wasting any more time on what she was supposed to do, and find what would truly make her happy.

With that, June left David's office and headed back to her own to call her sisters and let them know she was coming home.

CHAPTER THIRTY-TWO

As June packed, she'd quickly realized there was very little she wanted to bring from Greenwich to Wishing Cove. Other than a few pairs of jeans, sundresses, and sweaters, most of her tailored Connecticut clothes were impractical for a painter in the Pacific Northwest. Since David had never liked clutter displayed on the shelves, all her books and pottery were already in boxes, so it was only a matter of labeling them to be shipped.

The girls needed little more than their clothes and a few favorite stuffed animals. She and David had agreed to leave the contents of their bedroom so they'd feel at home when they came back to stay with him. June had said she would buy them new toys and decorate their room in Jasper's house, and they'd been excited by the idea. Maybe she'd even paint a mural on the wall.

*

A week later, June pulled her rental car through the gates of Jasper's estate and parked in front of the house. She hopped out, leaving the door open, and wandered to the end of the driveway, gazing out at the view of the ocean glittering in the sunshine, the wildflowers waving in the gentle breeze, the tall pines framing the entire picture. It was hard to believe she'd left all this behind; that she'd thought she could give it up forever.

June's eyes swung to Caleb's cottage, and she half expected to see him in his usual spot on the deck with a cup of tea in his hand. But there was no sign of him. In the whirlwind of packing, transferring her work over to Keith, and coordinating the handoff of her PTA duties, she hadn't told him she was coming.

June reached into her purse where his note was carefully folded in the side pocket. She'd pulled it out and read it about a hundred times on her journey west, but something had kept her from picking up the phone and calling him. She wanted to have this conversation in person. To look him in the eyes when they talked.

And now that she was here, and he was *right there*, only steps away, her body ached to pound on his door, throw herself in his arms, and tell him she didn't care about the past. As her feet automatically turned in that direction, Emma shifted in her sleep in the backseat of the car. Just like the first time they came to Wishing Cove, the girls had stayed up all night on the plane and fallen asleep on the drive.

June dragged her gaze from Caleb's cottage and turned her attention to getting the girls out of the car and into the house. Raven and Sierra came out to help her carry them upstairs to bed and unload the bags. After a quick shower to wash off her night on the airplane, June gathered with her sisters around the kitchen island.

She settled on her barstool and, for the first time in weeks, the tension drained from her shoulders and that persistent ache in her chest faded away. She'd missed the warmth and welcome of this house, with its bowl of stones and other treasures by the door, well-loved pine floors nobody worried about scratching, and comfortable throws scattered around in case there was a draft from the fireplace. She couldn't wait for her books and pottery to arrive so she could unpack them onto the shelves in the living room. She was never going to spend half an hour digging around in a pile of boxes every time she felt like reading again.

Sierra put a plate of warm blueberry muffins on the center island. That was something else June had missed when she was back east—having someone else do the cooking once in a while.

Of course, it would be up to her again when her sisters left, but there were a lot of bagged salads and pre-made meals from the grocery store hot bar in her future. June was entirely done with being the perfect wife and mother who prepared a nutritious two-course meal every night. The occasional pancakes and delivery pizza for dinner would be fine.

"Junie," Raven said, sliding onto the stool across from her. "I'm sorry for the way we acted when you went back to Connecticut."

Sierra sidled up next to Raven. "We know you gave up painting when you were young so you could support us, and we've never been very supportive of *you*."

June shook her head. She wished she could take back every word she'd hurled at her sisters when she'd left here. "I shouldn't have said those things to you. I didn't mean any of it."

"But you were right." Raven tore her muffin into tiny pieces. "Since we were kids, you've always been the one taking care of us. Mom checked out, and you were the one making sure we had our lunches and permissions slips, and that there was food in the house and the heat stayed on."

"You bought Raven her first camera and financially supported her internships with *National Geographic*." Sierra chimed in. "And I never could have afforded to study creative writing on my own… What if you never had to worry about us? Honestly— would you have become an accountant?"

June pressed her lips together. She didn't know anymore. She'd lived her whole life terrified of uncertainty, and none of it was her sisters' fault. "I don't regret anything. I'm so proud of both of you and your careers, and I wouldn't change a thing about any of it."

Sierra slid off her barstool and rounded the island to give June a hug. Raven followed and, soon, June was locked in a three-way embrace with her sisters, all of them crying and laughing at the same time.

Finally, June pulled away, wiping her eyes. "Speaking of your careers, summer is almost over. I guess you'll both be heading back to your real lives again soon." She hated to see her sisters go; the idea made her want to cry all over again.

"Actually…" Sierra grabbed her mug and crossed the kitchen to the coffee pot. "We were thinking we might stick around."

"Really?" June looked back and forth between her sisters. "For how long?"

Raven took a deep breath and blew it out slowly. "The *Wishing Cove Gazette* approached me about doing some work locally. It seems like a good option while I get these panic attacks under control. I think Will put in a good word for me with the editor."

"He did, huh?" June gave her sister a knowing smile. "But won't you miss traveling?"

"I'd like to get back out there eventually, but there's no rush. And when I do start traveling again, it will be nice to have a place to come home to."

Sierra made her way back to the kitchen island. "And someone special waiting when you get here."

"Maybe that, too," Raven said with a shy smile.

June turned to Sierra. "And what about your writer's block?"

Raven clapped her hands together. "It seems a certain handyman has managed to unblock Sierra." At that, she laughed and wrinkled her nose. "Wait, that came out sounding way dirtier than I intended."

"So, you're staying too?" June asked her middle sister.

Sierra took a sip of her coffee. "I was thinking I would. That is, if you don't mind having me."

"Of course not. But won't we be a distraction from your writing? The girls aren't exactly quiet and serene."

"No, it's been wonderful having them around all summer! I spent so many years focused on my novels, maybe at the expense of everything else." Sierra sank down on the barstool. "I guess it hit me when I turned thirty-five this year. I don't have a partner, or kids, or anything besides a cat who's staying with my neighbor and won't even notice I'm gone."

"I had no idea you wanted a family," June said.

"I didn't either. But being here with you both, and the girls—it made me realize what I'm missing. And it's probably where my writer's block was coming from. I've been writing about life instead of living it."

"But just because we're sticking around doesn't mean you need to take care of us," Raven cut in. "We want to help with the girls, and you need to start being a little selfish for a change."

"Well, I chucked my job and my marriage to move here and become a starving artist," June joked, "so, you guys might need to support *me* now." She waited for the little nagging fear of uncertainty to bubble up, but it never surfaced.

"Yeah, about that," Raven said, sitting up higher on her stool, glancing at Sierra.

"What is it?"

"Will heard from the appraisers about Jasper's paintings," Sierra said. "It turns out that we may have underestimated their worth a teeny bit."

"And by a teeny bit, Sierra means a *lot*," Raven chimed in. "Jasper may not have done much for us, but even if we only sell a few of his lesser-known pieces and keep the others to show in museums, Jasper made sure that we never have to worry about money again." And then Raven named an amount that left June's head spinning.

But while that kind of money meant she'd have the security she always wanted, June didn't need it in the same way she used to. More than the money, she realized, she'd always be grateful to Jasper for bringing her to Wishing Cove and inspiring her to start painting again. Would her painting career have launched earlier if he'd been in her life, mentoring her from the beginning?

Maybe. But then she wouldn't be the same person, wouldn't have the girls, and never would have met Caleb. Jasper had given her a second chance, and now she had the wisdom and life experience to appreciate every minute of it.

Starting right now.

With that, she hopped off her barstool. "Do you guys mind if I run down to the studio? The girls will probably sleep for a few more hours."

"Of course," Raven said, with a wink. "Tell Caleb we said hi."

"I'm not—" June started to argue, but then abruptly stopped talking. This was the first hour of her new life—might as well start by being honest. She ran a hand through her damp, tangled curls. "Do I look okay?"

"You look beautiful," Sierra said.

"We didn't tell Caleb you were coming, so he's in for quite a happy surprise," Raven added.

June took a deep breath, gave them both a hug, and headed down the hill.

*

Just like the first time she'd arrived in Wishing Cove, June stood in the middle of the studio, arms crossed in front of her, gazing at the half-finished canvas on the easel. But unlike that first morning, this painting was hers. The *studio* was hers. The awe in her chest wasn't about Jasper's work, but about her own.

This was her life now, and she was exactly where she was supposed to be.

She turned away from the easel, ready to go find Caleb, and as if her thoughts conjured him up, the door opened and he walked through it.

"*June?*" He stood frozen in the doorway with a pile of folded drop cloths under one arm, and an absolutely stunned look on his face.

Her heart crashed in her chest. She'd closed her eyes and seen that face a thousand times over the past few weeks, but now that it was in front of her, she realized just how much it felt like home.

Caleb took a tentative step into the room. "I had no idea you were back."

"It was all very last minute."

Caleb slowly lowered the drop cloths onto a table and, for the first time, June noticed he was dressed up—for Caleb, anyway—in black trousers and a pale blue button-up shirt.

"How long are you staying?" He rubbed his hand across the barely there stubble on his jaw. He'd shaved recently, which was unusual, too.

"For ever." June said. "I quit my job, we left David in Connecticut, and the girls start first grade at Wishing Cove Elementary in a couple of weeks."

Caleb's eyes crinkled around the corners as his mouth curved into a grin. "June, that's fantastic. You're really doing it."

"I got your painting. And your note."

"Yeah?" He shoved his hands into his pockets. "And what did you think?"

"I think… I need to apologize to you, Caleb."

"What? Why?"

"For blaming you for the accident. I jumped to conclusions because I was confused and afraid, and I'm sorry." June looked down at her hands. "But I still need to understand what happened. Why did you shut me out like that?"

"Jasper committed suicide."

June gasped. "Oh my God."

"I found out the morning of your show." He raked a hand through his hair. "And I obviously didn't handle it very well."

Of course he didn't. Who would handle news like that well? "I'm so sorry, Caleb."

"For what it's worth"—his copper-colored eyes met hers—"I'm dealing with it."

She knew that was his way of telling her he was managing his bipolar disorder, and his words tugged at her heart. She couldn't imagine how he must have felt, trying to hold it together after learning such terrible news about someone he loved. Worrying if he let himself fall apart, it might lead to a manic or depressive episode. It must be exhausting.

"For what it's worth, Caleb, it's okay if you're not dealing with it. It's an enormous, unfathomable loss, and it's okay to be completely toppled by it. It doesn't mean something is wrong with you."

"Yeah, I'm starting to figure that out." He gazed past her, out the window. "I spent so much of my life being hyper-vigilant about my moods, and maybe I lost sight of the fact that sometimes it's normal to experience intense feelings over something like this. I'm working on being a little more forgiving of myself." He sighed. "Letting people in has been a bit of learning curve, I guess you could say. But I should have been honest with you."

"I could have handled it, Caleb. What scared me was being shut out."

"I know. If I could go back and do it again, I'd do everything differently."

She felt an unexpected burn in her eyes as Caleb took a step toward her, so close she could smell that nutty Caleb-scent. God, she'd missed it. He reached out to brush a tear away, and her heart slammed into her ribcage. *I guess he still has that effect on me.* He always did, from that first moment he'd burst into the studio and found her standing right here.

June glanced from one end of the room to the other. This was where it had all started for the two of them. The wall of windows, the easel, the pile of paint tubes on the table. Her lips curved into a smile. There, in the corner, the broom she'd swung at him when she'd thought he was an intruder.

"Maybe we *can* do it all differently."

Caleb blinked, following her gaze to the broom, and understanding dawned in his eyes. "I guess we're right back here again."

June gave a watery laugh and shook her head ruefully. "So, if you walked into the studio and found a strange woman standing"—she shifted to the left— "right about *here*, what would you say?"

For a second, his eyes roamed over her, as if he were considering the question. Finally, he took a step forward, a smile tugging at his lips. He held out his right palm. "I'd say, hey, I'm Caleb," he said. "Welcome to Wishing Cove."

"June," she said, grasping his hand and gazing into those copper-colored eyes she knew as well as her own.

"It's so nice to meet you, June. If you need anything at all while you're here in Wishing Cove, you let me know."

"Well, now that you mention it…" She looked up at him, so close she could barely think straight. "I'd love to spend today with you. And tomorrow… and maybe every day after that…"

But Caleb didn't return her smile. "Shit, June. I can't." He let her hand go.

"Oh." June stumbled back a step. She couldn't have gotten this all wrong.

"I mean, I can't right *now*," he said, grabbing her by the shoulders before she moved out of reach. "I'm on my way to Starlake, for a meeting. I'm teaching a painting class."

"You're teaching? Caleb, that's amazing."

"Yeah." He met her eyes. "It's pretty exciting. It's a class for kids in the intensive outpatient program at the local psychiatric hospital. Art therapy for teens with bipolar disorder, major depressive disorder, and similar diagnoses. Emily recommended one of her colleagues who's an expert in art therapy to teach it with me. We're meeting at Starlake today to discuss the details. The class starts in two weeks."

June gaped at him. "Caleb, I'm so happy you're doing this."

"I'm sorry I have to leave now, though." He checked his watch and swore under his breath. "I'm about to be late."

"No, this is wonderful. You should go. Don't be late."

Caleb hesitated for a moment, and the muscles in his arms tightened almost imperceptibly. Finally, he let go of her. "Can I come by later?"

"Of course."

He took a step backward and finally turned and headed for the door. In the doorway, he paused and gave her a wave, and then he was gone.

June turned back to her easel but before she could move, the door behind her crashed open, and Caleb was striding toward her.

"Did you forget something?" she asked.

"No. Yes." He took her by the shoulders. "Just this." Then he leaned down and pulled her against him, pressing his mouth to hers. June wrapped her arms tightly around him, and kissed him back.

When they finally broke apart, breathing hard, Caleb pressed his forehead to hers. "I can't guarantee I won't have relapses, or that it will be easy. But I promise I'll always be honest with you. Starting right now." He gave her that smile she loved, and her heart slid right up into her throat. "I love you, June. The day you came to Wishing Cove was the best day of my life. And having Emma and Izzy here has been amazing. I'm grateful every day that I get to know them, and it breaks my heart that Jasper missed his chance."

There were the tears again, welling up and threatening to spill over. But they were happy tears, filled with hope for her future with this man who'd helped her find all the things she thought she'd lost for ever.

Love and art and possibility.

"I'd love to spend today with you," Caleb continued. "And tomorrow... and every day after that."

"I'll be right here," June said. And somewhere in her heart, the brightest, most vibrant hues took shape across a pure white canvas, brushed with bold, joyful strokes. With a smile, Caleb spun around and headed out of the studio.

June turned to the canvas propped on her easel, picked up a brush, and began the rest of her life.

A LETTER FROM MELISSA

Dear reader,

I want to say a huge thank you for choosing to read *Her Family Secret*. If you did enjoy it, and want to keep up to date with all my latest releases, just sign up at the following link. Your email address will never be shared and you can unsubscribe at any time.

www.bookouture.com/melissa-wiesner

In the fall of 2019, my family was invited to a wedding in Bellingham, Washington. I had never been to the Pacific Northwest before, so our family decided to make a vacation out of the trip. My husband, two children, and I spent a lovely week winding our way north from Seattle to Bellingham, stopping to hike, explore the cliffs along the ocean, and search for wishing rocks on the shore. Six months later, when the world shut down due to the COVID-19 pandemic and I found myself locked down with my family, my mind was often drawn back to those pine forests, fields of wildflowers, and sunsets over the Puget Sound. As I began to write this story, the Pacific Northwest seemed the absolutely perfect location for June to escape to and to find her inspiration as an artist.

I hope you loved exploring the Pacific Northwest with June in *Her Family Secret* and if you did I would be very grateful if you could write a review. I'd love to hear what you think, and it makes such a difference helping new readers to discover one of my books for the first time.

I love hearing from my readers—you can get in touch on my Facebook page, through Twitter, Goodreads, or my website.

Thanks,
Melissa Wiesner

MelissaWiesnerAuthor

@Melissa-Wiesner

www.melissawiesner.com

ACKNOWLEDGEMENTS

All the people who have impacted my writing are too numerous to name here, but I want to give thanks to a special few whose support on this journey made all the difference.

To my agent, Julie Dinneen, thank you for your wise and completely spot-on editorial feedback, for your patience, and for your continued support, encouragement, and occasional talks off the ledge.

Thank you to my editor, Caolinn Douglas, who has been nothing short of amazing to work with, and to the entire Bookouture team for all your work to bring this novel into the world. I'm so thrilled that my novel found a home with Bookouture.

I'd like to thank my many writers' groups and critique partners who taught me just about everything I know about writing, publishing, *why adverbs are bad* and, most importantly, about perseverance. A special thank you to Jody Holford, whose mentorship was absolutely invaluable when I was a brand-new writer with a lot of hope and very little experience. And to Maureen Marshall, for the incredibly honest and tough-love critique you gave me on my first novel. I would never have gotten this far if not for you.

Thank you to everyone who critiqued this book, particularly Megan McGee Lysaght, Lauren Alsten, Lainey Davis, Bella Ellwood-Clayton, Sara Whitney, Lindsay Jones, Eileen Emerson, Sammi Spizziri, and an extra special thanks to Katy James who read it twice!

To my mother, Gloria, thank you for handing me crayons and a sewing machine and letting me paint flowers on my walls and encouraging me to do all the creative things I wanted to do when I was a kid that eventually led me to become a published author today.

To my sister, Pam, thank you for being the absolute best aunt to my kids, and for the many, many hours that you spend with them to give me time to write. Thank you for doing this even when you didn't know I was writing a book and thought maybe I was having an affair because I seemed so distracted all the time.

Thank you to the Wiesners for welcoming me into your family, for your love and support, and for letting me build a writing retreat in your backyard!

To Jennie, Amie, and Scopel, thank you for always being thrilled for me and my writing career but never letting it go to my head. To my COVID "co-parent" Laura, thank you for helping me survive 2020. And to the MOMGs, thank you for helping me survive... everything.

And finally, to my husband, Sid, my first reader, my biggest fan, and my best friend... When I told you I was planning to write a novel, thank you for remaining calm, for nodding your head, and for saying, "Of course you will." You're my real-life romance hero. (And yes, I see you rolling your eyes because I'm being cheesy again.) I'm grateful every day to have you as my partner in life. I love you.